With You
All the Way

With You All the Way

CYNTHIA HAND

HARPER TEEN

An Imprint of HarperCollinsPublishers

Library of Congress Control Number: 2020950510
ISBN 978-0-06-269319-8

Typography by Jessie Gang
21 22 23 24 25 PC/LSCH 10 9 8 7 6 5 4 3 2 1
❖
First Edition

For Dan

*"One's destination is never a place,
but a new way of seeing things."*

—Henry Miller

1

"My mom isn't home," Leo says as he opens the door.

That's when I know that he wants to have sex.

"Oh" is all I can think to say.

"She's out of town until Tuesday." It's Friday afternoon. He definitely wants to have sex. We've been dating since February (this being mid-June), kissing a lot, making out whenever we can find somewhere private to hide away. Sex is the obvious next step.

"So we've got your place all to ourselves," I say giddily. I've been thinking about Leo all day, wondering when I would get to see him, daydreaming about the smooth warm feel of his lips against mine. When he texted that he wanted to hang out this afternoon, it was the best kind of surprise. And this, well, it feels like I'm having a sexy dream about Leo.

Only this is real.

Leo smiles, a little-kid-about-to-open-his-birthday-present type smile. "You could even—I don't know—stay the night?"

I laugh, that giggle I hate, the one I do so often around Leo. Stay the night. Wow. How can I even pull off being gone all night? My parents will notice if I don't come home. Pop will notice, anyway. Mom probably wouldn't notice if I went missing for a week.

"You could tell them you're sleeping over at a friend's house," Leo suggests. That's the obvious play. My best friend, Lucy, will go for it, too; she's so excited that I—quiet, nerdy Ada—finally have a verifiable love interest. At first they teased me that I made Leo up, this perfect boy I kept talking about. I had to practically beg Leo—who hates high school dances—to take me to prom, just to prove he was real. Ever since then my friends have been referring to Leo—popular, non-nerdy Leo—as "The Miracle." And this—him wanting to have sex with me, not just once, apparently, but all night long—seems miraculous, too.

I nod. Laugh again. "Okay."

His smile grows wider, kid-on-Christmas-morning level excited. "Okay? Really?"

I try to act like my heart isn't thudding in my chest. "I mean, Friday's family night, which is seriously sacred to my stepdad, but I can miss it. We're going out of town next week, so we're going to have a lot of family time, so—"

"I'm going to miss you," he says, "when you're in Hawaii."

I smile. "I'm going to miss you, too." Stupid compulsory family trip to Hawaii. "So yeah, I guess, I can stay the n—"

"So you really want to?" he asks.

"I do," I say breathlessly. I get out my phone and text Lucy, who enthusiastically agrees to be my alibi, and text Pop that I'm having a sleepover at Lucy's.

Have fun! Pop texts back.

Then Leo takes my hand and leads me toward what I'm guessing is his bedroom.

His house is in Santa Clara, a few train stops before San Jose. It isn't a large house. Three bedrooms, two baths. From the street it looks tiny, especially if I'm comparing it to my own house in Redwood City. If I'm being nice—and my default setting is nice, I can't seem to help it—I'd say it was "refreshingly minimal." When I picture myself as an artist (like Leo's mom, who's a famous local sculptor) I can imagine living in a house like this.

I've never seen Leo's room before. He's invited me over a few times since we started going out, but his mom was always home. There was some unspoken understanding between them that we wouldn't hang out in his bedroom, so we stayed in the kitchen or streamed movies on the living room sofa. Now, as we move down the hallway toward the inevitable (!!!) sex we're about to have, I pause to look at the framed photographs hanging on the wall. Most of them are of Leo and Diana with various people I assume are relatives. I point at the photo of a toddler with something bright red—beets? tomato sauce?—smeared all over his face. "Aw. Look at you."

He cringes. "My mom won't take it down. She loves to humiliate me."

"I think it's cute," I say.

"You're cute," he counters.

We come to a room crammed with tables and sculptures in various states of progression: his mom's studio. She works with wax

3

and clay in there and then takes it to a place in the city to cast it into bronze. I barely resist the urge to go inside and attempt to absorb some of her genius.

Leo, however, is not impressed. He tugs on my hand to get me moving again, toward a smaller bedroom at the end of the hall. His.

"Welcome." He ushers me inside. Closes the door. "Make yourself at home."

There's nowhere to sit but on his bed. I perch on the edge and fold my hands into my lap, gazing around at the various posters on the walls. Most of them are of swimmers. Leo's captain of the swim team at his school. By the look of it, he's obsessed with Michael Phelps, and this other guy with a huge tattoo that covers most of his left arm.

I wouldn't have pegged Leo for a posters-all-over-the-walls kind of guy.

"That's Caeleb Dressel," he explains almost shyly. "Two gold medals. Holds the world record in the hundred-meter butterfly."

"Nice." I try to seem appreciative, but it's weird to be admiring these spandex-clad older men. I can't imagine sleeping in here with their eyes on me. Or sleeping in here, period.

"So," says Leo.

"So," I say. My heart is skittering again. *I'm okay*, I tell myself. I'm sixteen, which I consider old enough to make a mature decision about it. Leo's seventeen. We've been dating for almost five months. I like Leo, really like him. I'm curious about what sex will be like. With Leo, like everything has been with Leo so far, it will probably be great.

"Do you want to listen to some music?" He reaches around me to turn on a speaker on the bedside table. Then he thumbs through his phone to find a soundtrack for the business at hand. The first song is about (you guessed it) having sex. It's a little cringey, how Leo obviously googled the best songs to have sex to. I hope there's not an entire playlist of sex songs.

Leo sits down next to me. We kiss. He buries one hand in the hair at the base of my neck, cradling my head. Kissing him is always so good. Delicious. I can't define what he tastes like, exactly, but it's not similar to any food or drink I know. Not sweet, but spicy isn't right, either. He tastes like Leo. Which I like.

After a few minutes he pushes me gently back onto the bed. I hang on to his shoulders. Leo has broad, muscly shoulders, from the swimming. He's a big guy—six three, solid, which is one other reason I like him. Leo being so big makes me feel smaller, in a good way.

His mouth is on my neck now. Goose bumps jump up along my arms. I tilt my head to give him better access. He moves to my ear. I predict he's going to stick his tongue in there. He's done that before, and I wasn't really a fan. I turn so he won't. Touch his face so I can pivot him back to my mouth. Kiss him again. Again. Exploring. Trying the different angles.

He moves on top of me, his large body stretching over mine. For a few seconds I feel smothered; he's too heavy, squashing me, but then he shifts his weight onto his arms and I can breathe again. His body against mine is familiar, but the way he's moving is new. The bulge— that solid bump that I know is his, uh, junk, what my mom would insist on calling his penis, because Mom refuses to be anything but technical and precise about naming things—presses against my thigh.

Oh god, I'm thinking about my mother. I squirm, and Leo pulls back. His face is so red it makes his eyebrows stand out against his skin, like furry caterpillars clinging to his forehead. It's distracting.

"You're beautiful," he mumbles.

"You too," I say automatically, and blush so hard it feels like my cheeks and neck have been scalded. Leo keeps kissing me and touching me, and I'm totally into it. At least my body is. My lower half seems to be transforming into hot liquid. There's a knot of sensation building between my legs. But the further along we get, the closer to the actual sex that's going to be happening any minute now, the more weirdly disconnected I feel. To the point where I can almost slip out of my body and float over us. See myself from the outside.

I'm wearing a red Harry Potter shirt from last year's trip to Orlando. It reads "9 ¾" on the front. It's childish—I can see that so clearly now—and unflattering, a size too big for me, because I prefer loose-fitting clothes. Leo is pulling this shirt up, exposing my very white, not-very-flat belly, and underneath he discovers a gray sports bra, which confounds him because it doesn't have any kind of hook or clasp. My mind whirls trying to remember what panties I'm wearing. Hopefully not the plain white cotton with the hole in the butt, which I should have thrown away months ago, but they're the most comfortable pair I own. Shit. It's probably those. My hair is tangled around my head. My chest heaves behind the sports bra, which is dark in places, because I'm so sweaty.

From this vantage point, the one in my imagination—seeing as how my eyes are actually squeezed shut—I know I'm not beautiful. Leo only said that to try to make me feel sexy. So I would want to have sex.

I do want to have sex, don't I?

Yes, I tell myself. *Relax. This is fine.*

But then Leo's hand is on the button of my shorts, and my upper half turns to ice. *Wait*, I think. *Wait*, and then I almost knock heads with him as I try to sit up.

He examines my face. "Hey. Are you okay?"

I swipe at a strand of hair that's clinging damply to my cheek. "I'm good. Sorry. Can we just take it slower?"

He nods. "Of course. Whatever you want."

"Okay." I lean in to kiss him again. We do that for a while, and the tension in my shoulders eases. He's very good at kissing, and I'm not so bad at it, either. It's not sloppy or teeth-banging. There's just the right amount of tongue involved. His arms feel solid around me. His hand squeezing my breast is good. I try to touch him, too, running my hands along his back, his swimmer's chest. Then lower.

"I love you," he says then, softly.

My hand stills. He's never said that before, the L-word. Neither of us have.

He says, "I should, uh, get some protection."

I blink up at him. Somehow I'm lying down again, although I don't know when that happened. "What?"

He spells it out for me. "A condom."

"Oh. Right. Yes." How responsible of us.

He gets up and goes out of the room. I wonder where he's going for this condom. Is he ransacking his mom's bedside table? Or the bathroom, where he has a stash for situations such as these? Has he done this before? We haven't talked about it. We really should have talked about it. At least then I would know what to expect.

I smooth my clothes back down over myself and take a steadying breath. The gray jersey sheets beneath me smell like fresh laundry detergent. I sit up. I'm surprised, actually, by how clean Leo's room is. There are no piles of dirty laundry like you'd find on the floor of my room. The carpet even has vacuum lines in it.

How long has he been planning this? Did he wake up this morning thinking *tonight's the night*? Did he tidy up and wash his sheets and hug his mom goodbye with a secret smile because he knew he was going to get laid? When all that time I was thinking that we were simply going to a movie this afternoon, then maybe we'd go back to his house, have dinner and talk art with Leo's mom, stream a show. Most of our relationship consists of watching various things together. And making out while his mom isn't looking.

But this.

It's unfair of him, springing this on me. I would have dressed better if I'd known, done something with my hair. Picked different underwear, at least. Shaved my legs.

Oh *god*. I haven't shaved my legs in days.

I glance around wildly like a razor is just going to magically materialize. Michael Phelps glares down at me from the walls. One of the posters reads, *FEARLESS. If you want to be the best, you have to do things other people aren't willing to do.*

And Leo just said he *loved* me. Was he being serious? Did he mean *love* the way you can say, *I love peanut butter cups?* Or the real way? Was I supposed to say it back? I like him, yes, so much, but could I say I love him? I mouth the words "I love you," and it feels fake. Maybe I could mean it in the peanut-butter-cup sense. But it's too late to respond now, anyway. He said he loved me, and I didn't say anything, and now we're on to the sex.

This is happening. I'm about to have sex.

Leo returns. He holds up a foil packet triumphantly. "Okay, let's do this."

That's when I know I can't do this.

"Actually, let's not." I stand up, eager to get off the bed.

His smile fades. "What? What happened?"

"Nothing. I . . ." I choose my next words very carefully. "I just don't want to go all the way. Not tonight. Okay?"

Now he looks like a little kid who's opened his Christmas present to discover a sweater. "But why not?"

"I'm not ready. I thought I was, but I'm not. Sorry," I tack on, and then hate myself for apologizing. I'm not supposed to be sorry. But I am.

Leo's frowning, but he says, "All right. I don't want to do it if you don't want to do it, obviously."

I smile. "Thanks."

Silence builds between us. A new song starts pouring out of the speaker, a song I know this time, a slow song by The Weeknd called "Earned It." Over Leo's shoulder I read another inspirational Michael Phelps poster. *You can't put a limit on anything. The more you dream, the farther you get.*

Leo puts the condom on the bedside table. "So what *do* you want to do?"

I wouldn't mind making out some more, but that could send a mixed message. Besides, my lower half is starting to ache, a tight but heavy, decidedly unpleasant feeling, like period cramps. I try to smile at him. "I don't know. Maybe we could watch something?"

"Sure," he says dully. "Whatever you want."

2

"I thought you were staying at Lucy's tonight," Pop says when I come into the kitchen later.

"I just wanted to be home." Things were awkward with Leo, so awkward that I finally said I wasn't feeling well—which wasn't really a lie—and he insisted on walking me to the train station.

"You're my little homebody," Pop says now with a smile. Like that's cute.

My five-year-old sister, Abby, is sitting at the counter coloring while Pop makes dinner. "What's a homebody?" Abby asks.

Pop continues dicing a stalk of celery. "A homebody is someone who loves to be home more than anywhere else."

"I like to be home," Abby announces. "But I also like to go places. Today we went on an African safari. I made a batik."

It takes me a second to realize that Abby is talking about the day camp she goes to during the summer, since Pop works nights at El

Camino Hospital in Mountain View, and Mom works days at Stanford Hospital in Palo Alto. Although to say that Mom works days is inaccurate. Mom works all the time.

Speaking of which: "Where's Mom?"

Pop keeps chopping vegetables. "She said she'd be home in time for dinner. It's family night, you know."

"I know." Normally I would stay and help him finish making the salad, but that could lead to conversations like "How was your day?" and I don't want to go there. So I grab a carrot and flee upstairs to my room. I close the door and go straight to my desk, where I take out my journal and art pencils and begin to sketch Leo.

I can still see him clearly in my mind's eye. That expression on his face when I said I didn't want to go all the way. The way his eyelids lowered, not squeezing into a squint or a glare, but dropping like protective shutters over his eyes. His eyebrows angled up at the inner edges, pressing together, causing two small bumps to appear in the space between them. The discontented downturn of his mouth.

My pencil practically dances over the paper, capturing that look. It takes me ten minutes, and the moment I finish I know it's one of the best sketches I've ever done. It illustrates the moment perfectly—the feeling in it, the tension. Strange how the worst experiences can lead to the best art. But that's life, I guess. Beauty in the pain.

I pick up the carrot I stole from Pop and crunch on it miserably. Clearly I've made a huge mistake here. Why didn't I want to have sex? Was it the *I love you* bit? Do I believe, deep down somewhere, that to "make love" you need to be *in love*, and I don't love Leo enough for that? Do I love Leo? I've never considered my feelings like that before: either love or not love. I like Leo. I love being with him. I'm attracted to him. Shouldn't that be enough?

Or was it the unshaved legs thing? The holey underwear? The sports bra? Am I so uncomfortable in my own skin that the idea of Leo seeing me naked is more than I can handle? I know I have body issues, but am I really that self-conscious?

Or maybe it was Michael Phelps.

Whatever the reason, it was the wrong call. Leo was offended. He might say it's all right and that he respects me and that he can wait, but he got instantly distant with me after I wanted to stop. He couldn't help it. He was disappointed.

Yeah, well. I'm disappointed, too.

I sign and date the sketch. It needs a title. I scrawl a word I like: *crestfallen*. That's what Leo was. His crest had definitely fallen. I snort, then erase the word carefully. *Not ready*, I write instead.

Not ready. I sigh. I flip back through the journal, past the pages and pages of sketches like this one, documenting the moments of my life as intimately as any diary would. There are so many drawings of Leo. Leo on the beach at Santa Cruz, the sea breeze ruffling his hair. Leo tying his shoe. Leo in swim trunks that one time we swam in his aboveground backyard pool, his back to me as he stood at the edge of the water, the muscles tightened as he prepared to dive in. He's beautiful. Built. Sexy. What is wrong with me?

I flip back a few more pages, to February and the first sketch I ever did of Leo, at his mother's show.

He was slumped in a chair to one side of the gallery, a modern teenage boy as Rodin's *Thinker*, rumpled hoodie, holes in his jeans, elbow propped on his knee and his chin in his hand. I knew after two seconds of seeing him that he was Diana Robinson's son. For a minute I just stood there, looking, internalizing his shapes and shading for this sketch, the one I'd do of him later. Then I actually went over and talked to him, a move so unlike my introverted self that thinking back on it surprises me every time. How was I so inexplicably brave that day?

"It must be weird" is what I said to him.

He looked up, startled. "Weird?"

"To be your mom's, like, muse." Almost all of Diana Robinson's sculptures featured a little boy doing something strangely adult: reading Proust, driving a car, shaving, fastening a cuff link to his sleeve. I'd recognized Leo from the back—that cowlick he has on the right side of his head. It's in every sculpture, that uncooperative swirl of hair.

"How did you . . ." Leo seemed confused at how I knew who he was, but then he glanced around and realized. "Uh, yeah. It's weird. Little bit."

We struck up a conversation, and at the end of it he asked me out. This still feels like the most improbable thing ever. A guy asking me out doesn't seem like something that is possible in my world, which consists of Notre Dame High School (Catholic, all girls), babysitting my little sister, hanging out with my big sister, and my art stuff (a largely solitary obsession). I'd never been asked out before. And then suddenly—bam—there was Leo. Athletic, affable Leo. Who likes me, maybe even *loves* me. Who wants to kiss me.

And other things.

God, I think. *What have I done?*

There's a single sharp rap on my bedroom door. Pop's voice. "Dinner."

"Okay," I call back faintly. "I'll be right down."

3

In the dining room I take my usual seat between Mom's chair and Afton's. Afton is eighteen and essentially a carbon copy of our mother—whip-smart, take-no-shit-from-anybody, and annoyingly gorgeous, with long ash-blond hair and hot-fire-blue eyes.

"I thought you were staying over at Lucy's," Afton says.

I shrug. "No."

"Did you get in a fight? What's going on?"

Normally I tell Afton everything of significance that happens in my life. But now is definitely not the time. Besides, just thinking about Leo is making my face feel hot and prickly.

"Nothing," I insist. I give a little shake of my head that means, *I'll tell you later.*

"Where's Mommy?" Abby asks, a welcome distraction from Afton's inquisitive gaze.

"She's not here." Afton smirks, a twist of her pink-petal lips. "What a shock, right?"

"I'm sure she'll be here any minute." Pop sets a steaming dish of meat in the center of the table, then a bowl of what looks like mashed potatoes with corn and peas in it. Meat and mashed potatoes. Not Pop's usual dinner offering.

"What is *that*?" Abby asks loudly, staring at the gravy-like substance surrounding the meat like it has oozed down from outer space.

"Is it . . . beef?" Afton's a ballet dancer. She's always careful with what she eats. As in, no red meat.

"*Nyama na irio*," Pop explains, like that explains it. "It's a Kenyan dish."

Ah. That does explain it. Pop recently took one of those DNA tests that tell you what ethnicities you're made up of. According to said test, Pop is 45 percent African (Nigerian, Kenyan), 26 percent European (British, Irish, Iberian), 14 percent South American (Columbian, Argentinian), 3 percent Native American, and then traces of other random stuff. Pop calls himself a "worldly specimen." Ever since he received the results, he's been researching and cooking meals from the different specific cultures he's related to. Last week was fish and chips. The week before: *arroz chaufa de mariscos*, a kind of spicy seafood and rice. And now this.

"I don't eat beef," Afton says, her perfect nose wrinkling.

Pop gestures grandly to the huge bowl of salad. "Knock yourself out. There's also bread."

"I don't eat bread."

Abby is similarly dubious. She crosses her arms. Her idea of fine cuisine is cucumber slices and chicken nuggets. "This looks yucky."

"It's basically steak, honey," Pop says. "You like steak. And you like potatoes, and you like corn, and you like peas."

"I don't like salad," Abby points out.

"You don't have to eat the salad," Pop says with a slight edge to his voice. "Come on, everyone. Eat up."

"But shouldn't we wait for Mom?" I ask. "It's family night."

"It's getting cold." Pop grabs Abby's plate and scoops a big dollop of potatoes onto it. Next comes the meat and gravy stuff. I'm about to warn him to ladle it next to—as opposed to on top of—Abby's potatoes. Abby doesn't like her foods to touch. But it's too late; he pours it right over the top.

Abby's bottom lip starts to tremble. "I don't think I like it."

Pop doesn't give up. "This is a meal from our *ancestors*, Abbycakes. This food is in your blood."

In the meantime I've dished myself up a generous portion. This food isn't in my blood like it is Abby's, being that Pop is my stepfather and not biologically related to Afton and me, but he's been around since I was seven. He feels like my real father in every way that counts. I don't even remember much of the time before Pop came along, when I had a different father, the one Afton and I have an awkward visit with about twice a year.

"It's in my *blood*?" Abby cries in horror. "What does that even mean?"

I wish I had such an interesting combination of ethnicities in my blood, but Mom took a DNA test, too, to discover that she is 90 percent European. Mostly German. Which explains the blond hair, I guess.

My phone vibrates in my pocket. I sneak it out—Pop disapproves of phone use at the dinner table—and check my texts. There's a new one from Leo, a photo of his long legs stretched out in front of him on his couch, sneakers on the coffee table, behind them the television paused on one of the shows we always watch together.

I wish you could have stayed, it says.

My chest tightens. It seems so silly now. Cringey. Cowardly. It's just sex, isn't it? Does it have to be such a big deal?

I glance up at Pop. He's busy trying to calm Abby, who's working herself into a full-blown tantrum over the food.

Me too, I text Leo quickly.

You're missing out on this. He texts me another photo of himself on the couch, his lip stuck out in a playful pout. Also he's not wearing a shirt.

He sends me photos like that a lot—Hot Leo—always a few minutes before he posts them to his social media. I'm flattered that he wants me to see them first.

I text back a sad emoji, followed by, *Sorry about before.*

Don't worry about it. You're ready when you're ready.

Relief fills me. He isn't mad. I can still salvage this. It's only Friday, after all. Our family is leaving for our trip on Sunday, but that still leaves all of Saturday and Saturday night.

Maybe I could be ready tomorrow. I hold my breath as I type the words. It feels bold, but I can be bold, I tell myself sternly. Remember how I was the one to approach Leo in the first place? I can take charge of my sexual destiny.

It takes him an agonizing few seconds to respond. *I have a swim meet tomorrow afternoon and dinner with some friends after.*

I'm about to type something else but then Pop bellows, "Enough!" and I thrust my phone under my seat cushion.

It isn't like Pop to yell.

"What about a corn dog?" he says more quietly, trying to get back into his loving-parent mode, love and logic and all that, but his voice comes out tight and strangled.

I look quickly around the table. Pop is standing next to Abby, jaw clenched. He turns and walks stiffly toward the refrigerator to fetch Abby a corn dog out of the freezer that he can microwave. Abby's gnawing on a hunk of bread. Afton is meticulously picking at her salad. She meets my eyes and raises her perfectly shaped eyebrows as if to say, *What an awesome family night we're having.*

That's when my phone rings. Loudly.

Pop swivels. "No phones at the table! Ada! You know that!"

"Yeah, Ada," Abby says. "You know that."

"I know, I know. I'm sorry." I hold up the phone like it's a grenade about to go off, mashing at buttons to make it be quiet, and then I realize who's calling me. "Wait. It's Mom."

Everything goes silent except for the ringing phone. Then Pop says, "Well, answer it."

So I do. "Mom?"

"Hi, Ada. This is Ruthie, actually."

"Oh, hi, Ruthie." Ruthie is Mom's assistant. Ruthie does all the normal-person things for my mother so Mom can focus on the genius-doctor things. Ruthie shops for Mom's clothes and purchases wedding gifts and birthday presents for people as needed, and she organizes Mom's schedule. It's Ruthie who reminds my mother when I have an art show or Afton has a ballet recital, Ruthie who gently orders Mom to go home when it becomes clear that she hasn't left Stanford Hospital for days. Or to wash her hair.

Or eat something. Because genius doctors can't be bothered by such mundane details.

It's also Ruthie who calls to make excuses whenever Mom needs to get out of something.

"Is everything okay?" I ask slowly.

"Oh, yes. Everything is fine. Dr. Bloom wanted me to tell you that she's going to be here late. She's working really hard on her presentation for the Hawaii conference, and—"

"How late?" I ask.

Ruthie sounds confused. "What?"

"How late is she going to be there?"

"Oh. How late, do you think?" My mother must be standing right there, because Ruthie is apparently asking her. There's a pause as Ruthie listens to the answer. "She says to go ahead and have dinner without her. She'll try to be there to read stories to Abby at bedtime, but don't wait up, just in case. Okay?"

"Okay," I say. Everybody is staring at me. "Thanks, Ruthie."

"You bet. Good night."

I hang up the phone. I don't need to tell the rest of my family what Ruthie relayed to me—that much is obvious from the fact that Ruthie called at all. Why couldn't Mom just call herself and tell us? And why have Ruthie call me, and not Pop?

"Where's Mommy?" Abby asks in a small voice. "Is she going to miss our special dinner from our ancestors?"

"She's trying to get everything ready to go to Hawaii," Pop says, the picture of calm again. Nothing in his face or his voice suggests that he's upset. But something feels decidedly off.

Abby picks up her fork and absentmindedly starts to eat the

nyama na irio without complaint. "What part of Hawaii again?" she asks after a while.

"Where we're going is the one called the Big Island, because it's the biggest." Pop sits down and takes a bite of the food. Then he gets up again and crosses with his plate to the microwave. Pop likes his food so hot it'd burn off the taste buds of normal humans. "You're going to love it there, honey. I promise."

"And you're going, too, right, Poppy?" Abby asks.

"We're all going," I answer for him. Every June, for as far back as I can remember (except for the one summer when nobody went anywhere), our mother has dragged us to the yearly conference of the Society of Thoracic Surgeons. The conference is held in a different place each year, but it's always with the same people—heart surgeons, basically, and their families. Normally I look forward to this trip. But things have been heating up so much with Leo lately, and it feels impossible to go a whole week without seeing him. We can text and video chat, but it won't be the same. There will be an entire ocean between us.

"When are we going?" Abby asks.

"The day after tomorrow. Your mommy is going to do a big talk in front of a lot of people, so she needs to practice what she's going to say. That's why she's missing dinner." Pop retrieves his plate from the microwave and comes back to the table. "But I know she really wishes she could be here."

"Okay," says Abby. She's used to Mom's absence. We all are. "Dr. Bloom" is always busy, but she's busy for a good reason. Every single day she spends away from us at the hospital, my mother saves lives, and that means she doesn't completely belong to us. It's like she belongs to the world.

Even Abby, at age five, has come to accept this.

"Ada," Pop says gently. "No phones at the table, please."

I'm still clutching my phone. I stick it in my pocket. "Sorry. It will never happen again, I swear."

He snorts. "You just need to make sure you don't experience all of your relationships via text, all right? Embrace the real. Be physically there. Okay?"

I try not to roll my eyes. "My relationships are sufficiently real, thank you, Pop." If only he knew. But I would never in a million years tell him.

"But you *were* texting your boyfriend," Afton remarks.

I turn my head to give Afton a sharp look. "Not that it's any of your business." Subtext: shut up. "But yes."

Pop chews for a minute thoughtfully. "How's that going, by the way? That's where you were today, right? With Leo?"

"Yeah. We went to a movie. And then . . . his house for a while."

Afton's right eyebrow lifts. "Oh, so before you went over to Lucy's."

Frick. "Right. Before I went to Lucy's, I was at Leo's house. For a while. And then I went to Lucy's." There's that stupid catch in my voice that happens whenever I try to lie.

"Interesting," says Afton with a knowing smile.

"How long have you two been dating now?" Pop asks obliviously.

"Like six months?" Afton supplies for me.

"Almost five," I correct her, making a mental note to murder her later.

Pop nods. "You must really like this Leo guy."

"Six months is serious," Afton says.

I would almost prefer that the conversation return to the yelling about food or Mom blowing us off. Almost. "Five months," I say again. "And yes. We're serious, I guess."

"It's kind of weird, though," Afton continues. "You've been together five whole months and he hasn't been over here once to meet your family. I mean, you even went to prom together, but you met him there instead of having him pick you up."

"He doesn't have a car—" I start to protest, but Afton cuts me off.

"Ada, are you ashamed of us?" The side of her mouth quirks up.

"No!" I burst out. "It's not like that. It's just that he's really busy with swimming all the time, and it's a long way to come from San Jose—it takes forever."

"But you go to his house," she points out.

"I like going to his house." It's quiet and nice, just him and his brilliant mom, when at home it feels like I have so much to deal with all the time.

"Well, you should bring him over for dinner sometime," Pop says. "We're all curious to meet him."

"Yeah!" Abby exclaims, brown eyes wide with excitement. "We could find out who his ancestors are and cook *them*! But don't kiss him in front of me. That would make me throw up." She pretends to gag.

"Uh, Abby, that's not what I—" Pop starts.

"How about tomorrow night?" Afton claps her hands together like this is the best idea ever. "That'd be so fun."

"I can't tomorrow night," I say, holding Afton's gaze. "I'm going to Leo's swim meet, and then we're having dinner with some of his friends."

22

I don't know why I say this. The idea only solidifies as the words are leaving my mouth. But it's a good idea, I realize, and my voice is steady, because that's suddenly what I'm going to do: surprise Leo at his swim meet. Be the supportive girlfriend and cheer him on. Tag along with his friends to dinner—I've met some of his friends before, and they were, well, friendly. They won't mind. I'm sure Leo won't mind. And then afterward we can go back to his empty house, and try again. This time with shaved legs and sexier underwear and better music.

"That sounds fun," says Pop.

4

"That sounds terrible," Afton says later. "No wonder you choked."

She's sitting cross-legged on the bed with my left foot in her lap, painting my toenails a deep shade of pink. I have just finished spilling my guts about Leo, the entire humiliating story complete with the sordid details: the music, the posters, the holey underwear, and the unfortunate confession of love that I still don't know how to feel about.

"I totally choked," I agree. "But I'm over it. I'm ready now. I've got a plan."

"Are you sure you still want to do it?" Afton switches to my other foot. "I mean, there's a case to be made for waiting. No need to, like, rush these things."

"You did it when you were sixteen," I point out.

"Yes, but it was in a *garage*, remember, with this boy I hardly knew whose sister was in my ballet class. And it—the sex, I mean—wasn't very good." Afton sets the bottle of nail polish on the bedside table and leans back against the headboard, remembering. "But at least he spread a blanket out on the floor next to the washing machine." She smiles almost sadly. "And he said I was the most beautiful girl he'd ever seen."

Yeah, yeah, she's beautiful. Tell us something we don't know. I'm already familiar with this story—Afton told me right after it happened. I also know that Afton's second time had been later that same year, with a college boy at a party in San Francisco. Afton didn't say much about that, but afterward she seemed to form a negative opinion of college boys in general, and she and I took the bus to a Planned Parenthood in Blossom Hill for Plan B. The third time was with Logan, Afton's current boyfriend. Logan counted for sexy times three through like a hundred, over a year of hooking up regularly, usually at his place or the back of his car, but one time they apparently did it in Pop's camper trailer parked next to the house.

In other words: Afton is well-versed in sex.

Right then we hear the garage door opening. Mom coming home. I glance at the clock; it's after eleven. Abby has been asleep for hours. Pop read her stories and then went into his den downstairs and shut the door. He likes to read, comic books mostly, a bit of high fantasy thrown in now and then. It's one of the ways we connected, early on. He heard that I liked art and let me borrow these old-school graphic novels about elves, but not like cutesy Santa elves—sexy badass elves who rode wolves and were descended from aliens. I loved it.

We listen as Mom creeps up the stairs and passes my room on her way to her and Pop's bedroom. After a while we hear the water in the master bathroom go on: she's taking a shower. She didn't bother to stop by the den to apologize to Pop for missing family night, even though she knows he's still up. Pop must have heard the garage door, too. But he didn't come out to talk to her.

I get a sinking sensation in the pit of my stomach. They aren't fighting, so far as I know. But they aren't exactly getting along.

Dear God, I think, even though I don't know if I exactly believe in God. *Please don't let them break up.*

"So tell me about this plan of yours," Afton says to disrupt the silence that's fallen over us.

I tell her. It's embarrassing, talking about sex with my big sister. But the upside is that by the end of the conversation, my first-time-having-sex plan is much more solid than "show up at Leo's swim meet." Granted, it involves my sister explaining the delicate art of grooming one's bikini area.

"Why do boys even think hair down there is gross?" I complain, pushing aside my earlier freak-out over my unshaved legs. "I mean, I don't want to look like a little girl, do I? That's creepy."

"It's a societal norm," Afton says, shrugging. "Like we're supposed to be Barbies."

"I hate the patriarchy," I sigh.

"I know. But we still have to live in it. I knew this girl at school who hooked up at a party one time, and afterward the guys in our circle started calling her 'Hairy Mary.'"

"Ugh. Boys are awful."

Afton nods. "Boys suck." She looks genuinely upset for a minute.

"Not our boyfriends, though," I add.

She only smiles sadly. I wonder if she's thinking about that other

26

party, the one with the college boys. She didn't tell me what happened or act like it was any big deal, but I think it weighs on her sometimes, whatever it was. She's not like me, eager to blab all about my feelings. Afton's always kept her feelings to herself, mostly. Probably because she doesn't want people to find out that she's not perfect. Only she kind of *is* perfect.

I try to lighten the mood. "Well, this shaving/waxing thing doesn't make any sense, because boys also seemed to be grossed out by vaginas. It's like an insult now. *You're such a vagina. Your face looks like a vagina.*"

Afton snorts. "Like the penis is so attractive. You know that phase where boys draw penises on everything?"

"That's a phase?"

"You're right. It might not be a phase. They always think it's so funny, drawing that, but if girls went around drawing pictures of vaginas, everybody would be horrified. Vaginas are no laughing matter."

My vagina definitely doesn't feel like a joke. It feels like a goddess who occasionally demands a blood sacrifice.

"But you should still probably shave," Afton says. Then she also makes me commit to going underwear shopping first thing in the morning. She finishes up her big-sister advice session by telling me about some kind of how-to sex website that Afton swears is a total game-changer that I flat-out refuse to investigate.

"Some things should just come naturally," I say as I rummage through my closet, holding up various tops while Afton gives each a thumbs-up or thumbs-down. "Without, you know, like an app."

Afton makes a face at the next top I show her. "No. Definitely not that one."

"I like this one," I protest. It's a purple tee with various pens and pencils drawn on the front, along with the words, "Draw, Paint, Create." "It's like my favorite shirt."

"It's not even a little bit sexy." Afton reaches into the closet around me and pulls out another shirt, this one wine-colored with a V-neck that I didn't even remember I owned. "This would look amazing on you. It'll set off the hidden red tones in your hair."

I close the closet door to access the full-length mirror on the back of it. We both examine our reflections for a minute. Afton is too skinny, Pop regularly says. Which we all know is not really a thing. I can't help but focus on my own image in the mirror behind my sister. I'm horrifyingly tall—I've been five eleven since I was thirteen, looming over the other students in my class. Wide shoulders. No hips to speak of. Legs like tree trunks. Also, I'm not skinny. I'm not overweight, according to my parents, who are both health-care professionals. I am simply, for lack of a better term, "big boned."

So Afton took after our gorgeous and enigmatic mother, and I took after our father, the caveman. Life is unfair.

I take the wine-colored tee from Afton and hold it up to my chest. "Weird. There *are* red tones in my hair." Normally I just think of it as being the color of straw.

"See? You're not the only one with artistic ability," Afton says.

"I guess not."

"Wear it with the jean shorts," she adds. "And put on some mascara. Waterproof, in case you cry or something."

"Why would I cry?"

"It hurts the first time."

Oh. Right. "How bad is it?"

Afton shrugs. "I don't know how well you tolerate pain. On a scale of one to ten, I'd give it a six. But I'm such a delicate flower, as you know."

I try to imagine a part of my body *tearing*. I'm not even sure that's what really happens down there, or what the point is. The most I know about the hymen is that it's named after the Greek god of marriage. That's seriously messed up. I begin to feel nervous again. What *is* my tolerance for pain?

"It's normal pain, though, right?" I say. "Everybody has sex."

"Not everybody," says Afton faintly.

"Right. Not old people."

Afton stifles a laugh. "I think old people do occasionally have sex, Ada."

"Stop. You're ruining it."

Afton grabs my hand. She's being uncharacteristically serious about this all of a sudden. "All I'm saying is, you can wait, if you want."

I pull my hand away. "What, you don't think I'm mature enough?" This is something we argue about a lot, whether I'm "old enough" to do certain things that Afton does.

Afton sighs. "You're not immature. You're just sixteen, and—"

"But you think you were more mature when you were sixteen."

"I think my first time was a mistake," Afton says softly.

I stare at her. "You do?"

"Come on, it was ridiculous," Afton admits. "It was in a *garage*. It wasn't romantic or sweet or special. And my second time, I—" She gets that look like she tastes something terrible. "Sometimes I want to have a long talk with sixteen-year-old me and tell her to make better choices."

"But you still have sex with Logan," I say.

Afton's blue eyes cloud over in a way that makes me think maybe sex with Logan isn't so great, either. "Yes."

"Is that a mistake?"

"No. But that's because I know Logan, and—"

"And I know Leo. We've been dating for six months."

"Wait, isn't it more like five months?" Afton asks.

"The point is, this is a fine choice." I fold the wine-colored shirt and the jean shorts carefully and set them on top of my dresser for tomorrow. "It's *my* choice. I'm choosing to have sex. With my boyfriend. Who I . . . really like. In a bed. Not in a garage."

"Okay, fine." Afton starts flipping through my shirts again, even though we already chose the one I would wear. Her movements are brisk, jerky. Upset again.

"I'm sorry," I murmur. "I didn't mean to—"

"It's fine." She smiles tightly. Subtext: it's not fine, but she doesn't want to talk about it anymore. "I'm happy for you," she says.

But she doesn't sound very happy.

5

My best date with Leo was like six weeks ago. Normally our "dates" are just hanging out at his place, but this time we actually went somewhere together. There's a boardwalk in Santa Cruz with amusement park rides and a long stretch of beach. We spent the first couple hours playing mini golf, of all things, at this indoor pirate-themed golf course. Leo was good at golf. I sucked, but I enjoyed Leo trying to console me every time I missed a shot, a little kiss, a hug, a touch. And I blamed him, of course, for keeping me so distracted.

"I just wanted you to feel good about yourself," I told him as we scarfed down some pizza for lunch later. "I had to lose so you could feel like you were winning."

"Is that right?" His honey-brown eyes were full of light and humor. He reached across the table and took my pizza-grease-stained hand in his. He has large hands, like big blocks on the ends of his arms. An artist's eye is trained to recognize shapes, and to mine, Leo's hand is made of solid squares and rectangles. But gentle.

"That's right."

"In that case, thank you," he said, and actually lifted my hand to his mouth and kissed it. "You're my good-luck charm, I guess."

But it was me who felt like I was winning.

He made me feel brave. Like if a guy like Leo liked me, I must be doing something right. And that made me feel like I could do anything. Be anything. Strong. Fearless. Attractive. Cool. The way I always saw Afton, but me this time. Me.

So then I went on the boardwalk rides with Leo, even though I don't like rides. I got tossed into the air, screaming in a fun way. I was whisked and whipped by a roller coaster, swung by one ride, spun by another, and I didn't barf, not once.

Leo played some of the carnival games, and because he's good at everything, he won more often than he lost. I was his good-luck charm.

But the best part was at the end: when we walked along the beach, holding cotton-candy-sticky hands. We didn't talk much. We took off our shoes and rolled up our pant legs and made a set of footprints in the sand, side by side. We played for a while—like kids, I guess—a kind of tag with the water, back and forth, laughing when it almost caught us. Then we let it catch us, and stood kissing while the waves rolled past our legs. Salt on Leo's lips. Golden glints in his tawny hair. The water shining as the sun began to set.

If my life has a top ten list, this is in the top three. Leo on the beach. It's the image that keeps coming back as I lie in bed tonight, thinking about tomorrow and the sex I'm determined to have, no matter what now, so Leo will be happy. I'll be happy, too, of course—this isn't all for him. I still don't know if I love Leo, like from-the-heart love him, but maybe I do. I think about the day on the beach and it makes me feel all warm inside. Tingly. Nice. That could be love. Maybe I'm putting too much pressure on the word.

What I do know is that I'm ready this time. Seriously. I'm ready.

Because Leo is a miracle, I tell myself.

And I want to believe.

6

Saturday afternoon. I'm nervous as I make my way into the pool area where (after some light internet stalking) I figured out that Leo's swim meet was being held. But it's a good nervous. I feel prepared this time. Ready, like I said. I even feel pretty. My hair has been tamed and braided over one shoulder. I'm wearing some light makeup and the prearranged outfit and a pair of strappy sandals that show off the pedicure Afton gave me. The shoes are Afton's, too. We don't have the same size bodies, so we've never been able to share clothes, but we do have the same size feet: seven and a half.

I trot those strappy sandals up to a seat in the bleachers. From above I spot Leo right away. His cowlick is covered by a swim cap, and his eyes with goggles, but I still recognize him by his height and the chest-forward way he strides along the edge of the pool. He's wearing a black Speedo with a bright blue letter Q on the side—Q for

Quicksilver, the name of his swim team.

I don't try to get his attention, and I don't text to tell him I'm here. I don't want him to know yet. I've been imagining a moment while he's swimming when he'll look up, and then he'll see me here, and I will wave and cheer, and he will smile and swim even faster.

He's gorgeous in the water, graceful in a way he isn't on solid ground. I compose a half dozen mental sketches of him swimming, the shapes filling my mind: the double arcs of his arms sluicing through the crystalline liquid, his legs trailing behind, the fierce set of his mouth as he pushes forward. I can almost understand his preoccupation with Michael Phelps. There's something mesmerizing about watching Leo do what he does best.

But he never looks up. When he's in the water he's completely focused, and when he's out of the water he concentrates on his teammates, encouraging them, calling out their names.

"Go, Kayla!" he screams during one of the girls' races. "You've got this, Kayla! You're killing it, Kayla! Go!"

I wonder if the swimmers can even hear what people shout at them, or if their ears are full of water. I guess it doesn't matter. The point is that people are cheering them on.

I feel proud when Leo wins first place in his division, like my presence has brought him good luck, like that day on the boardwalk. I'm happy for him, of course, but I'm also happy because now tonight's sex can be a celebration of his awesomeness. If he lost, it might feel like consolation sex, which sounds like less fun. The only problem is that I can't stay the night. My family is leaving for Hawaii at nine a.m. tomorrow morning.

Hawaii is turning out to be a major inconvenience in my life.

I wait until the meet is completely over—the medals handed out and everything—before approaching Leo. Outside the men's locker room I pause a moment to reapply my lip balm. I want my lips to be soft and smooth against his when we kiss. My heart is beating fast again. But good fast.

"Hello there," I imagine myself saying as he comes out. Or maybe I'll try to come up with something bold like I said that first day in his mother's gallery, like, "It must be exhausting, being that good at swimming."

This is it: I hear his voice from the hall that connects the men's and the women's locker rooms. He's talking to someone. He's laughing. This is my big moment.

I adjust my braid and check my breath: minty. The strappy sandals looked amazing. My toenails are gorgeous. This is as good as it gets. My body tenses. My feet start to walk around the corner to reveal myself.

"You know," Leo's saying, "my mom's out of town until Tuesday."

Something about the way he says it freezes my breath inside me. It's exactly the same—the same cadence to his voice, the same words, the same undercurrent beneath them.

My mom's out of town until Tuesday.

But my body is already moving around the corner, and I can't stop it, so I keep walking, and instantly get an eyeful of my boyfriend—my miracle, mine—leaning in to kiss another girl. They are both angled in perfect profile: Leo's sharp straight nose, his full lips, his cowlick. The girl's delicate chin. She's one of the swimmers, her hair still wet, leaving damp trails across the shoulder of her sweatshirt.

"That sounds promising," she says to Leo after they've kissed for an uncomfortable amount of time. "So we'll have your house all to ourselves." She has to crane her neck to smile up at him. Because she's so petite.

"You could even stay the night," he says.

"Wait." I find my voice. "That might get a little crowded."

I say this without even thinking, and much louder than I intend to. Leo and the girl swing to face me. Leo's eyes widen so dramatically I could laugh, if I thought I'd ever be capable of laughter again.

"Ada," he says, sounding breathless, but then he was just sucking face with someone else. There wasn't a lot of time for breathing properly.

I should say something scathing. That crowded comment was pretty good, but now I need something that will brutally cut him off at the knees. Something truly devastating.

"I wanted to surprise you," I state hoarsely. "You look . . . surprised." Epic fail. I spin around and stagger for the exit. The strappy sandals might be good for looking sexy, but they are shit for running.

And even worse, Leo is running after me. Alongside me, I realize. Talking to me. Although I'm not really registering what he's saying.

"Ada, stop!" he exclaims as I reach the main door. He pulls me away from the line of people leaving the pool. "Please stop. Talk to me."

I stop, if only because he said please. "I can't think of anything to say."

"I'm sorry if that hurt you just now," he begins.

"*If?* You're my boyfriend, and you were—"

Cheating. That's the word for it. Leo is cheating on me. I've been cheated on.

"No, it's not like that." He shakes his head, his honey-brown eyes sorrowful, like this is all a tragic misunderstanding. I feel an improbable flash of hope, like maybe it isn't like that—Leo cheating on me. Maybe I'm misinterpreting things somehow.

"We never established that I was your boyfriend, Ada," Leo says. "We didn't talk about being exclusive. I'm seeing now that we probably should have."

I let out an incredulous, unladylike snort. "We've been dating for six months!" I exclaim, even though it's only been five.

"I wouldn't call it dating," he says. "Do people even say that anymore?"

God. This is worse than cheating. This is Leo saying that I was never important enough to him to classify as his girlfriend. But I can't bring myself to believe that. Every moment I've spent with Leo lately suggests otherwise.

"Is this because I wouldn't have sex with you?" I whisper. "I turned you down last night, so for tonight you thought you'd find a girl who'd actually put out?"

What does that even mean, put out? Put out what, exactly?

"Oh my god, no!" Leo says in disgust. "How could you think that?"

I gesture impatiently toward the locker rooms, where the other girl is still standing there with an increasingly hurt expression.

"No," Leo protests. "I don't care that you didn't want to have sex with me. I mean, I was hoping you would, but it's fine. You weren't ready. I was okay with that."

"So you just—I don't know—found a girl who *was* ready?"

"I'm not assuming that she's going to have sex with me. I thought

I'd see what happens, go with it, you know."

"Oh, I know," I say. "But she—"

"I actually think you'd really like Kayla," he continues, the most nonsensical thing he's said so far. "Did you see her swim today? She's got the best form of any girl on the team. And she's really funny. She—"

"Please stop talking about Kayla," I say.

"Okay." He nods. Clears his throat. "I just think if you got to know her—"

"You said you loved me," I say, again too loudly, and someone passing by catches the words and hoots at us. We both redden. I cross my arms over my chest. "That was yesterday, that you said that. Less than twenty-four hours ago."

"I know. I didn't mean—"

"So you meant it like the way a person says they love peanut butter cups."

His eyebrows squeeze together in confusion. "I don't like peanut butter."

I close my eyes for a few seconds. "Fine. So maybe the way a person says they love a good cheeseburger." My stomach turns at the thought. The chlorine smell of the pool is so strong it makes me feel dizzy. I lean against the wall and take a deep breath.

Leo scratches at the back of his neck. "Yeah, I guess I meant it that way. I do like you, Ada. Really. You have to believe me. I meant it, what I said."

"So I'm the cheeseburger in this scenario. And she—" I gesture again toward the locker rooms.

"Kayla," he fills in.

"Thank you. Kayla. She's the shrimp cocktail."

"Actually, I'm allergic to shrimp," he says.

"Goodbye, Leo," I say. I push off from the wall and run for the door.

This time he doesn't run after me.

I'm halfway through the parking lot when I think of more I want to say. About how if you kiss someone regularly, if you go on (I do the calculations in my head) twenty or possibly twenty-one dates with a boy, over the course of five fucking months, it should be safe to assume that he's your boyfriend. And about honesty. And about communicating your expectations.

I turn around and march back to tell him this, to make sure that he understands I don't accept his half-assed excuses. But then I see Leo walking with the other girl—the hilarious and talented Kayla—and his arm is around her, and he's clearly trying to talk her down, too. And for some reason I duck behind a car to eavesdrop on them.

"I met her at one of my mom's art shows," Leo says as they pass me crouched behind a VW Bug. "I think she got a crush on me because she was obsessed with my mom's sculptures—and so many of them are of me. She's a nice girl, but we don't actually have a lot in common."

Subtext: unlike Kayla, who clearly has so much in common with Leo. Kayla is likable. A good swimmer. Funny. Athletic. Undeniably attractive.

"She looked upset," Kayla murmurs. "I felt so bad for her."

Oh, and great, Kayla is nice, too.

Leo smiles, a kid-seeing-a-baby-kitten type smile, because he's come to the same conclusion. "That's so sweet. You're a really good person, Kayla."

It's too much. I stand up. "You know what, fuck you, Leo," I scream, and everybody in the parking lot turns to stare at us. I shoot a killing glare at Kayla, nice or not. "And fuck you, too."

I've never said that before to anyone: *fuck you.*

Which is literally about sex.

Which is something I'm not going to be having anytime soon.

7

When I arrive home an hour later, I've calmed down a little, but not a lot. My first stop is the kitchen, where I find Afton and Abby at the table watching *Moana* on Abby's iPad in preparation for Hawaii. Pop is out somewhere, thank god, because this afternoon's developments call for drastic action. I grab a heavy-duty trash bag out of the pantry and head upstairs. A few minutes later I come down again lugging the trash bag, which is now full. I slip out the back door and into the yard.

By the time Afton comes outside to see what's going on, I'm halfway through the process of building a fire in the large cast iron bowl our family uses as a firepit. I found some firewood in the garage and gathered up dry grass and weeds to use as kindling. Once I have a good fire going, I open the trash bag and pull out a shirt. Leo's. It's a blue-and-green-plaid flannel. It's comfy. Even holding it away from myself I can detect Leo's boy smell on it, mixed with his musky cologne. Which I used to think was sexy. I used to hold this shirt to my face and breathe in and think about him.

I throw the shirt on the fire.

Afton sidesteps over and puts her hand on my shoulder, to let me know she's on board with whatever. "So we hate Leo now?"

I stare into the flames. "Yes."

"What happened at the swim meet?"

"I surprised him." I take another shirt from the trash bag. The wine-colored tee. I took it off upstairs. Afton instinctively reaches out to stop me from burning it, but she's too late. Onto the fire it goes.

"You surprised him, and . . ." prompts Afton.

"And he was kissing Kayla," I say.

Afton obviously doesn't know who Kayla is, but she understands sisterly loyalty. "Well then, screw Leo."

I smile grimly. "I think Kayla's got that covered."

I burn several other things in quick succession: photos of Leo and of Leo and me together, a few ripped-out pages from my sketchbook, the pair of red lacy underwear I bought today, so new they haven't been washed yet, the dried rose corsage I wore at prom a few weeks ago, followed by my prom dress, which takes a surprisingly short time to burn. Lace, it turns out, is highly combustible.

Then I get to the final item, the stuffed white horse that Leo won for me at the boardwalk at Santa Cruz. I hold it up and gaze into its glass-marble eyes.

Afton takes a step closer. "You don't have to—"

I toss the horse into the fire. It smokes and smokes, horrible black puffs that smell awful, like when something plastic ends up on the heating coil of the dishwasher. Then the wind shifts and blows the smoke directly at us.

"We're probably inhaling toxic chemicals right now," Afton says, but I don't move out of the path of the smoke. The horse finally catches fire and burns, its ears blackening, first one and then the other. Then the entire thing kind of melts into a sludge.

I cough. I'm being melodramatic. I know that. But I can't shake the urge to destroy everything in my life that has ever touched Leo. Those things are tainted now. They need to be cleansed.

"Did the horse have a name?" Afton asks somberly.

"Bucky."

"Farewell, Bucky the horse," Afton says.

The screen door bangs. It's Abby holding a bag of marshmallows. "Can we have s'mores?"

"Why not?" I say.

We put more wood on the fire until it's burning cleanly again. Then we find chocolate and graham crackers and settle around the firepit, roasting marshmallows on the metal poles we use for camping. Abby soon gets bored and goes back inside. Afton and I stay and watch the fire go through its stages, first hot and fierce and a little bit out of control, then steady and warm, then glowing embers. I scooch my chair close to the fire like I'm cold, even though it's 75 degrees outside. I wrap my arms around myself and stare into the flickering glow.

"Are you going to live?" Afton asks after a while. This is something Mom used to say when we were little and fell off our bikes or skinned our knees.

I scoff. "I'm not going to die over a boy, thank you very much."

"That's quite sensible of you."

I stir through the coals with a fire poker. "This whole time he was hooking up with other girls." It feels like a joke, like a bad plot twist in a movie, so predictable, so clichéd, that it couldn't be true.

"He's an asshole," Afton says.

"Yes, yes, he is," I agree wholeheartedly.

"So really it's a good thing."

I turn to look at my sister. "What? What's good about it?"

"That you didn't sleep with him. You deserve for your first time to be better than my first time. It should be special."

She's right, and I know it, but this also feels like an I-told-you-so.

"It *was* special," I snap. "I thought he loved me."

Afton arches an eyebrow at me. "Yeah, and yesterday you were freaked out about that because you didn't feel the same. But today you're pissed because he clearly didn't love you. The point is, it wasn't right between you."

My face burns. Leo doesn't love me. He never did. Sure, it's true that I don't love him, either, but that doesn't seem like an important distinction at the moment. I think about the way he told Kayla how we met. That's all I was to him. One of his mom's art groupies. A walking compliment. A fangirl.

Afton reads my expression and backpedals. "I get that it hurts, though. It's the principle of the thing, or whatever. I know."

"How would you know?" Afton's never been dumped. She's never been cheated on. Her boyfriend clearly adores her and doesn't have a difficult time with the definition of the word *boyfriend*. This kind of thing would never happen to Afton.

"I know because . . ." She stops herself, because she sees I'm right. "Trust me, it would have been a mistake, sleeping with Leo. You would have regretted it. So you should be glad."

"I'm a lot of things right now, but glad isn't one of them." What I am is tired of Afton telling me how to feel. Some part of my brain understands that my sister is only trying to help, but another part wants to punch her in her perfect upturned nose. Especially since Leo isn't here to get his nose punched. "You can't ask me to be happy about this, okay?"

"I get that," she says. "But in my experience—"

I hold up a hand. "This isn't your experience. It's *my* experience."

"Okay, but I—"

"I'm not you, Afton!" I burst out before she can get fully into the big-sister lecture on changing my perspective. "I'm not . . ."

Perfect is the word I don't say, the word that sticks in my mouth, because I know Afton won't like that. Perfect people hate to be called out on being perfect. Because being perfect isn't perfect. A perfect person needs to have just the right amount of flaws.

"What?" Afton's eyes become ice. "A slut? Is that what you're about to say?"

"No!" I say immediately, shocked. I've been taught never to say *slut*. The word feels dangerous in my head. "No. I did not say that."

"It seems like you were about to say it."

"I wasn't."

"That's not fair." Now Afton's cheeks are each stained with a blotch of nearly neon pink. She stands up and starts to pace. "It's not like I'm promiscuous, Ada. Yes, I've been with three guys in two years. And yes, the first two were big mistakes—you don't even know—but that's why I've been trying to tell you that you aren't ready for—"

"You don't get to tell me what I'm ready for," I interject. "I'm not like you," I say again.

Afton turns to face me. "How are you not like me? Enlighten me."

I scoff. She's got to be kidding me. "I mean, outside of the obvious differences. Everything always works out for you. That's not me. I have to think things through first. I *did* think this through. And tonight with Leo, it was going to be the one part of my life that I did right. This wasn't the same as hooking up with a stranger in a garage, or some rando boy at a party because you had too many wine coolers."

Afton stares at me silently for a minute. "Well, I'm sorry your plan to be better than me didn't work out the way you wanted it to."

She stalks off toward the house.

"That's not what I meant," I say, too late for Afton to hear. I shiver. The fire has burned out.

8

All day I replay our first conversation, from when Leo and I met, about a million times in my head. How I recognized him. How I went up and asked him if it was weird being his mom's muse. How I told him that I was an artist, too, and he seemed genuinely interested. Because of course he did. Leo, if nothing else, knows how to deal with artists.

Then after we talked for a while, he asked, "So do you know my mom?"

I'd stared at him blankly, unsure of how to answer his question because it seemed so obvious. Of course I knew her. That was why I was there. "Yeah, I'm a huge fan," I said finally.

I actually said that I was a *fan*. That's the word I used. God.

"I mean, have you met her, in real life?" he asked.

"Oh. No," I said, my cheeks heating. "I just admire her enormously."

"You should meet her."

"That's not necessary," I protested, but he'd already grabbed my hand and was towing me over to where his mother stood in the back corner, next to a woman in a white linen dress who was drinking a glass of red wine. I was momentarily distracted from my panic by the feel of Leo's enormous fingers enclosing mine. He pulled me right up to Diana Robinson like it was no biggie. Which I guess it wasn't, for him.

"There you are, Leo," Diana said, as if he hadn't been parked in a chair directly in her line of sight the entire evening. "And who's this?"

All eyes turned to me expectantly. Even Leo didn't know my name at this point. I had forgotten to tell him.

"I'm Ada," I got out with difficulty. "Ada Bloom."

"She's an artist," Leo said.

Diana smiled, a real smile, as warm as Leo's hand that I was still inexplicably holding. "Ada Bloom is an artist's name."

"Thank you." With my free hand I tucked a strand of flyaway straw hair behind my ear. Looking at Diana was like looking at a piece of art herself. She was wearing a little black dress with a beaded necklace that sparkled under the gallery lights; her bobbed hair waved around her face in something that reminded me of flapper fashion from the twenties; her lips a bright, well-defined red, the same color as her heels. I wished I'd worn nicer clothes. I was wearing fricking jeans and my purple art shirt, topped by a somewhat ratty gray cardigan my grandmother had knitted for me years ago.

And Diana Robinson was looking at me.

"I'm a . . . huge fan," I breathed. "I mean, I love your work. Every time I look at one of your sculptures, I see a detail I never noticed before."

"Oh? Like what?" she asked, but not like she was challenging me. Like she genuinely wanted to know.

I turned and pointed at the nearest statue: kid Leo reading Proust. "Like his shoelace on the left foot. It's about to come untied. So many people would just make it so the shoelaces are the way you'd expect them to be, tied up neat, or maybe untied, because he's a little kid. But about to become untied is kind of brilliant."

I was talking too much. It's a problem.

The woman in the white dress made a noise in the back of her throat. "You have a sharp eye. Do you sculpt?"

"I draw," I explained. "Portraits, mostly."

"Well, I'd love to see your work sometime," she said.

This is something people say all the time, when they find out that you're an artist: I'd love to see your work. Which always feels to me a bit presumptuous. Sharing your work is like showing people a piece of you. An intimate piece. But with this woman, the request felt different.

"Me," I said. "Why?"

Diana Robinson chuckled. "She's the gallery owner."

"Oh." My eyes widened. "Oh. Well, I don't have anything I could . . . I'm not a professional artist or anything. I'm not—"

"But you obviously will be," the woman said. "Take my card."

I was worried she was going to spill red wine on her white dress while she dug into her bag, but she didn't. She handed me a simple, heavy card, where cleanly printed in silver letters was the name Eileen Watts, Watts Gallery, and her phone number and email address.

Later I taped the card to my bedroom wall, where I always look at it and think, *Someday.*

"What else?" Leo asked after the conversation with Diana and Eileen moved to other things and I kind of backed away.

"Else?"

The corner of his mouth lifted. "What other details did you notice?"

I bit my lip. "Let's see. You have a mole on the side of your neck. Not anything big or hairy or gross, just a little dot halfway up on the left side."

He turned his head and pulled back the collar of his hoodie to reveal the mole, just where I said it would be.

"Your second toe is a tiny bit longer than your big toe," I said.

He grinned. I smiled, too, but I was embarrassed. Here I was describing parts of his body like I knew what was underneath his clothes.

"I promise I'm not a stalker," I said. "I just pay attention to your mom's work."

"What else?" he said.

I laughed. It was the first time I'd ever used that laugh, the nervous one, which doesn't really sound like me. I mentioned the cowlick.

"Do you want to come over to my house sometime?" Leo said then.

"Yes," I squeaked.

God. I was so pathetic. I was so naive. I was so wrong.

9

I've been comforting myself by imagining a scenario in which Leo shows up on my front lawn and shouts *I'm sorry* up at my window, like a scene in a romantic comedy. He'll also yell that he's made a terrible mistake, and if I will just forgive him he'll make it up to me, and Kayla doesn't mean anything to him. Then I plan to open my window and scream back, *You don't mean anything to me, either! Go away, loser!* and slam the window shut again. No kissing and making up for me. I don't require a happy ending, only some small form of petty vengeance.

But, sadly, Leo never appears.

"What's up with you?" Pop asks. "You're being quieter than usual."

"I'm a quiet person," I say, although that's not entirely true. I'm only quiet around people I don't know. Around Pop I'm generally talkative. "I'm fine."

Pop and Abby are in my bedroom, helping me pack for Hawaii. Although helping is not quite what Abby is doing. She keeps bouncing on the bed and suggesting weird stuff for me to bring, like my large wooden art easel that won't have a prayer of fitting in my suitcase, or the white feather boa that's draped over one of my bedposts, a leftover from a birthday party years ago. "To remind you of home," Abby says, flinging it around my neck.

"We're only going to be gone for like a week," I remind her.

"How many days is a week?" Abby wants to know.

"Seven. But we're going to be gone nine, counting the travel days."

Abby counts it out on her fingers. "Nine days is a lot," she decides.

Yes, it is. Thank god. It's just what I need, nine days with an entire ocean between me and Leo. "I won't get homesick, Abby. Trust me."

"It's too bad you burned up Bucky," Abby adds mournfully. "You could have brought him instead. He was snuggly."

"Bucky?" Pop looks confused.

"Ada got mad at her horse," Abby explains. "I don't think it was his fault, but she burned him up anyway, in the firepit, because Leo's an asshole."

Pop's mouth opens, but no words emerge. He turns to me, eyebrows raised.

I cringe and hold my hands up, like I surrender, arrest me. "I don't want to talk about it?"

Thankfully that's when Afton struts into the room—without so much as knocking, of course—and everyone's attention shifts. Because all Afton has covering her body is a bright red bikini.

"Um, why are you wearing your underwears?" Abby asks.

A legitimate question.

"Oh no, that's too little to be underwear," I say. "I'm not sure what that is, actually. I don't think it's clothing."

"What, is this too *slutty* for you?" Afton says archly.

"Whoa!" Pop exclaims. "You know we don't use that word."

"Oh, grow up," I mutter to Afton.

"I am grown up. Unlike you, who is so very immature."

"Are you two having a fight?" Abby asks.

"God, that's hurting my eyes," Pop says, looking away like Afton's bikini has become the sun, too bright to stare at directly.

"Aren't you cold?" asks Abby.

"Well, yes." Afton runs her hands up and down her arms, where there are, in fact, goose bumps. "But I won't be cold in Hawaii."

If she's trying to prove some sort of point, I'm not sure what it is.

"You're not wearing that in Hawaii, young lady," Pop says. "You'll give your mother a heart attack."

Afton gives him a cool, assessing look. "I'm legally an adult, sorry. I can wear what I want, when I want. And when did you and Mom become such prudes?"

Pop looks even more shocked than he did when his five-year-old cheerfully uttered the word *asshole*. Afton has never mouthed off to him before. He stares at her in stunned bewilderment.

Afton pretends not to notice. She turns to me, holding up a hanger that has a different bathing suit on it, a white one-piece with a neckline that plunges nearly to the belly button. "Which one?"

"What are you doing? There's no need to take things out on Pop."

"Oh, come on." Afton turns to gaze at herself in the mirror on my closet door. "I'm feeling the red. It's less *careful*, you know? Less boring."

Oh, so Afton's calling me boring. I grab my robe and throw it unceremoniously at my sister. "Get out of my room. No one here wants to see that."

Afton scoffs but retreats to her own bedroom, slamming the door behind her.

"All right, what exactly is going on here?" asks Pop.

"Afton and Ada are having a fight!" exclaims Abby excitedly.

I wave my little sister off. "Not really. Afton's just digging up drama. We'll be fine."

"Did something happen with Leo?" Pop looks worried.

I consider telling him and decide against it. I always assumed I could talk to Pop about anything. But, it turns out, not this. If I think about the look on his face if I confess it all, it feels like too much, for both of us. I swallow down a lump in my throat. "Seriously, Pop, I don't want to get into it. Let's just pack, okay?"

I can see in his eyes that he's deciding whether to push or not, to try to make me tell him or leave it. In the end he goes with leaving it. "Okay. But I'm here if you need me, Ada. I'd be happy to bestow my relationship wisdom upon you. Ask, and you shall receive."

"Maybe later," I say lightly.

Pop finally drops it and returns to organizing my luggage. He likes to roll the clothes into neat little tubes, which somehow allows him to cram more into the carry-on suitcase than should be physically possible. My mom always makes our family travel with carry-ons only. She doesn't like to wait for luggage at the airport.

"Wait," Pop says after a minute. "Don't you have a swimsuit?"

I shake my head. "I don't own one."

"Ada!" he exclaims like I am personally offending him with my appalling lack of swimwear. "We live in California."

"I'm aware."

"You can go to the beach any time you want."

I shrug. The beach makes me think of Santa Cruz. Which makes me think of Leo.

"We have a *pool*," Pop says.

"I know. I swam in it, like twice, when we first moved here." That was around the time Abby was born. Swimming just isn't my thing. Especially now. God. I never want to set eyes on a pool again. Because that of course also makes me think of Leo.

It's a good thing that I'm escaping to Hawaii, which is made up entirely of pools and beaches.

Pop huffs. "How do you not own a single swimsuit?"

"I used to." It was black, if I remember correctly, with a white diagonal stripe across the chest. I grew out of it and never got around to procuring a new one. That time I swam in Leo's pool, I did it in my underwear. Which felt bold and sexy at the time. I swallow. "I could get one—maybe, somewhere . . . before tomorrow morning. Hmm. This seems unlikely."

Pop apparently decides it's not important. "No worries. If there's one thing a person can buy in Hawaii, it's a bathing suit." He sighs wistfully. "I love Hawaii. Your mother and I had our honeymoon in Kauai."

"I remember. I was mad because you didn't take us."

"We had a beautiful time there. One morning we got up early, just as the sun was coming up, and we went paddleboarding. It was so tranquil out there on the water. It was an almost spiritual experience."

That sounds amazing. It also sounds like just what I need. "You'll have to teach me," I say.

His faraway gaze focuses on me. "Teach you?"

"How to paddleboard."

His mouth tightens. "Oh. About that," he says quietly. "I'm not coming this time."

"Not coming paddleboarding?"

"Not coming. To Hawaii. We've had a last-minute change to the schedule."

I stare at Pop breathlessly. "What? But you always come to the STS conference."

"I can't this time. It turns out that they need me at work."

Abby stops jumping on the bed and flops down onto the bedspread. "Wait, why can't you come, Poppy?"

He strokes her hair. After taking a minute to consider, he says, "Well, you know that I'm a nurse."

Not just a nurse, really, but the best emergency room nurse at El Camino Mountain View. But let's be modest about it.

"And June is when people start doing more dangerous things like hiking and camping and rock climbing, and they end up needing emergency care more often than usual," he continues. "And what would those people do if Poppy were on vacation when they needed help?"

"The same thing people do when they need surgery when Mom's on vacation," comes Afton's voice from the doorway. This time she's wearing a pajama shirt and boxers, thank god. "They get it done by somebody else, and they're fine."

"And you always come to the STS conference," I say again. "Plus, you've been working so hard lately. You could use the R and R."

"What's R and R?" asks Abby, adorably, because she can't fully pronounce her *R*'s yet.

"Rest and relaxation." Pop rubs at his eyes like he's tired just thinking about work, which proves my point, but he's already saying no even though he knows I'm right. "I'm sorry, girls. We're short staffed this year. I can't get away."

Afton and I exchange tense glances, the friction between us momentarily placed on hold while we assess this new information. I don't believe his flimsy excuse about work for a second. This has to be about Mom. Maybe they even had a fight between last night and now, one that we don't know about. Maybe they're breaking up.

"What does Mom think about you not going?" Afton asks, because she's come to the same conclusion.

"She understands. Of course she does," Pop answers a bit sadly.

This is not good. Not good at all. "But, Pop—" I start.

"You probably don't even want to go to the conference," Afton theorizes.

"That's silly," Pop says. "Why wouldn't I want to go?"

I can think of a reason: Because Hawaii is where he and Mom were in all kinds of intense, beautiful love, and they're not in that kind of love anymore.

"Because you hate having to spend an entire week with a bunch of judgmental, stuck-up surgeons who think nurses are morons, and male nurses are even worse," says Afton.

Pop's face goes slightly red. "No. That's not—"

"Then why?" Afton asks sharply.

"I told you," he says. "I have to work."

"But this year is Hawaii. You love Hawaii." I hate that my voice is a whine, but I can't help it. Pop is my favorite person. I know it shouldn't be a kind of competition between who I like best in my family, but if I'm being honest, there's no contest. It's Pop. Not Mom or Afton or even Abby.

Pop is my rock.

"I do love Hawaii," he sighs, agreeing with me but not agreeing. "You girls are going to have so much fun."

10

"Hey, I'm sorry about what I said yesterday," I try out as an apology Sunday morning. The plane is about to lift off from SFO. Afton and I are stuck sitting together, seats 17 A and B, respectively, and while I'm still moderately pissed off at my older sister, for reasons I can't quite articulate, I don't think I can endure the entire six-hour flight with the two of us actively fighting. So I'm waving the white flag. Being the bigger person. Making nice.

Afton pulls out a compact and reapplies her lipstick. "What part?"

"What?"

"What part of what you said, exactly, are you sorry for?" She presses her lips together to blot them and clicks the compact closed.

"Um, all of it?"

"Hmm. Okay." Afton starts texting someone. Probably Logan.

Because Afton, lucky her, still has a boyfriend.

"You're not supposed to use your phone right now," I say. "It interferes with the plane's radar or something."

Afton sighs and puts her phone back into her purse, but she doesn't turn it off or put it into airplane mode first. The plane starts to pick up speed. I try to steady my breathing as it thrusts itself into the air. I've never loved flying. I don't like being in tight, enclosed spaces where, if something were to go horribly wrong, I'd be trapped with no way of escape. I only get through it by reminding myself that it's temporary.

But this is a six-hour flight.

"Have you heard from Leo?" Afton stares out the little window as the ground drops away beneath us. She has the window seat. She always gets the window seat, and I always get the aisle. This feels like a metaphor for something.

I exhale through my mouth slowly before I answer. "No. And I don't want to hear from him, ever again."

"Good," says Afton.

So we're on speaking terms again. I sigh in relief. "The thing that kills me is how he always said the right things, all that progressive, woke, feminist bullshit about respecting me and liking me for who I was, but underneath that he was just a cliché of a douchebag, after all." I've also been taught not to say the word *douchebag*, because the reason it's supposed to be an insult is that it's associated only with women. The same way that *pussy* is a slur. But the word *asshole* just isn't covering it when it comes to Leo. "So you were right. It's a good thing."

"Right," says Afton vaguely.

"This trip is just what I need," I say, almost cheerful now. "Even if Pop's not coming."

We haven't talked about that yet, Pop not coming and what it could mean. Because we haven't been talking.

"And even if it is for the stupid conference," I add.

"Excuse me," comes our mother's voice from the seat in front of us, making us both jump. "This conference is going to be amazing." She shifts to a higher-pitched voice to represent us: "Thank you, Mom, for taking us on this wonderful adventure."

"Thank you, Mom," Afton and I drone in unison.

"That's better." Mom obviously thinks the conference is super exciting. For the rest of us, the conference largely consists of waiting for Mom to become available after the meetings and social mingling she's expecting to do, punctuated by a few touristy trips they book in advance for the families—like the time we took a boat ride through the bayou when the conference was in New Orleans. Or the Vatican in Rome. Or the Christ the Redeemer statue in Brazil. But the food is usually good, and we always stay in the best hotels. This time the conference is at a Hilton that has like twenty swimming pools and its own lagoon and a myriad of gift shops and restaurants. I looked it up online earlier, and it seems like a literal paradise, swaying palm trees and gleaming blue water.

I want to play with watercolors. And I want to go paddleboarding, to find that "spiritual experience" Pop was talking about. And I want to try to forget that Leo ever existed.

"Maybe you could find some cute boy to have sex with," Afton says then. "I've heard rebound sex is awesome."

I peer around the seat to see if Mom is still listening, but she has her noise-canceling headphones on again. She's working—still, perpetually working—hunched over her laptop with the presentation for the conference open on the screen. It's weird how she can do that: pop in for a tiny part of a conversation, to prove that she's participating, I guess, and then disappear into her own world again. Next to her, Abby is also wearing headphones, watching a movie on her tablet with the subtitles on. When I asked her why earlier, she said that she was teaching herself to read.

"I don't want to have rebound sex," I whisper to Afton stiffly.

Afton twists a long strand of her hair around her finger and releases it. "What? You said you were ready. Maybe in Hawaii there will be a boy you'll want to get busy with. You never know."

I'm about to argue that yes, in fact, I do know, but that's when I realize that Afton doesn't mean it. She's perfectly aware that I'm not considering having sex anymore. She's just trying to mess with me, because she thinks we're still fighting. Because she's still mad.

Why is she still mad?

"Look, I said I was sorry," I say in exasperation.

"And I said it's okay."

"Meaning that it's okay, you forgive me?"

Afton regards me coolly. "Meaning that it's okay that you're sorry."

Oh. That's not the same thing at all.

"Ladies and gentlemen, the captain has turned off the fasten seat belt sign," says a voice from the speaker over our heads. "Please feel free to move about the cabin."

Afton unbuckles her seat belt, wriggles out of her jacket, and reclines her chair as far back as it will go. Then she rolls up her jacket into a makeshift pillow, pops on an eye mask, and curls against the gray plastic wall. Conversation apparently over.

I poke her. "You're supposed to have your seat belt on."

She lifts the mask. "The seat belt sign is off."

"Yes, but you're supposed to keep it on while you're seated. In case of turbulence."

Afton stares at me for a long minute. Then she says, still totally straight-faced but I can tell this time that she absolutely means it: "Oh, Ada. Don't be such a fucking square."

I inhale so sharply I can hear the air sucking into my lungs. What's happening to us? We've never been the kind of sisters who try to hurt each other. We argue sometimes, give each other crap, of course, when called upon, but it always felt like we were on the same team. Sisters. Best friends.

"All righty, then," I murmur, blinking fast because my eyes have started to burn. *Bitch*, I think, but I know that if I say that there will be a real showdown, and I won't be the winner.

Afton slides the eye mask back into place and appears to go to sleep.

I stare at her peaceful face. It's not fair. I didn't actually call her a slut yesterday. Maybe she thought I was implying it, but I didn't mean it that way. And I'd just had my heart broken—sort of. I was upset.

The air thingy on the ceiling starts making a whistling sound, and I reach up and twist it until it stops. At that exact moment the plane rises and drops suddenly, like it's riding a wave. Once, and then twice. Instantly I become very aware of everything else around me: the baby crying a few rows behind us. A tray rattling. The smell of burnt coffee wafting out of the back.

The plane dips again. My stomach lurches.

"Ladies and gentlemen," comes the captain's voice from the speaker. "We seem to be experiencing a bit of rough air. We'll be through it and on to smoother skies shortly, but in the meantime, take your seats and fasten your seat belts."

Afton shifts and murmurs something unintelligible.

I clutch at the armrest. The seat belt light goes on, accompanied by a perky ding.

Turbulence ahead.

11

Thankfully by the time we actually reach Hawaii, Afton and I are both in better moods. It's hard to maintain a foul mood in Hawaii. It's too beautiful to sulk.

"This hotel is ah-mazing!" I exclaim as we drag our suitcases through the door of our suite. The room has all the major amenities: big-screen TV, mini refrigerator, bar. Tropical but tasteful decor. Fluffy white comforters on the queen beds, which sport high-thread-count Egyptian cotton sheets. Granite countertops in the spacious bathroom. A walk-in closet. A Keurig. A large mahogany desk. It's definitely a contender for one of the best rooms we've ever stayed in, and we've stayed in some epic hotels.

But what makes it *ah-mazing* is the view.

The far wall is one big window—well, a sliding glass door that opens to the balcony and one big window. Palm trees frame the glass, their silhouettes dark against the bright sky. The water shimmers blue and silver in the distance against the rich green of the hotel lawn.

Right away I go out on the balcony. Our room is on the sixth floor, and far below me there's a long stretch of close manicured grass and a twisting stream (part of a golf course?), then a paved path that leads to the beach and a gentle hill topped by two benches and a large statue of Buddha that gleams white in the afternoon sun.

My fingers itch for the brand-new set of watercolors I brought along.

"We should go rub his belly." Afton steps up beside me. She tilts her head back and breathes deeply, taking in the fragrant sea air.

It's all going to be okay now, I think. The trip will be what we both need. I'll get some distance between me and Leo, spend some time in the sun, paint a bunch of landscapes, relax, eat, drink, and be merry, and yesterday's humiliation will fade away like it never happened. Afton will forgive me for the offensive thing that I didn't actually say, and we'll go back to normal.

"I don't see any cute boys I want to have sex with," I say with an exaggerated sigh.

Afton's perfect forehead creases in the middle. I hold my breath, waiting to see if she'll take my comment for what it is: a tentative peace offering.

"Well, we only just got here," she says after a minute. "There's still time."

Of course she doesn't mean it. I certainly don't mean it. But we act like we do.

Satisfied that I'm making progress with her, I go back inside. The connecting door to Mom's room has been flung open, and Abby is jumping between Afton's bed and mine.

"This . . . is . . . nice," Abby gasps.

I nod. "You're right, bug. This is nice."

"Dinner's in an hour," comes our mother's voice from the other room. "We need to get cleaned up and head right over."

I go to the door of Mom's room and watch her unpack. She's spent the entire day in grimy airports and on bumpy airplanes and in a less-than-stellar taxi, but she manages to look completely put together, the top half of her bobbed blond hair pulled back in a tortoiseshell barrette, her sweater set and khaki pants still crisp and unwrinkled. She carefully hangs up a row of her expensive, tasteful blouses in the closet, two pairs of pressed black slacks, a little black cocktail dress, and a black formal gown for the awards night at the end of the week. There's a lot of black in my mother's wardrobe, because it matches everything so she doesn't have to give it too much thought.

"Do we have to have dinner with the entire group?" Afton protests from behind me. "This is supposed to be a vacation."

"We always have dinner with the entire group the first night." Mom crosses back to her suitcase and withdraws a silk robe I've never seen before. It's white with a red-and-black cherry blossom pattern on it.

"That's pretty," I say.

"What's pretty?" Afton comes around me and over to inspect the robe. She strokes the fabric down one of the arms. "Ooh, shiny."

"Thanks," Mom says stiffly, and hangs the robe up with her dresses and shirts. She has never been good at taking a compliment, even about her clothes. "Ruthie found it at Nordstrom's last week."

"We could get room service," says Afton.

I don't even know why she's trying to get out of dinner. It's like she doesn't know Mom at all.

"No," Mom says flatly.

See.

"You could say I wasn't feeling well," Afton suggests.

"We always have dinner all together the first night," Mom says again.

"Will there be ice cream?" Abby inquires.

"I bet there will be pineapple," I say. Pineapple is Abby's self-proclaimed favorite fruit. "And there might be—I don't know—some *cute boys* for us to assess at dinner," I direct at Afton.

"Cute boys?" Mom frowns at us. "But don't you both have boy-friends?"

I stopped trying to keep Mom up to date on the current happenings of my life a long time ago. I don't enlighten her this time, either. I'm not in the mood for a speech about how heartbreak is a natural part of life, or about what a strong and capable woman I am, and how I don't need another person—a boy, especially—to be my awesome self. Mom is great at those kinds of speeches, and it all sounds wonderful and encouraging if you feel like you really are those things, strong, capable, independent, but otherwise it feels like you're even more destined to fail.

The corner of Afton's mouth turns up in the ghost of a smile. "Okay, fine, if there will be cute boys there," she says, like I'm doing her a favor. "I'll get dressed."

The Hilton Waikoloa Village is so large they have a tram for the guests to ride from one part to the others, and a little boat, too, that you can get around in. Our family is staying in the Ocean Tower at the far side. We take the tram to where dinner is supposed to be—the "Grand Staircase," an outdoor space at the bottom of some impressive marble stairs. The room is like a giant garden trellis that sticks out into the lagoon, a waterfall cascading in the background and soft, indistinguishable ukulele music floating through the air. The sun is going down when we arrive, a flare of orange against the distant indigo ocean.

I take a quick photo on my phone to re-create later in watercolor.

"Oh my dog," breathes Abby—her curse of choice. She gazes in wonder at the row of buffet tables off to one side. "Look! There's pineapple *and* ice cream."

"Hello! Good to see you!" Mom starts calling out to her colleagues before we are even halfway down the stairs. "How have you been?"

I brace myself for awkwardness. I've grown up seeing these people every year—the same faces, the same voices, the same air kisses and hugs. Mostly the group is composed of older couples who've been coming to the conference since forever, their children already grown. At forty-six, Mom is one of the younger members of the Society of Thoracic Surgeons. This means that Afton and I have been cooed over and had our cheeks pinched a lot over the past—I do some quick math—eleven STS conferences. You just kind of have to grin and bear it.

"Oh my goodness!" a lady exclaims as Mom ushers us down the rest of the stairs. "Are these your girls?"

"I mean, who else would we be?" Afton mutters under her breath.

Mom gives her a look that's a warning shot. Afton and I both step forward, pushing Abby out in front of us like a sacrificial offering.

"Hello," we say in unison. "Good to see you!"

The next half hour is pretty much this process over and over ad nauseum, until everyone separates into their smaller circles—those colleagues they hang out with every year. Mom's inner circle is made up of the following:

Jerry Jacobi, who is supposedly a brilliant doctor, but inevitably drinks too much at these events and starts talking too loudly, and then his wife, Penny, starts giggling nervously and making excuses for him, and then their daughter, Kate (a divorcée in her late thirties) starts rolling her eyes like she wishes she were far, far away from her mortifying parents.

Max Ahmed, the chief of surgery from somewhere on the East Coast, accompanied by his wife, Amala, and their eleven-year-old granddaughter, Siri, who never stops talking about her YouTube channel.

Marjorie Pearson, an eighty-nine-year-old badass single lady who was one of the first black women ever to study heart surgery at Princeton. I kind of want to be her, minus the cutting-people-open part. She retired years ago, so she doesn't really participate in the conference-y part of the conference so much as she comes to hang out with old friends and go on all the excursions.

And finally there's Billy Wong, his wife, Jenny, and their kids: nine-year-old Peter and six-year-old Josie. We know Billy and his family well because we see them all year round; Billy practices cardiology at Stanford with my mom. He and Mom did their residencies at UC Davis at the same time. Mom calls Billy her "work husband," and she technically spends more time with Billy than she does with Pop. Or us.

I like Billy. He's upbeat and funny and nice. He's one of the good ones, Mom says.

We spend about a half hour chatting and catching up with Mom's circle. Everyone expresses surprise and dismay that Pop isn't here. Mom explains why Pop had to stay behind so smoothly, and with real regret in her voice, too, that it makes me feel instantly better about the Pop situation. Mom's not a liar, or any kind of amazing actress.

Maybe things at home are fine.

Afton and I could simply be paranoid.

Finally Dr. Asaju (the surgeon in charge of the conference) calls everyone to order, and we take our seats.

"I'd like to welcome the members of the Society of Thoracic Surgeons to our thirty-sixth annual conference," Dr. Asaju begins. "I hope this week will be informative, restful, and most of all, inspiring. I look forward to seeing you all bright and early tomorrow morning at the conference center directly behind us. Please pick up your name badges, your schedules, and your tote bags first thing. There will be pastries and coffee available in every room for the morning session. Lunches will be provided in one of the ballrooms, but you're on your own for dinner until awards night at the end of the week."

Afton heaves a sigh, and I have to agree. Awards night is the worst. We all have to dress in formalwear and sit through like a dozen awards for things we don't know anything about. It's the most grueling part of the trip, every time.

Dr. Asaju presses his hands together in a prayer-like gesture. "Now I'll stop talking, because I know you've all traveled a long way today and want to get settled in. Enjoy the conference," he concludes. "Let's eat!"

"Yay!" cheers Abby, and I'm right there with her. I haven't eaten since the plane.

We beeline for the buffet. There's so much food I don't know where to start: Three different salads, pasta, rice, and potatoes. Beef. Chicken. Fish. Hawaiian-style pork. Piles of dinner rolls and giant bowls of fruit salad. And the dessert table stacked high with cheesecakes and pineapple upside-down cakes and a Hawaiian type of coconut pudding and cookies and brownies and parfait.

"You'd think none of these doctors ever heard of a heart attack before," Afton says as we make our way through the line.

"Right?" But we're both secretly thrilled. Mom and Pop have always been woefully inadequate parents when it comes to dessert.

We load our plates and eat like we're starving, go back again for multiple desserts, and then sit making small talk with our bellies way too full.

"Hey, where's Michael?" Afton asks out of the blue.

I'd almost forgotten about Michael—Billy and Jenny's oldest child. Michael is in college. He's also a carbon copy of Billy the way Afton is a replica of Mom—tall and slim, with the same dark hair and friendly smile as Billy. Afton had a crush on Michael off and on over the years, but a crush from afar, of course, because he's so much older than she is.

Billy smiles regretfully. "I don't think Michael's going to make it this year. I booked him a ticket, but he just graduated, and he's got his hands full with a summer internship." He glances around the table like, *These kids today, right?*

"I always thought he was a bright young man. What now?" Marjorie asks.

Billy's face breaks into a proud smile. "Med school."

The whole table practically ejaculates at this utterly foreseeable news. "Following in Papa's footsteps, eh?" beams Max.

"Not entirely." Mom is the one talking now, waving around her forkful of cheesecake. "Michael wants to be a family practitioner."

"Oh dear." That's obviously the incorrect career path for Michael.

They all discuss better possibilities for a while: if not surgery, because of course not everyone is born to cut, then something specialized, oncology or podiatry or prosthodontics. I tune out until the topic suddenly shifts to how Afton has recently graduated, too, from high school.

"With honors," Mom adds. "Top of her class."

"Congratulations," says Max. "Where do you intend to go to university?"

Afton glances up from where she's been texting someone under the table. Probably Logan again. "I've been accepted to Stanford," she answers demurely. We're lucky that way. Because Mom teaches as well as practices medicine at Stanford Hospital, getting into Stanford is kind of a given.

"Ah, so your mother will be able to keep her eye on you," says Marjorie.

I try not to smile at the idea of Mom ever keeping her eye on Afton.

"Do you also want to get into medicine?" asks Marjorie.

Afton frowns, still texting. "No, I'm thinking pre-law."

"And how about you?" Marjorie turns her attention to me.

"Oh." I hate this question. I like a lot of things, and it's so much pressure to try to choose just one. "I want to be an artist?" I say finally.

"I mean, I *am* an artist. I work in charcoal, mostly, but I also sculpt and do watercolors and some oils and . . . So in college I think I want to study art, obviously, and maybe history, which is my other great love, so maybe that will turn into some kind of academic form of employment . . . but I also love reading, so maybe literature? I'm also thinking about getting into writing comics."

"She's only sixteen," Mom interjects. "She has a few years to pick a respectable profession."

By which she means a job that could make me some decent money. Like not-art, or anything creative or fanciful or that I actually care about.

"I want to be a diplomat," chimes in Abby, and the whole table melts at her utter precociousness, and then the spotlight is blessedly off me.

I scoot my chair closer to Afton, who puts her phone away with a sigh. She looks bored. "See any cute guys?" I ask quietly as the conversation at the table moves on to medical topics again.

She drops her chin into her hand. "No. I'm sorry Michael's not here."

I'm not sorry. The last thing I need is Afton suggesting that I sleep with a much older college boy who happens to be the son of my mom's closest colleague. Not that such a thing would even be possible. Michael Wong's way out of my league.

But then, I think, so was Leo. Maybe that was the real problem all along.

"I thought you didn't approve of college boys," I remind Afton.

She tugs her hand through her long waterfall of pale hair and settles it over one shoulder, her expression neutral. "He just graduated, so he's not a college boy anymore. And have you ever taken a good look at Michael Wong's ass?"

"Uh, no, can't say that I have." It feels wrong, reducing a person to the state of their backside.

"It's perfection. Too bad for you, Ada. Michael would be the perfect rebound."

"Uh-huh." She's definitely still messing with me. But I'm determined to go along with it. "Yes, it's terrible that he couldn't make it this year," I say fake-mournfully. "He might have been just what the doctor prescribed."

We peruse the other tables. There are, quite simply, no eligible males our own age.

I sigh. "This is pathetic. You'd think there'd be a hot guy on the waitstaff, but no."

"Poor, poor Ada," Afton says, patting my shoulder. Then she spots a familiar face a few tables back. "Oh, wait. Look, there's Nick Kelly. But isn't he, like, twelve?"

"He's the same age as me—well, a little younger," I correct her. "He always has his birthday at the conference, remember? He'll be sixteen this week."

She smirks. "Do you remember when Nick got lost in Rio?"

"Yeah." I was ten that year, and Nick going missing in the middle of this enormous city in a country where none of us spoke the language and the adults all losing their shit over it had been a welcome piece of drama in my life at the time.

"Where is he?" I look around.

"Two tables over, one down," Afton directs, staring at him over my shoulder. Then she seems to come to some kind of decision. "No," she concludes. "He's not fuckable."

"Hey, that's not nice," I protest, although I'm not surprised by this verdict. When Nick was thirteen, he smelled funny and was so thin I worried that he was starving to death—"a beanpole" is how Marjorie Pearson labeled him, as in "Where's the beanpole? Better keep an eye on that kid"—but Nick's not so bad. "When did you become a mean girl?" I ask Afton.

She actually looks mildly ashamed now that I've called her out. "You're right. I guess we shouldn't judge the book by its cover."

I sneak a peek at Nick Kelly. He's staring at his phone below the table, probably playing a game, though, instead of texting. Nick and I are the same age, but ironically I don't know him as well as I know Jerry or Marjorie or any of the other grown-ups. I consider myself a shy person, an introvert, but Nick is worse—or maybe not shy so much as too preoccupied by his own thing to bother getting to know anyone else. No matter where we go in the world, Paris or New Orleans or Shanghai, Nick mostly stays in the hotel room playing video games.

He looks like it, too. Look up the word *gamer* in the dictionary, and there will be a rough approximation of Nicholas Kelly. His skin is pale, like he's never been touched by the rays of the sun. He's filled out a little since the beanpole days, but he's still too thin—too thin can be a thing with boys. *Undernourished* is the word I'd use. His Adam's apple sticks out like it's trying to poke through the skin of his neck. We're supposed to be dressed up for this dinner, but he's wearing khaki shorts and a faded old T-shirt that has something *Fortnite* on it. His red-brown hair is uncombed and so long it almost covers his eyes. His shoulders have a weird hunch.

Afton's right. I can't imagine sex with Nick.

For all of two seconds I get a flash of Leo on the virtual movie screen in the back of my brain. His red face hovering over mine. "I love you," he whispers.

"Fuck you," I whisper back. I've never been big into swearing before the past twenty-four hours happened. At least not out-loud swearing. But now it's like that word won't leave my brain.

"Looks like you'll have to spend this vacation in celibate self-reflection, after all," says Afton sympathetically.

"Yeah, I'm very disappointed." I try to shove thoughts of Leo away. It's hard to stop thinking about someone when you've done nothing but think about them for the longest time. "I've heard rebound sex is awesome. Wait, have *you* ever had rebound sex?"

"Well, no," she admits. "Not yet."

"So how would you know?"

"What are you talking about?" asks Abby then, loudly.

"Yes, what are you two scheming over there?" asks Mom, her mouth pinched up. She must have heard me say an inappropriate word or two. She disapproves, of course, but she doesn't like to parent us in public—Mom relishes the idea that her children are well-behaved without being threatened or bribed. I think she's proud that we're so self-governing. Even if she had very little to do with it.

"Nothing," Afton says swiftly.

"Yeah, it's nothing," I concur.

12

That night I dream that Leo leads me into a room I don't know. It has a concrete floor. Shelves with sports equipment and cardboard boxes. A bicycle leaning against the wall.

It doesn't make sense, but it's a dream, so I don't question it.

"Here," Dream Leo says, and whips his arms to spread a red-plaid blanket on the floor next to a washing machine.

It's a garage, I realize dimly as he reclines on the blanket and I slip down next to him.

His hand brushes my cheek, tucks a strand of hair behind my ear. "You're the most beautiful girl I've ever seen."

I run a quick hand up my calf to check. My legs are smooth as a baby's butt this time. This could actually work.

But then it happens exactly the way it did before. Kissing. Touching. His fingers on the button of my shorts. My breath seizing up in my chest. Sitting up.

Stopping us.

"Wait," I gasp, and it's so frustrating I feel this way that I want to cry. "Afton's right. I can't do this. I'm not ready."

There's the look on his face: the one I sketched before. The shuttered eyelids. The frown. And then the frown becomes a sneer.

"Oh, Ada," Leo says. "Don't be such a fucking square."

I wake up in darkness, the kind of velvety black that makes me feel swallowed whole. For a few seconds I have no idea where I am, and I can hear the ocean, the shushing of waves. Then my eyes adjust. I remember I'm in Hawaii. It's a clear night, the sky a deep blue outside the wall of windows, punctuated by the ebony shapes of the palm trees.

I turn to look at Afton in the bed next to mine, but she's not there. After dinner she set out on her own and hadn't come back by the time Mom put Abby to bed and closed the door between our rooms. I fumble for my phone and check the time: it's not quite one in the morning.

I open the texts and stare at her last text conversation with me, all from before our fight. Most of our texts are silly: a string of emojis or funny remarks to show one another how brilliantly sarcastic we both are. I can't shake the sense that everything's going wrong. Leo. Mom and Pop. Afton, where she seems fine one minute, pissed off the next, and is now missing. She's a big girl, I tell myself as my finger hovers over the screen of my phone, tempted to check up on her. Afton is fierce and fearless. She always has been. She can handle herself.

Plus, the words *don't be a fucking square* are still stinging in my brain.

So I tell myself that I am not my sister's keeper. And I roll over and try to go back to sleep.

The next morning Mom comes into our room predictably early, towing a sleepy-eyed Abby behind her. "I have to go now," Mom says briskly.

I turn over to check for Afton. She's there, in the bed next to mine, all that's visible a long trail of wheat-colored hair sticking out from under the comforter.

"You're in charge of the munchkin," Mom says.

You would think it would fall on Afton, as the oldest, to be the caretaker of our younger sibling. But Afton made it clear from the very first day Mom and Pop brought Abby home from the hospital that she was not remotely interested in childcare, whereas I was super excited to hold the new baby and feed her and help change her diapers. And those roles just kind of stuck.

"Okay," I mumble sleepily, because Mom is clearly talking to me.

"Don't charge things to the room," she reminds me. Mom likes to keep the room charges for business expenses only, which is a pain. Instead she lays a hundred-dollar bill on my nightstand, her standard allowance to cover my and Abby's expenses for the day. Then she goes out the door of our room, leaving the door to the other room open so we can access Abby's luggage.

Abby trundles onto my bed and curls up beside me, so warm that I quickly become too hot, but I don't move her. She's quiet for a few minutes, snuggling, but then she decides that she wants to watch cartoons. And then she decides she's hungry. She bounces around making so much noise there isn't really a choice but to get up. She even drags Afton out of bed. Eventually we all get dressed and wander down to the outdoor café on the ground floor, where Afton and I discover the joys of Kona coffee, feed muffin crumbs to the crowd of tiny birds that's zipping in and out of the patio area, and watch the hotel guests run to catch the tram.

The entire time we're eating I'm biting back the words *Where were you?* because it really is a mystery to me, what Afton could have been doing out so late, but to ask her would put me back into the fucking square category. So I don't ask. And she doesn't enlighten me.

"What should we do today?" I say instead, and dig around in my bag until I find the brochure with the hotel activities listed on it. I slide it across the table to Abby. I'm thinking something quiet and physical, some way to get a little exercise after the whole day of sitting and eating we had yesterday. Something preferably without much in the way of walking along beaches or swimming in pools.

Like paddleboarding. This single activity refuses to leave my brain. Paddleboarding. That's when I'm going to truly feel better about everything.

"I want to do *that*." Abby puts a tiny finger down on the brochure and then lifts it again so I can see what she's referring to: a picture of a young Hawaiian woman hula dancing in front of a group of older ladies.

My first mistake, I realize immediately, was asking the five-year-old what we should do.

"That looks fun, but what about this?" I point at a picture of the lagoon, where it shows a family in a four-person boat, and another couple in a kayak, and a girl standing on a paddleboard in the distance. "We might even get to see a sea turtle. Wouldn't that be awesome?"

"No," Abby says. "I want to dance."

I hold in a sigh. I can't think of anything less fun than towering over a group of women all watching me try to move my nonexistent hips. "Well, that's a class, isn't it?" I try to redirect. "We probably had to sign up beforehand."

Afton, who's again been texting all through breakfast, suddenly picks up the brochure and inspects it. "There's a hula class that starts at ten today—perfect timing, actually. It says walk-ins are welcome. And you get one class a day free with your stay."

"Yay, we're going to dance!" Abby exclaims.

I give my older sister a tight smile. "Thank you, Afton. You're so helpful." I turn to the younger one. "I don't know, kid. Maybe we could try the hula class another day. . . ." Tomorrow we're going to take a day trip to the other side of the island, but after that we'll have some free time.

"I want to dance *now*," Abby says, the edge of a whine I am all too familiar with creeping into her voice. "Please?"

"Okay," I sigh. "But—"

"I could take her," Afton says lightly.

I stare at her.

Afton slides her phone into her pocket, which signifies that she's serious. "I wouldn't mind moving my hips a little."

"Really? You want to take Abby to hula class?"

"I want to dance," repeats Abby.

Afton shrugs. "It's not like I have anything better to do."

"O-kay," I say slowly. "If you're sure . . ."

"You're not the only one who can take care of her, you know," she says.

"Do I know that, though?" I ask sarcastically. Afton does babysit sometimes. But when she does, it's always as a favor, to me, or to Mom or Pop. Whereas when I take care of Abby, it's because it's my unspoken responsibility.

"I take care of *you*," Afton says, and that's mostly true. While I've always taken care of Abby, Afton has always looked out for me. Until lately, anyway.

"I missed you last night," I murmur. Asking, without technically asking, where she was.

Her face gives away nothing. "I was just wandering around. Thinking."

"Thinking about what?"

"Oh, you know. This and that." She stands up. "We better get going. The tram's about to leave. See you later." She throws her cup and the empty acai bowls into the nearest trash, then grabs Abby's hand, and the two of them run the fifty feet or so to the tram stop. I wave as they get in, but they aren't watching me. The tram beeps its warning that it's about to move, and then it whooshes away.

Just like that, I'm alone.

For a few minutes I sit there, clutching my lukewarm coffee, unsure of what to do. The reality of what's just happened slowly sinks in. I am verifiably alone. Afton has given me a gift, and to make such a generous offer, to take Abby off my hands, she must be over her drama. That's the best news of all.

I find myself smiling. Not that I don't love my little sister, but it's so rare to have time to myself. I still have that hundred-dollar bill in my pocket, crisp and promising. I can do whatever I want. I can go back to the room and sleep some more, although I suddenly don't feel even a little bit tired. I can explore the resort without having to answer to anybody else.

I examine the brochure again. Then I text Mom (who ironically likes to be kept informed of what we're doing during the day) that Abby and Afton have gone to a hula class, and I am going to try paddleboarding.

Don't get burned, she texts back.

I am already picturing myself on the lagoon, not with Abby sitting on the board in front of me, making her little-kid observations and perpetually about to tip us over, always needing something, like a drink or her life jacket adjusted or for me to find the sunglasses that had been on her face two seconds ago, but alone, blessedly, sweetly alone. The water lapping at the board. The sun on my shoulders. The breeze in my hair.

Abruptly I realize that, in the magnificent paddleboarding scenario I'm creating in my head, I'm obviously wearing a swimsuit, and I still don't have one.

I'm going to have to shop for a swimsuit.

My elation at being free from all of my responsibilities fades as quickly as it came. I dislike shopping. I flat-out hate shopping for a swimsuit. If there are circles in hell, I am sure one of them is made up entirely of an endless row of dressing rooms and three-way mirrors.

Suddenly hula dancing doesn't seem like that terrible of an option.

"Do you know where I can buy a bathing suit?" I ask the girl working at the café.

She nods. "There's a gift shop in each of the five buildings—this one's right there, see it? And there are several different shops located at the Lagoon Tower."

I thank her and trudge off toward the gift shop that's closest, where the offering of women's bathing suits turns out to be a single rack of two-pieces, which definitely won't work. My bare stomach is no one else's business but mine. My mind drifts back to Leo, his bedroom, Michael Phelps judging me from above, but I jerk my attention back to the business at hand. Focus. Shopping. None of these suits are in my size. I walk to the Palace Tower, the next building over, but it's the same story there.

The walk to the Promenade takes longer. I could catch the tram, but it seems lazy to ride between buildings in one hotel, and by walking I'm less likely to run into anybody who knows me from the conference and get held up making awkward conversation.

At the Promenade there's another small store off the front lobby, and this one has one-pieces, but only stocks smalls and mediums.

This is discrimination, I think, annoyed. I'm wasting all this beautiful time to myself on a quest that's starting to feel impossible. What if I can't find a swimsuit? Pop said it would be easy, but what if it's only easy for men like Pop? What if nobody on this island has ever conceived of a female being a size large?

I could go in my underwear, like I did at Leo's pool that day. I have a black bra and briefs that I might be able to get away with. But that would be like wearing a two-piece, which we've already established is a no-go, and besides, people would probably be able to tell. Mom definitely wouldn't be too keen on the idea of me walking around in front of all of her esteemed colleagues in my bra and panties.

I could wear a shirt over it, I consider. And shorts. But regular clothes in the water would feel uncomfortable and gross.

Desperate now, I take the tram to the Lagoon Tower. When I get off the train there's a large set of stairs leading down to the spa and the cultural center, a sign helpfully informs me. The cultural center is where Afton and Abby are learning hula. I check my phone; about thirty minutes have passed since I last saw my sisters. I don't know how long the class is. I'm overcome by the panicky feeling that they're going to come bounding up the stairs at any moment, and then Afton will dump Abby off on me and leave me exactly where I started.

I duck into a shop—the girl was right; there are several shops here. I don't even really care which one.

"Can I help you?" asks a guy folding shirts in the corner.

"I need a swimsuit," I mumble.

"Sure," he says cheerfully. "Back wall."

The entire back wall is stocked with bathing suits of many shapes and colors and styles, and, most importantly, sizes. I breathe in a sigh of relief when I discover a board shirt—like a wet suit top with short sleeves—which would cover my cavewoman shoulders and also extend down to cover my belly. It's white with hibiscus flowers on it, it's a size large, and I immediately love it.

On the next rack there's a selection of separate tops and bottoms, also available in large.

I pick a bright green top like a sports bra (okay, a two-piece, but no one is ever going to see, on account of the board shirt) and a matching boy-shorts bottom. I bring all three items straight to the checkout counter and lay them out carefully in front of the guy who helped me earlier.

"Would you like to try these on first?" he asks. "We have a dressing room."

I shake my head. "I'm good."

He rings me up. The total is ninety-two fifty. I slide the hundred-dollar bill across the counter.

In a minute I'm standing outside the store again, waiting for the tram. This time I am faced with more than the fear that my sisters are going to spontaneously appear before me and spoil my solitary fun. To get back on track with my paddleboarding plan, I'll need to change and apply sunscreen and do something with my unruly hair. I also forgot my sunglasses.

I have to go to our room. Which is at the opposite end of the resort. Then I have to hurry and dress and prepare myself and make my way to the paddleboard rental place. Which is where I am now.

It's going to eat into so much more of my precious time, but I don't have a better option. I consider buying new sunscreen and sunglasses and getting dressed at the store after all, but then I remember I only have seven dollars and fifty cents.

So I do the only thing I can do: I get on the tram and go back to the room.

I don't waste any time when I get there. I want to hurry, in case Afton and Abby come back soon. I feel mildly guilty about trying to avoid them, but I want my time alone to be more than just a shopping excursion. I want to freaking paddleboard. I grab my hairbrush and the tube of sunblock that's sitting out on the dresser and turn to go into the walk-in closet, where I can get dressed and stand in front of the mirror to apply the sunscreen.

But then I hear the noise.

It's a noise I've heard in R-rated movies and a couple of uncomfortable nights when Mom and Pop were in a certain kind of mood, since I unfortunately share a wall with their bedroom. That kind of noise.

Don't be silly, I tell myself. It's a hotel. There are bound to be occasional sexy times noises in a hotel. But it sounds . . . close. It almost sounds like it's coming from Mom and Abby's room.

I go to the door, which is open a crack, and I peer inside.

It's dark in the room, the only light spilling in through a small wedge of window, the rest entirely blocked by curtains. But I can see well enough to make out a figure in the middle of my mother's bed. A woman.

A woman with blond hair.

Wearing her new white robe with red-and-black flowers on it. Straddling a dark-haired man.

Her back is to me, but of course I know who it is.

My mother.

13

Everything in my brain screeches to a halt. It's horrible, and it's definitely scarring me for life, but I can't tear my gaze away from the strangers on the bed. No, I correct myself. Not strangers. My mother, on the bed, acting like she's having sex.

Because she is having sex.

My mother is having sex. With someone who is not Pop.

I finally manage to unfreeze myself and back away. They haven't seen me. From their angle they can't see the door to the adjoining room. They don't know I'm here.

I creep slowly, carefully, to the door leading out. I open it with such excruciating slowness that it feels like it takes five full minutes. Then I'm outside on the long outdoor walkway, and everything feels like a different world out there. Blue sky stretches overhead, not a cloud in it. People stroll around in bathing suits and saris and wrapped in fluffy white towels. Birds sing in the trees. Kids laugh and race each other and parents yell, "Slow down!"

The door shuts behind me with the tiniest, softest click.

I stand there like I've been turned to stone.

Everything that I was most afraid of—the worst thing that I could possibly imagine—is happening. It has happened. *It's over*, I think, although I don't know what the *it* is that I'm referring to.

Mom and Pop.

My childhood, perhaps.

Happiness in general.

Someone comes out of the room next door. It's not Mom—she's still busy, I imagine, but the sudden noise and movement jolts me into action. I can't stay here. I can't be here. I have to go.

So I start running.

I don't know where I'm going. I run to the end of the hall, and when I get there I run down a set of stairs, and down and down, floor after floor, until I think I hit the ground floor, but I actually go one lower. There's a laundry room down there, and a series of vending machines and the lockers where you can get a towel for the pool. I run past them, push out onto a set of steps that leads into the sun again, run and almost fall into a big sparkling pool I've never seen before. Beyond the pool is a row of white plastic reclining deck chairs, and a paved path that leads away from the building.

I sprint down the path. My brain isn't working yet; it's just recycling a few crucial words and focusing on getting air into my lungs: *my mother*, gasp, *my mother*, gasp, *my mother having sex*, a kind of rhythm that takes me farther and farther away from the room, away from the Ocean Tower, away, away, from my mother and whoever

91

it is, past a long string of pools connected by slides and stairs, past a wedding chapel, over a series of little bridges, past sunbathers and toddlers splashing and squealing, past a restaurant with people eating at outdoor tables and an aquarium where they apparently keep dolphins. Past another large pool and a waterfall and . . .

And then I have to stop. I've reached the end of the resort. I've run from Ocean to Lagoon. There's nowhere else to go.

Normally that kind of running would kill me, or at the very least lame me for a significant amount of time, but I don't even feel winded. My heart is pumping so hard I can feel my pulse throbbing in my neck. My legs feel like they aren't even connected to my body; they're simultaneously numb and tingling, light as feathers and heavy as sacks of rocks. My head swims with the image of my mother in the white robe, and then settles into a kind of woozy blankness that I welcome.

I turn around and go back along the path, willing my breath to slow, trying to cool down. Clear my thoughts. Understand what it means. And what it means is this:

My mother is having an affair.

I immediately think of Pop. Pop's gentle voice. Pop's funny laugh. Pop.

I need to be calm. But . . . Pop.

It's over, I think again. It hurts to swallow. I stop walking and press my hand to the space just below my ribs. Pain stabs at my side. I'm suddenly dizzy. I become aware that a lady with a stroller is trying to pass me on the path, but I'm blocking her somehow and can't get my body to respond correctly to even the most basic of commands. I finally stagger to one side and sit down on a patch of short, sandy grass, trying to get my bearings.

That's when I notice where I am.

The lagoon. More specifically, I'm sitting right in front of the rental shack for the lagoon.

Paddleboards, a sign reads in large letters on the back of the shack. *Ten dollars per hour.*

I choke on a laugh. It isn't remotely funny, but I can't help it. I panicked and ran for my life and somehow ended up practically in the line to rent a paddleboard—my plan all along. I laugh again, and then my laugh becomes a dry sob.

I put my hand over my mouth. Poor Pop. How could she do it?

I mean, seriously, how? Not just how could she cheat on her spectacularly smart and sweet and good-looking husband, but how could she bring some man back to the room she shares with us? How could she know we wouldn't come back and catch her? How could she be so careless? Or does she even care if we find out?

My heartbeat picks up again. I have another thought, an important one.

Afton and Abby could be headed back to the room right now. My sisters might be about to walk in on Mom having sex.

I fumble in my pockets and find my phone in one of them. My hands shake as I make the call. The phone rings and rings, then goes to voice mail. I don't know what else to do, so I try again. And again.

On the fourth time Afton picks up. "What's up?" She sounds normal, almost cheerful. She doesn't live in this world yet, the world where Mom is a cheater and everything we've been suspecting is true: Mom and Pop aren't in love anymore. They're done.

"Are you finished with hula? Where are you?" I ask between pants.

"Just wandering around."

"Don't go back to the room," I say.

Her voice sharpens. "What? Why?"

"Abby's with you, right?"

"Are you okay, Ada? Your voice sounds funny."

"I'm fine." I clear my throat. "Where are you? Come meet me for lunch somewhere."

"They're serving lunch free in the Promenade," she reminds me.

I shudder. I do not want to go to the convention center, not with all those people who knew Mom. And maybe by now she's done . . . doing that . . . what she was doing . . . and she will head back there, too.

"No, that's always sandwiches," I say. "Abby hates sandwiches. You should bring her to the lagoon. There's a restaurant where I'm at. It's called"—I swivel around to see the sign—"the Lagoon Grill." Another thought occurs to me. "Hey, do you have money?"

"Didn't Mom give you some?" Afton asks.

"I spent it. I have like seven dollars." But money is the least of my problems.

"Okay, sit tight," Afton says. "We'll be right there."

14

My very first memory, ever, is of a car accident. I was about three, I think. Dad (my original father, not Pop) was driving us to pick up Afton from somewhere, on a freeway between San Jose and San Francisco, the world pleasantly zooming by outside the window. Then Dad had to merge. He looked over his right shoulder to check that the other lane was clear, and what he didn't realize was that the cars ahead of us had all stopped.

"Aaron!" my mom screamed, and then my dad had about ten seconds to go from seventy-five miles per hour to zero.

He slammed on the brakes. That's the first real part of what I remember, actually, the sensation of being flung violently forward, so hard that I got a hairline fracture on my collarbone from the force of me hitting the straps of my car seat. And then there was my mother screaming again, and me screaming, too, knowing as the car in front of us rushed toward the windshield that we weren't going to stop in time. Then BAM—the impact—the sheer loudness of it was terrible, that huge, sickening bang, compounded by the crunch and crack of glass, the pop of the airbags.

And then everything, for a few seconds, anyway, was totally still. Dust floated in the air.

The blinker was still on, and it went click. Click. Click.

I could hear my own breathing. In and out. In and out.

Then Mom scrambled out of her seat belt and reached over to me, her hand touching my face. "Are you okay, honey? Are you hurt?"

I shook my head. Something *was* hurt, of course, but I didn't feel it yet.

My dad coughed. "Shit," I remember he said. "The car is totaled."

Mom turned on him with an expression I'd never seen on her face, before or since. "You," she said, gasping for air, at first, but then starting to yell. "You asshole! You could have killed us!"

"I didn't see!" he bellowed back. "It wasn't my fault!"

"We could have died!" she screamed.

We were fine, relatively speaking. But it was obvious to me even at three that there was something really wrong with my parents, who shouted at each other until the police showed up. My mother was like a different person in that memory, so angry when I knew her to be cool and collected most of the time. In that moment, the world shifted from being safe to being scary. It became a place where people could get hurt. They could die. They could change.

Seeing my mother today, betraying Pop, it feels exactly the same way.

My world has stopped, but my body still keeps going, and something breaks.

15

It feels like forever before Afton and Abby arrive at the Lagoon Grill. By that time I've calmed myself. I even feel embarrassed at how dramatically I reacted. All the running. The hyperventilating. The huge emotions and hopeless thoughts. The flashback to a freaking car accident, for freak's sake. I've pulled it together now. Still, seeing my sisters coming toward me holding hands, their faces both so innocent of the things I know, I feel my eyes burn. But I somehow manage to smile. "Hey! How was hula?" I ask Abby.

"Fun!" She beams up at me. "And Josie and her mom and brothers were there too! And we learned a new song." She proceeds to sing an off-key ditty about the ocean and the silvery moon, but stops midway through to inform us that she's hungry now, and we should probably feed her.

"How are you?" Afton asks, squinting at my face.

I nod. "Fine. Let's get her something to eat."

We find a table that overlooks the dolphin tank. It turns out that most of the things on the menu are sandwiches.

"I don't like sandwiches," says Abby.

"I know." I scan the menu. "How about a burger?"

"I don't like burgers."

"How about a nice green salad?"

"Salad is rabbit food," she says with a sniff.

"But you're a little rabbit, aren't you?" Afton says, and wiggles her nose.

Abby giggles. "No. I'm a girl, silly."

"How about a salad . . . with pineapple in it?" I offer.

Sold.

I order a Hawaiian bacon BBQ burger for myself, which is an epically bad idea. My head feels full, but my body feels empty, and it seems in the moment like maybe if I eat something familiar, like a burger, things in my world will return to normal.

But instead the burger instantly gives me a horrible stomachache.

Abby picks at her salad and after about four bites announces that she's done. I don't try to argue. On average we can only get my little sister to eat about one full meal a day, and she did that at breakfast. I tell her that she can go over and look at the dolphins, and away she goes, half skipping, half running to the edge of the dolphin tank.

Afton and I stay at the table. Afton uses her debit card to pay for the meal.

"Are you okay?" she asks me. "You look . . . weirder than normal."

I don't say anything right away. It doesn't feel like there's anything I can say.

And then Afton says, "I'm sorry, okay?"

I blink at her. "What?"

"I'm sorry I've been kind of mean to you. I know you're going through a thing. It just hurt my feelings when you called me a—"

"I didn't call you a slut!" I exclaim. "I was going to say that you're perfect, and no, I didn't exactly mean that as a compliment, but I did not say slut, because I would never say that and I don't think you are."

"Oh," she says. "Okay. Well, I'm not perfect."

"Oh, I know," I say.

She smiles. "Right. Anyway. I'm sorry."

"I'm sorry, too," I say, but this topic feels like a lifetime ago. We're on to more serious catastrophes now; she just doesn't know it yet. I take a shuddering breath. I have to tell her. She's my sister, and this is about her, too. She should know.

But it feels like I'm about to tell her that someone—or something, I guess—*has* died, and the dead thing is this fanciful notion we've been holding on to for so long of our family as this secure little unit. Mom and Pop and Afton and Abby and me. Our family. And that idea was basically stabbed through the heart the moment I peeked through the adjoining door of our hotel room.

But I'm being dramatic. Again. Because of course, she and I both knew deep down that something like this might be coming.

"I need to tell you something," Afton says, which short-circuits my brain for a minute, because what could she possibly have to tell me? "Logan and I broke up."

I blink at her. "What? No."

"It was a mutual thing," she explains. "Amicable. Friendly. He was thinking about going to Stanford, but then he decided he wanted to go with Dartmouth instead."

Wow. Dartmouth. Logan always struck me as a smart guy. He'd

have to be, for Afton to be interested in him. "Where's Dartmouth, again?"

"New Hampshire," she says with a sigh. "We agreed that the long-distance thing was probably not going to work, and we should just call it good, you know, quit while we're ahead, make a clean break of it, et cetera, clichés."

"When did this happen? I mean, when did you break up?"

She looks simultaneously guilty and sad. "Friday."

I feel like she punched me, which makes my stomach hurt even worse than the terrible hamburger. "Friday. As in two days ago."

"Yeah. I thought I was fine with it, that it was a mature decision and all that, but I haven't exactly been fine. I've been . . ." She searches for the word. "Struggling."

"You didn't tell me."

Her eyes meet mine. "You had your own thing going on."

The way she's been acting makes a lot more sense now. Also: I am a crappy sister. "I'm sorry. You should have told me. I mean, we broke up with our boyfriends on the same weekend."

"Yes, we did," she says with a hint of a smile. "But we're both going to be okay now. Trust me on this. We're going to be great. You'll see."

In this moment I know this as an absolute fact: I can't tell her about Mom and the affair.

If I tell Afton, not only will I ruin Hawaii for her and all the optimism she's feeling about how fricking great we're going to be, but she'll feel like we have to do something. I know her. She'll want to confront Mom. And if we confront Mom, the only thing that will happen is that Mom will feel like *she* has to do something. And the only something that she can really do is, like, confess. And then she'll probably split up from Pop. They'll get divorced.

I can't imagine life without Pop. Or Abby. Because Abby goes with Pop.

I'm a terrible liar. My face is an open book, Pop always says. My voice does the catch thing. But this time I manage to pull it off. "You're right," I say steadily. "We're going to be great."

Abby comes running up to us, grinning and chattering, cheeks flushed with excitement, eyes bright with her simple five-year-old delight in the fact that dolphins are a thing that exist. "Oh my dog, I want to swim with the dolphins! Can I, Ada? Can I swim with the dolphins like those people are doing?"

Afton stands up. "Let's go see, Abby-cakes." She holds out her hand to our little sister, who grabs it. "I'll babysit," Afton says, another generous gift to me. "We'll talk more later."

Or we won't talk more later, which is what I'd currently prefer. Not until I figure out how I'm going to deal with this. Alone. All by myself.

But I can *do this*, I think. I can act like I don't know anything. Like I didn't see anything. Like it didn't even happen. I have to.

"Let's go pretend we're mermaids," Afton's saying as she pulls Abby toward the dolphin tanks. "Under the sea."

16

I spend the next several hours alone, thinking until I think I'll drive myself insane.

It's at this point that I ask myself the question: Who? Who was it? It was dark in that room, and I never saw the man's face. I only got a glimpse of the back of his head. I struggle to call up the image. Dark hair, cut short. Wide bare shoulders narrowing to a trim waist.

I shudder with revulsion.

One thing is for certain: it wasn't Pop, changing his mind about not coming on the trip, Popping in to surprise us all.

Pop is black. And this guy wasn't black.

So *who* was it?

I make a mental list of possibilities, starting with the men in Mom's circle:

Jerry. He has dark hair but, ugh, no. Jerry is way older, and not in the best shape. The man I saw was definitely not Jerry with his shirt off.

Max Ahmed. Max also has dark hair. But Max is so quiet, so reserved and so proper all the time. I can't grasp the idea of a universe in which Max would cheat on his wife.

Billy Wong. But he's so attentive to his family, which I've always appreciated, in contrast to Mom. Last year at the awards dinner I caught Billy mouthing the words "I love you" to his wife across the crowded room. I can't imagine Billy doing . . . that.

Which only leaves the hundreds of other doctors at this conference, men who only my mother has met. Men I don't know.

Tearful and frustrated, I stretch out in one of those white rope hammocks that are scattered around the resort and try to talk myself into taking a nap, so I'll have a few hours of relief from the torturous rat maze that my mind is turning into, but I can't make myself sleep. After I give up on that, I stand on the hillside and watch a couple get married in the outdoor chapel.

Because I am apparently a glutton for punishment.

I'm not close enough to hear what the bride and groom are saying, but I know they're making promises to each other. Like promises to be faithful. As in, to refrain from having sex with anyone else. It must be so easy to believe those promises, I think mournfully as I watch them, when you're young and you're in love.

Of course I wouldn't know anything about that. The whole thing with Leo is now so clearly unimportant and childish and silly. I didn't love Leo. I liked him, sure, and I loved the idea of him, and that's not the same. But I believed that true love existed, out there in the world, that it was a real thing. That it was possible.

I believed that because of Mom and Pop.

They got married at a vineyard in wine country when I was eight years old and Afton was ten and Abby didn't exist yet. It was sunny that day, and the air smelled of lavender. Mom wore a simple white cotton dress, a circle of wildflowers pinned to the crown of her head, and cowboy boots because she thought they would be funny and more comfortable than heels. She smiled all day long, from morning until night, even when she knew she was having her picture taken. Mom hates to smile for pictures because she thinks smiling makes her eyes get small and squinty. Her doctor profile picture on the hospital website, for example, is of her staring almost solemnly at the camera, her eyes as wide as they'll go, her lips turning up in the tiniest possible version of a smile. But that day, on her wedding day, she smiled with her teeth.

I wonder if Mom smiles at this other man like that. I don't want to imagine it, even though I've seen her doing so much worse. There's a part of my brain that refuses to accept that what happened this morning was real. *It was dark in there*, this part of me whispers urgently in the back of my mind. Maybe I didn't see what I thought I saw. Maybe I misinterpreted it somehow. It tries to make me doubt everything, because it wants to cling to the stubborn belief that Mom would never cheat on Pop. Mom can be distant sometimes, she can be neglectful in her own distracted intellectual sort of way, and she can be careless with a person's feelings because feelings are not her forte. But I don't want to admit that she could be so horribly disloyal to us all, so dishonest, so repulsive and ugly and bad. *That's not her*, I keep thinking, over and over. *That's not Mom.*

But clearly I'm wrong. Clearly I don't know my mother at all.

Clearly the promises she made that one sunny day don't mean

anything to her, and there's nothing I can do about that. I am completely useless. The only thing I can do that has any value is to keep Afton and Abby from finding out. I can protect my sisters. And possibly Pop. If he doesn't already know.

But maybe this is why he refused to come to Hawaii.

My phone buzzes at my hip. A text from Mom.

All done for the day. A group of us is getting together for dinner at seven. Meet you back at the room at six?

I squeeze my eyes shut against the desire to hurl my phone into the nearest body of water. There are a lot of bodies of water around to choose from, but I resist the urge. It wouldn't be fair to take my anger out on my innocent, well-meaning cell phone.

My fingers are cold, and for some reason the phone won't register my touch. I rub my hands together, open and close my fists, take a deep breath, and try again.

Actually, I'm not feeling well, I type shakily. *I think I'm sick.*

I'm a coward. I hate myself for it. But I know I can't do it, not tonight. I can't have dinner with Mom and Afton and Abby and everyone in our group and pretend like I don't know.

I send the text.

What kind of sick? my mother texts back immediately.

Of course she wants to know the exact symptoms I'm experiencing.

Stomach, I reply.

Did you vomit?

I bite my lip. She won't let me stay in tonight if I only have an upset stomach. She'll make me take a Pepto or a Tums and go with them anyway. She has this thing about participating.

Yes, I text back. A lie. The first of many, I think, about this thing

I am not supposed to know. The first in a lifetime. But what choice do I have?

Are you at the room?

I cringe at the phone. Shit. *Yes.*

I'll come check your vitals.

I tuck the phone back into my pocket, my heart drumming in my ears again, and start walking fast, calling myself a moron the entire way back, because I was so incredibly brainless to tell her I'm sick, and she's a doctor and she'll know I'm not really sick, won't she, and even if she doesn't know I've made it up, she'll be actually examining me and how am I going to be that close to her, look into her eyes, and hide what I know? She'll figure out that something's up in two seconds flat. She'll demand to know what it is. She and Afton are so alike that way.

But I can't think of what else to do. I'm on an island two thousand miles from home. I don't have a car or money or a good excuse.

I have to go back to the room.

I quicken my pace, and within a few minutes I'm standing at the base of the Ocean Tower. I stare up at it for a minute, wondering which window is ours. They all look the same, but some of them have the curtains drawn and some don't.

I wonder if they opened the curtains, afterward, while I was running away as fast as I could. I wonder if Mom went out onto the balcony in her new sexy robe—it's sexy, why didn't I notice that before, why wasn't I suspicious that she brought a sexy robe with her on a business trip?—and I wonder if she stared out at the ocean perfectly happy with where she was and what she'd just done with someone who wasn't Pop.

I feel a sudden stabbing pain in my stomach, followed by an awful pressure, and then I veer off the sidewalk and throw up in the bushes. Out comes the half-digested Hawaiian bacon BBQ burger. I kneel down in the dirt for a few minutes, wiping my mouth on the hem of my shirt.

I guess I won't have to lie about the vomiting, after all.

"Whoa, are you okay?" comes a voice.

I look up. Standing a few feet away is Nick Kelly. He's been swimming. His hair is slicked back, and he has a towel wrapped around his skinny waist.

"Hi, Nick," I say numbly. "I'm fine."

"Are you sure?" His face is arranged in the classic expression of worry, eyebrows arcing upward, wide, sympathetic eyes, slack mouth. "That was . . . a lot of puke."

"I'm okay, really." I straighten. Nick takes a step forward like he'd like to help, but that would involve touching me, and he's not sure he ought to touch me. I would laugh at how awkward we are, but I'm too worn out. "I should go in, though."

He walks along with me to the door of the building and holds it open for me.

"Do you want me to call anyone? My dad's a doctor. He could come look you over." He scratches the back of his neck. "Wow. That was a dumb idea, sorry. I realize that everybody here is a doctor. Should I call your mom?"

"She knows. She's coming." My stomach rolls again, but I keep it down this time. Barely. "I need to go in."

"Okay. Feel better, Ada," he says.

But I know I won't.

17

Morning again. My first whole day in which I know about Mom. We have one of those tour things, to the other side of the island.

"What's on the other side of the island?" Abby asks at breakfast as I stand behind her, attempting to wrestle her hair into submission. Abby has long blond hair, but a darker, sandier blond than Afton's or mine, and it's curly, like mine but way, way more.

"A volcano," I answer. I am trying—so very hard—to act like everything's normal. Jokes and all.

Abby's mouth drops open. "Shut up."

"No, it's true. And today we're going to see it up close." I finish braiding Abby's hair, tie it off, and check my phone. "It's almost time to go." Right on time, the tram arrives. "Come on, Abby." I take Abby's hand. "Are you coming?" I ask Afton.

"Of course she's coming," Abby answers. "She's not stupid, is she? She can't not see a volcano. Duh."

"We don't say stupid, Abby," I say. "And we don't say duh."

Abby scoffs.

Afton has her phone out, texting again. Always texting. Phone at the table, in flagrant violation of the family rules, but then Pop's not here to enforce them.

I'm trying not to think about Pop.

The tram starts to beep. It's about to leave.

"Let's go, Afton!" Abby cries, and Afton throws her phone back into her bag. We all sprint to the tram. We barely make it, but we do.

"Where are we going?" Afton asks as we're whooshed away.

I tilt my head to look at her. "Uh, the volcano?"

She closes her eyes like I am annoying her greatly. Afton's never been what you'd call a morning person. "I mean, where are we going to start this wonderful trip to a real-live volcano?"

"Oh. There's like a parking lot for buses where we'll meet up. Off the floor under the front lobby." Clearly she did not read through the folder of helpful information about the conference that was left for us in our room. With the stuff about schedules and the outings we're taking and what we're supposed to bring and where we're supposed to be. I, of course, have read the folder cover to cover.

Abby is frowning. "The volcano's not alive, is it?"

"No."

"Afton said it was a real-live volcano." Abby looks troubled. It's difficult to say what kind of worries pass through my baby sister's head.

"I didn't mean it was alive," Afton clarifies. "Hey, look."

She points to outside, where in the center of its own small island there's a large gray bird with a yellow Mohawk. I take a quick picture.

Because that's my normal behavior. I see a pretty thing, I take a picture. For painting purposes.

Abby spends a few seconds in appreciation of the startling bird. "I'm going to call him Walter," she says. Then she tugs at my arm. "Is this the kind of island where they have to throw people into the volcano to appease the gods?"

I frown. "How do you even know about that?"

She shrugs. "Well, is it?"

"No. I don't think there are any more islands like that. Or if there ever were islands like that, outside of the movies."

"Good," she breathes. "I don't want to become a human sacrifice. Poppy would miss me."

I reach over and smooth down her curly hair. "And I would miss you."

She nods, accepting my love for her so simply it hurts. "And Afton would miss me."

Afton nods. "I would."

"Although not as much as Ada," Abby says, and neither of us argue the point.

"And Mom would miss you," I add, because that, too, is something Normal-Ada would say. Because Normal-Ada would of course include Mom in our happy family.

"Mom would be sad, that's true," Abby says, and it's wild to me that even at five years old, my sister seems to understand that there's a difference. Between missing someone and being sad that they're gone. Or maybe that's my own messed-up thought and not Abby's.

"I miss Poppy already." Abby sighs and leans her head against the window as the palm trees and tropical foliage whiz past. "I wish he was going to see the volcano."

Afton's gaze catches mine. I look away.

"I know," I murmur around the lump in my throat. "I miss him, too."

The first people we see when we climb up onto the tour bus are the Wongs, minus Billy, who's back at the conference center with Mom. Jenny Wong and her kids are occupying the first two seats on the left side of the aisle, and she's leaned over tying one of Josie's shoes as Afton, Abby, and I clamber up the steps. I'm usually happy to run into Jenny, because it means that Josie will also be there, so Abby will have somebody her own age to play with, i.e., less work for me. Plus, more often than not, Jenny offers to take care of Abby, too, and give me some time to myself.

But this time my stomach clenches, seeing Jenny, thinking that it's possible—possible but not probable, I tell myself—that it was Billy I saw with Mom yesterday. Which still makes me want to throw up. So I try to slip us past her unnoticed, but then Abby of course sees them and yells, "Hi, Josie!" and Jenny looks up.

"Hi, Abby!" she greets my little sister warmly. Afton's already scooted by her and headed straight for the back of the bus. Afton prefers the back. I like the front. Usually we compromise and sit somewhere in the middle.

Jenny turns to me. "Hello, Ada. We missed you last night at dinner. Are you feeling okay today?"

She says this like she's concerned about me, but also like she's a tad worried that a sick person might be about to hang out around her kids all day.

"I'm feeling much better," I mumble. "It was something I ate. I'm okay now."

A lie. Yesterday was what I imagine it would be like to watch your house burn down, all of your childhood treasures and family heirlooms turning to ash and you just standing there helplessly watching it happen. Knowing that things are never going to be the same again. Knowing that you are going to have to live someplace else now.

But today I'm past being sad. Today I'm officially pissed off. Which is the opposite of okay.

Jenny nods obliviously, smiling like she's relieved. "Well, I'm glad you've recovered. It would be no fun to be stuck in the hotel room when you're supposed be out and about enjoying Hawaii."

"Yeah," I agree. "No fun."

I debated playing the sick card again today. But last night was bad enough. I barely made it back to the room and into my bed before Mom arrived in full doctor mode, ready to diagnose and treat my mystery illness. I closed my eyes and pretended to be too sick to look at her as she took my temperature, felt my glands, and made me change into a clean shirt. (Apparently mine had a splattering of Hawaiian bacon BBQ burger on it.) Then she gave me a bottle of cold lemon soda she'd picked up at the gift shop on the way over from the convention center, and petted my head in a maternal fashion for a few minutes, and concluded her business by saying I needed rest. There wasn't much to do for food poisoning except to make sure I didn't get dehydrated.

"It's best to let it run its course," she instructed. "If you feel like you need to vomit, don't fight it." She emptied out the ice bucket and stuck it on the bedside table for exactly that purpose: puking. "You'll feel better," she said, "if you just get it all out."

I wish that were true.

After she was gone again I closed the curtains, trying to not even glance in the direction of the door to the adjoining room, watched brainless TV for a while, and finally went to sleep. I woke up this morning still alone. Mom had moved Afton over to her room to share a bed with Abby. A precaution in case I had the stomach flu and not an incident with a bad hamburger.

Or a bad mother, I thought bitterly when Mom bustled in again and put her hand against my forehead.

"How do you feel?" she asked.

I knew that if I said I didn't feel well still, she'd confine me to the room and examine me over and over again throughout the day. I'd have to keep lying and pretending that the mere sight of my mother didn't fill me with revulsion.

I also didn't want to be hanging out in that room a second more than I had to.

So I said I was fine and chose to go on the field trip. If I went on this little excursion, I wouldn't see Mom all day. That was good enough for me.

"Um, can Abby sit with Josie?" I ask Jenny.

"Of course," Jenny answers. "We always love to hang out with Abby."

"There's going to be a volcano!" Abby exclaims. "But don't worry; they're not going to throw anybody to the dogs."

"That's good to know, sweetie," says Jenny, laughing.

I mumble a thank-you, instruct Abby to stay with the Wongs, and flee farther back in the bus in search of Afton.

"Hey, Ada," says a voice, and there is Nick Kelly again, staring up at me from beneath his shaggy hair in the same slightly worried way he looked at me yesterday. "Are you feeling better?"

"Oh, hi, Nick," I say. "Yeah. I'm good."

A lie. A lie.

"Good. You can sit here, if you want." He gestures to the empty seat beside him.

"Thanks, but I'm sitting with my sister," I say, and hurry past him, but when I get to the back of the bus, I find Afton already sitting with Kate Jacobi.

It's for the best, I tell myself even though my feelings are kind of hurt that she didn't save me a place. I probably should stay well away from Afton until I have this Mom-having-an-affair thing under wraps in my brain.

I throw myself down into an empty seat a couple rows in front of her and stuff my bag under the seat. Then I slump so I'm out of sight of everyone else. I try to force myself to relax. I gaze out the window into the hotel parking lot, where shuttles and minivans and taxis are zooming in and out like bees in a flower garden. Everyone so busy and centered on our own little worlds.

The engine for the bus suddenly roars to life.

"Aloha, everybody!" booms a voice. "My name is Kahoni, which means 'the kiss,' but don't get any ideas, okay, unless you're a really pretty lady, and then I guess I don't mind. I'm going to be driving you today to some very special places on the Big Island. Are you ready to have some fun and learn about Hawaiian history and culture?"

There's a chorus of weak yeses from all over the bus.

"Aw, you can do better than that," says Kahoni, and everyone tries again, louder. "Okay then, let's go!" he laughs, and the bus lurches forward.

We ride through the endless sea of desolate black rock for a couple hours as our driver pal Kahoni gives us the lowdown on Hawaiian history. Eventually we stop at a rest area where they let us out in a flat grassy park with picnic tables scattered around. They hand out bento boxes for lunch.

I don't know where to sit. Eating with Afton or Jenny Wong and her family feels like a bad idea, considering how much I've got bottled up inside. So I make sure Abby is settled in with them and then lurk around for a few minutes before walking over and slapping my bento box down on Nick Kelly's table.

Sweet, clueless Nick.

He's playing a game on his phone with earphones on. I assume he's the safest bet for a quiet, no-fuss dining experience.

I'm wrong. He pulls his headphones down around his neck the instant I sit across from him. "Hi."

"Hi. Can I join you?"

"Let me think." He looks deliberately thoughtful for a second, then smiles, a flash of crooked teeth. "Okay, just this once."

"Thanks."

It's quiet for a minute. Then Nick says, "White people suck."

I swear, that's what he says.

I stare at him. I mean, Nick is about as typical a Caucasian teenage boy as they come. "Uh, what's that?"

He points with his thumb at Kahoni a few tables away. "You know, how the white explorers brought mosquitoes to these islands?

Oh, and tuberculosis. Rats. Syphilis. If you ask me, Captain Cook had it coming."

I haven't been paying attention to Kahoni's history lesson. I've been too busy stewing over my own disasters.

"I did think it was interesting, though, when he said they traded nails for sex with the native women," Nick adds.

And we're back to talking about sex. Everybody is so fixated on sex.

I sigh.

"Nails, like, iron nails. Like what you build houses with," he continues.

I'm not sure what I can say to that.

"You don't talk a lot, do you?" he says.

"I'm just trying to eat, I guess."

"Right. Sorry. I'm not usually this loquacious, either." His cheeks turn pink, then his ears. "Sorry. I'll let you eat. The food's actually better than it looks."

I pull off the lid of the bento box and stare inside. There are three compartments: one that holds a piece of fried chicken, another with a bunch of unidentifiable chunks of meat, and the third a large pile of white rice with shredded seaweed on top and what look like two large, bloated zombie fingers, but what turn out to be a type of purple potato.

I spear a zombie finger with my fork and eat it. It's not bad, so I move on to the mystery meat, which I decide is teriyaki pork.

"Nene," Nick says then.

It's like we're not even speaking the same language.

"What's nene?" I ask.

"Hawaii's state bird. It's a goose, actually."

I promptly spit the meat back into my napkin, and then it's Nick who's staring at me strangely. "You don't like it?"

"I didn't sign on to eat a goose!"

His eyebrows come together and then smooth as he starts to laugh. He points behind me. I turn. About five feet away a group of birds with black-and-white stripes are strutting around in the grass. Nene. On the lawn. Not on my plate.

"Oh," I say. "Oh, thank god."

Nick keeps laughing, until it's hard for me not to laugh, too, in spite of everything. It *is* pretty funny. We laugh, and the geese honk, and for like five seconds I actually forget that my life is being turned upside down, and then Nick goes back to his phone and his game, and I resume eating the mystery meat, which is still, probably, pork.

After that Nick decides we're buddies, and I don't argue. He gravitates toward me whenever we stop, first at Rainbow Falls, which is gorgeous but crowded, and then to a beach where the sand is pure black. From the pier, Nick points out a sea turtle. But I can't find it.

"I love turtles." I squint to find the shape under the water, but all I see is reflections of light and gleams of darkness.

"What kind of turtles?"

I shrug. "Big ones. Small ones. Tortoises. Little snappers. They're the best." Something about turtles just speaks to me. I like their weird textures, their mix of being kind of rough and reptilian but also beautiful, somehow. Their quiet. Their steady intelligent eyes.

"Which ninja turtle are you?" Nick asks, a bit of a non sequitur. "You strike me as a Raphael," he says. "Maybe a Leonardo."

I don't know the ninja turtles—they were before, and possibly after, my time—so I go with the OG artists. "Raphael was good—I like his portraits more than the religious stuff. Michelangelo's genius kind of intimidates me—I could never accomplish what he did. But Donatello, now he's approachable. He was interested in real people, not only ideas or storybook figures. He was a sculptor, and I'm not very good in that medium, but something about his work—I don't know—it transfixes me. I get Donatello."

The neural pathways of my brain immediately lead to me another sculptor: Diana Robinson, and from there, straight to Leo. Calling me his mom's groupie. Saying that we didn't have anything in common. If anyone asked me about my feelings for Leo at this point, I'd say I was over it now, it was yesterday's news, but still, my chest gives a painful squeeze when I think of what he said about me.

But, again, I also recognize it for what it is: a minor bump in the hazardous road that's become my life lately.

Nick smiles at me obliviously. "That's right, you like art."

"Yes. I like art." I spot Afton walking along the beach with the Wongs, keeping up with them but looking at her phone. Something about her expression catches at me. Wistful? Resigned?

"Sometime," Nick is saying.

"Huh?" I didn't catch the first part of his sentence. Or any of the past two or three sentences before that.

"I said, you'll have to show me your work. Sometime."

"Oh. Okay, sure," I say, but I don't mean it.

I turn my attention back to Afton. She catches me looking at her and frowns for just a second, like a single cloud passing in front of the sun, before she smiles at something Mrs. Wong says. Guilt lies heavy in my gut. I want to tell her. I really, really do.

But I'm not going to.

18

My keep-Afton-away strategy doesn't work, however, because not even a half hour later she approaches me outside the restrooms at Volcanoes National Park. "What's going on with you?" she asks immediately.

Shit.

"Nothing is going on with me," I spit out. Another lie.

"Still thinking about Leo?"

"No, I am not thinking about Leo at all, except now I am, thank you very much." It's a good cover, I realize, acting like I'm upset over the stupid breakup. It explains things that I need to explain. Like the way my teeth are grinding together right now.

"You should talk to Mom about it."

I snort. "Mom. Mom doesn't even know I broke up with my boyfriend. Does she know *you* broke up with your boyfriend?"

"Not yet," Afton says lightly. "She's busy."

"She seems to make time for the things she cares about, though," I say bitterly.

"Yeah," Afton says, because she thinks I'm actually saying something good about Mom. "She's had some interesting breakups. She could give you some perspective on the subject."

"I don't want Mom's perspective," I mutter.

"That time I . . . after my first time, in the garage, I talked to her," Afton says.

I sit up straighter. "You told Mom about having sex?"

Afton nods.

I scoff. "What did she do?"

"Oh, she wasn't exactly happy about it," Afton remembers. "But she hugged me. She talked me through it, even. She's not as good as Pop about these kinds of things, maybe, but she's capable of the parenting thing. When forced. You should talk to her."

I wonder how long it will be before I can even comfortably be present in the same room with my mother again. This morning, before she left the hotel, I thought about calling her out. And then, while Abby and Afton and I were having breakfast, Mom texted me asking about what we were planning on doing today (she didn't read the folder, either, apparently), and I was so tempted to text her back, *Oh, nothing, just hanging out in the room. Or do you and whoever-it-was need it again? It seemed like you were pretty busy in there yesterday.*

And then I imagined Mom staring down at her phone, horrified, almost as shocked as I was yesterday, sick with knowing that she's caught. Terrified that I know who she really is now. Dreading that she's going to have to look me in the face at some point and finally tell me the truth.

That might make me feel somewhat better. If she could feel just a little bit of what I am feeling. If she would fess up to it. If she'd say she's sorry. If she promised not to do it again.

But if we all put our cards on the table, I can still only see one probable outcome: divorce—a word I associate with a few hazy memories of voices screaming at each other from behind closed doors and the silhouette of a man holding a suitcase. And this time the man with the suitcase will be Pop. My jaw clenches at the thought. I'll be damned—yes, damned, I decide, which feels like an older person's word, but I embrace it—I'll be *damned* if I lose Pop because my mother is a selfish slut.

There it is. The word. I mean it this time. We aren't supposed to use the word *slut* because that's what men used to call women who dared to have sex outside of their control. There are a lot of words for it: *strumpet, hussy, tramp, skank, ho.* Any woman who might possibly enjoy sex and actually want to participate in the act, who hooked up with more than one partner—there must be something wrong with a woman like that. She should be punished. *Slut.*

But I can't think of another word. My mother has betrayed us with sex.

And why? Why would she do it? It isn't like she's sex starved. She and Pop have sex. She isn't one of those repressed and lonely housewives from the fifties who never really had a choice but to get married to the first available beefcake and have babies and do her marital duty. Mom is a modern woman. A freaking surgeon. She cuts people open and takes them apart and then puts them back together. My mother is a titan. She's a badass.

So why can't she also be a decent person? Is that so much to ask?

121

Mom always talks about how Afton and I (and Abby, eventually) need to be strong and good, as people but also as women. She likes to say we need to be the change the world needs—something ripped off from Gandhi, I think. She expects us to do our best, and we do. We get straight As. We participate in the requisite extracurricular activities, and we excel in those, too. We have been model children.

And all this time, Mom has been screwing around.

I really, really want to hate her.

"Ada?" Afton prompts quietly.

"Why is sex such a big deal?" I ask, more to myself than to my sister.

"Oh. Right. I used to think it wasn't a big deal," Afton says. "I used to see sex as a purely physical thing, something programed into our animal brain, or whatever. I didn't think it had to mean anything. I was pretty eager to cash in my V-Card. But now—"

"I guess I couldn't possibly understand," I snap, "because I'm a naive little virgin."

She cocks her head, confused at my sudden attitude. "What couldn't you possibly understand?"

"Why everyone around me feels like sex is the thing to do."

Her cheeks get pink. "Everyone?"

"Well, you told me I need to find some cute boy to sleep with so I could get over Leo."

And just like that, we're back to fighting. And it's my fault.

"You know I didn't mean it like that," Afton says, her eyes dropping like *I've* embarrassed *her* somehow. "I was just—"

"I think you did mean it. Otherwise you wouldn't have said it. Because that's exactly what you would do."

Afton's mouth snaps closed so hard her teeth click. "Hey. Don't be a bitch."

Oh, so now *she's* calling *me* a bitch. "Who, me?" I pretend to look around. "I guess it's better than me being a fucking square, though, right?"

Afton's eyes narrow. She stares at me silently for a minute. Then she says, "Where is your *new* boyfriend, anyway?"

I bristle. "Nick is not my boyfriend. We're just hanging out."

"You've been hanging out all day."

"It's nothing. He was nice to me last night when I was sick."

"Yes, I was wondering about that. *Were* you sick last night?" she asks, blue eyes sharp on me. "Really? Because I think you were faking it to get out of having dinner with everyone. And that's normally my move." She sighs. "I don't want to fight anymore. I don't know what bug crawled up your butt today, but it's not okay for you to just puke your rage all over me. Why are you even so mad? I mean, I get that you're still steamed about Leo, or at least I would be. But you don't have to take it out on me."

She's right. It's Mom I'm really pissed at. I should apologize. I know that. I should be an adult about it. But I also still see the common sense in getting Afton to stay away from me. It's a painful push and pull with us, like turning magnets toward and away from each other. I want to draw her in, confide in her, work it through with her, get her advice, get her sympathy, get her support. And I also want to push her away so she doesn't get hurt.

Sisterhood is complicated.

And in some irrational way I do blame Afton. If Afton hadn't taken Abby to hula class—if they hadn't both insisted on freaking hula, instead of paddleboarding like I wanted, none of this would have happened. I'd still be blissfully unaware of what is going on with Mom.

But I can't say any of this, so I have to think up another reason.

I start with the obvious. "You didn't tell me about you and Logan breaking up."

She frowns. "Well, like I said before, you had your own thing—"

"A good sister would have told me. We always tell each other everything. I told you about Leo. And if you'd told me about Logan, then we could have—I don't know—commiserated. But instead you just let me babble on and on about all the things I was feeling."

"I was trying to be supportive," she says tightly.

"Well, don't. Also you didn't save me a seat."

"A seat?"

"Today, when we got to the bus. I thought we were going to sit together, but no, you sat with Kate."

She gives a little confused shake of her head, like what the hell am I talking about? "I thought you were going to stay up front with Abby."

"But I didn't. And you don't even like Kate. And you were sitting on the inside, by the window."

"So? I always sit by the window."

"So you must have sat down first. And then Kate came to sit down next to you, and you didn't say, 'Sorry, I'm saving this for my sister.' Which would have been the sisterly thing to do."

She looks tired. "Maybe I'm not that good at being sisterly."

"I know, right?" I say wryly. "Anyway. That's why I'm hanging out with Nick."

"Well, awesome," she says sarcastically. "He obviously likes you."

"He's being nice. That's all."

"Maybe he could be more than nice."

I scoff. "So you're single now. How about *you* look for some cute boy to hook up with? It should be easy for you. You're so fricking beautiful. There's got to be someone around here who—"

That's when I spot him.

Michael Wong.

As in, Billy and Jenny's oldest kid. The one who just graduated from college. The one with the supposedly amazing ass. He's walking around with Abby and Peter and Josie, chatting with Jenny.

"Oh look, there's Michael," I say slowly, surprised and confused because Billy said at dinner that first night that Michael wasn't coming to Hawaii. "What's he doing here?"

"The same thing as the rest of us," Afton says. "Getting dragged along by his parents."

We're both staring at Michael, and it's like he feels it. He turns, smiles in our direction, and mouths the word *hi*.

Afton lifts her hand in the lamest wave ever. And then she actually blushes.

I give a disbelieving laugh. "Well. Okay. You should get on that. You said yourself that Michael would be the perfect rebound." I look around. All that's out there at the moment is a tangle of rain forest, so thick I can't see anything beyond the crush of trees and bushes around us. Which feels like my current mood. "I mean, it could be awkward, if anyone found out you were getting busy with Mom's . . . colleague's much older son. But who cares? It's what animals do, right? I say go for it."

"He's sweet, actually," Afton says coolly. She smooths her hair over her shoulder. "He doesn't seem to get how hot he is, and I like that in a guy. And he's very smart."

"Plus he has the stellar ass," I fill in.

"True. We have a lot in common."

Of course perfect people have a lot in common. Because they're perfect.

"So I assume you're going to have sex with him," I say. "Like, it's no joke anymore, right?"

We lock eyes in some kind of impasse where we're both thinking better of mean things we want to say. "Who says I haven't already?" she says finally.

"That'd be impressively fast, even for you," I snap.

"Yeah, well, I'm nothing if not efficient."

Right then Nick comes out of the bathroom, shaking his hands to dry them. He looks around and sees me. His eyes actually light up, and he starts walking over.

In that moment, I know Afton's right. Shit. Nick likes me. As in, he's interested in me, romantically speaking. I can tell by the way his walk changes, shoulders straightening, more self-conscious, like he's deliberately trying to be smooth. He brushes his hair to one side and tucks it behind his ear. He smiles. Shit shit. He thinks I'm interested in him, too. I'd assumed he was simply being friendly. I wasn't paying attention. But now I see, in that flash of insight you have sometimes, that all this time he's been flirting with me, in his nerd way. Because he likes me.

"Aw, he's cute," says Afton archly. "Like a little puppy."

I turn to her. "If you could refrain from speaking to me for the rest of the day, that'd be swell, thanks."

Her eyes narrow. "Fine."

"Fine," I agree. Another F-word.

She stalks off. Probably to go find poor unsuspecting Michael.

Nick is almost upon me. Ten more steps, and he'll be here, wagging his tail.

But instead of greeting him, instead of being nice the way he is nice, I decide I have enough to deal with. I don't even really know Nick, and I've had enough drama with boys this week, thanks.

I don't need a puppy.

So I turn my back on him. And I walk the other way.

19

The first major crush I ever had, a couple years before Leo came along in the art gallery that fateful day last year, was literally the boy next door. His name was Darius, some wise Bible name, which suited him because Darius was quiet. Like me, I thought. I'd see him bringing in groceries with his mother, her monologuing, him following behind her silently, back and forth to the car. I'd see him mowing the lawn. Putting up Christmas lights. Taking out the trash. I'd watch him walking to the bus stop (to a different school than mine, since mine was all girls), and while the other boys would be laughing and teasing each other and trying to act cool, Darius would just *be* cool by default. When he did speak, the other kids listened. I liked the sound of his voice, too, the low, gentle timbre of it, although I never caught what he said. I was never close enough to hear.

I started drawing him. His face. Ears. Hands. The way a

long-sleeved tee draped across his shoulders. The shoes he wore. I'd always made quick sketches of people, but I did so many of Darius that year that Pop finally noticed. "Is that the boy next door?" he asked one morning at the breakfast table, leaning over my sketchbook, and I blushed so hard I could have passed out, and Pop said, "Oh. So that's how it is."

That's so how it was.

Pop said, "That's a good likeness," which felt like a perfect summation of my feelings at that point. "You should ask him out."

"You should probably stay out of my love life," I said.

"Fair enough." We dropped the subject until it came up again, naturally, a few weeks later when we were in SF at a Giants game. I was just sitting there watching the game, minding my own business, when suddenly Pop poked me in the shoulder.

"Look over there," he said, and gestured very subtly with his head to two rows ahead of us, where Darius was sitting with his family. "Now's your moment, Ada. You could go over and talk to him."

But that was impossible. "What would I even say?"

"You'd say, 'Hi, I'm Ada. I live next door.'"

I shook my head. "He knows I live next door."

"You'd go from there," Pop said.

But go from there to what? *I think you're cute? Nice weather we're having?*

"Now you have something in common to talk about," Pop said.

I stared at him blankly.

"You both like baseball," Pop explained.

Oh.

"So go talk to him," Pop said. "Carpe diem. You go, girl."

I shook my head again. "I . . . I can't."

Pop shrugged. "Your call. I guess everybody has to go through unrequited love at some point. I get that. If you don't even try, that's safer. And that way he doesn't get messed up by, you know, reality—people can stay perfect if you never get to know who they are. But it's not very satisfying. I'd want something better for you. Something real."

"You've got to be the first dad in history who *wants* his teenage daughter to talk to boys," I pointed out. Then, out of the blue, I pictured Darius and me standing in my room, Darius turning to look at my art on the walls.

"These are great," he'd say in his deep voice.

And then he'd be startled, because he would have spotted a drawing of himself. And I'd be embarrassed, because I'd essentially been creeping on him, I guess, but then I could tell that he was flattered. He liked it.

"You're really talented," he would say, and I'd breathe, "Thanks," and then who knows what would happen, in my room, with the door shut and Darius whispering that he liked my work.

"I'm not saying you should make out with the guy," Pop said loudly. "I just don't want you to miss out on the best parts of life because you're afraid of getting hurt."

Essentially Pop was calling me a coward. I knew that. And I also knew that my daydream would never happen if I didn't start by actually talking to Darius. So I stood up.

"You got this," Pop said.

"We both like baseball," I whispered to myself as I awkwardly stepped sideways around a bunch of people to reach the aisle. Then

I went forward a couple of rows and stood for a minute watching Darius as he was watching the game. He was wearing a black-and-orange Giants jersey with his own last name (OLIVERA) printed on the back, and the number 07. A shirt that meant that he was more than just the casual baseball enthusiast. He was a real fan.

Not like me, who came to one or two games a year. I barely understood the rules of baseball. I was mostly there for the food and because Pop loved it.

I couldn't possibly talk to Darius about baseball, I decided. So what could I say?

"Do you need to get in?" asked the lady at the end of the row, who I realized all at once was Darius's mother.

"I just came over to say hi," I said.

She frowned. She clearly didn't have a clue who I was.

"I'm your neighbor," I explained. Maybe if I talked to Darius's mother, I could then somehow work my way up to Darius himself. (Which is sort of the way it worked out with Leo, too, now that I think of it.) "From next door. Ada Bloom?"

"Oh." Her frown didn't go away. "Oh, that's nice. Hi."

"Hi."

Something happened on the field. Everybody lurched to their feet, cheering.

Mrs. Olivera looked put out that she'd missed the action. "Well, it's good to see you, Ava. Thanks for stopping by."

I didn't care that she got my name wrong or that she made it sound like I was one of those solicitors who ring your doorbell to talk you into buying solar panels. I was trying to figure out how to ask her if she wanted to have dinner: her family and my family. Something about how we never get to know our neighbors these days, and how sad I thought that was. But she wasn't looking at me anymore.

I would have given up right then, but that's when Darius glanced over, and his eyes brightened like I was the person he most wanted to see. He even smiled. *Smiled.* At me.

I could have passed out.

Then he got up and edged his way over to me.

"Hi," I practiced under my breath. "Enjoying the game?"

He stepped into the aisle with me.

"Hi," I said breathlessly.

"I'll take two," he said in that soft, rich voice of his, and reached behind me to give the hot dog guy his money. Because he was *buying hot dogs, dummy.*

Then, hot dogs in hand, he went back to his seat.

It was so much more than him not recognizing me. He didn't even register that I was there.

I did not exist in his world.

I hurried back to my seat.

"How'd it go?" Pop asked as I slumped into place beside him again. He saw the look on my face. "That well, huh?"

"Do me a favor, okay?"

"Anything. Within reason, of course."

"Don't give me any more advice about boys."

"Okay."

"Like ever."

"Okay."

"I mean it."

"I got it."

"Good."

That was the first time I think I realized that I wasn't that kind of girl, the ones that boys look at and want to kiss. Like they all apparently wanted to kiss Afton at the first sight of her long blond hair. They just didn't see me that way. If they saw me at all.

I was—my stomach churned at the revelation—unkissable.

I would never have thought the word unfuckable, but that, too.

Until Leo, that is. But that was a fluke. Or not. The more I think about it, the more I think that maybe Leo wasn't that interested in having sex with me. Maybe he was simply interested in having sex. Which is not the same thing. Not the same thing at all.

20

Obviously I don't sit with Nick on the bus after I snub him, or when we stop again, this time for dinner at a huge buffet-style restaurant. I lurk in the corner of the dining room, justifying how rude I was by reminding myself that I'm not fit company for anybody. My breakup with Leo is less than forty-eight hours old. My parents' marriage is imploding. I'm keeping a huge secret from my sister. I'm over here remembering Darius, of all people, who I haven't thought about in a long, long time.

I'm a hot mess.

The look on Nick's face, though, was awful. I just caught, as I was turning around, the way his eyes clouded over, this smile dropping from his face. It was way worse than my "I'll take two, please," moment with Darius, because I did it to him deliberately. But I tell myself I'm actually doing Nick a favor by rejecting him. Sometimes, according to one of Pop's favorite songs, you've got to be cruel to be kind.

I'm feeling moderately okay about this decision until they bring out the birthday cake, a small, round pineapple upside-down cake with a blazing candle in the center.

It's his birthday.

Kahoni sets the cake on the table in front of Nick. Everybody starts to sing off-key. Nick hunches over the flickering candle with a look of bemused embarrassment. He doesn't look at me, even though I'm sure he knows I'm here. He looks at everyone *but* me.

Because I hurt his feelings. I made him feel small and stupid. On his birthday.

That was a dick move. I am a dick.

"How old are you?" Kahoni asks after the singing dies down and Nick blows out the candles. Nick mumbles an answer. I can't hear it, but I know what it is: he's sixteen, the same as me now.

"Sweet sixteen!" Kahoni says, clapping him on the back again.

"Have you ever been kissed?" asks a red-faced woman at the next table—Penny Jacobi, because of course it is. She looks like she had too much wine at dinner. "Well, have you?

Nick stares at her incredulously, like Penny just asked him if he's ever walked on the moon. "You mean, like, romantically?"

"Well, I don't mean by your mother." Penny smirks.

Nick doesn't have a mother that I know of. Everyone calls his dad a "confirmed bachelor," whatever that means. Nick's mother must have been in the picture at some point, but what happened to her, I don't know.

"No," Nick murmurs. "I've never been kissed."

135

"Maybe we could fix that." Penny giggles and looks around. "Who wants to kiss this young man on his birthday?"

Silence.

"What, no takers? Oh, come on, he's not that bad-looking!" slurs Penny. "Who will volunteer?"

Every girl of a remotely eligible age turns away. I'd like to say I'm different, that I stand up then and give the Jacobis the finger and plant a big fat kiss on Nick's surprised lips in front of everyone.

But I don't. I just sit there, keeping my head down, hoping I don't catch Penny's eye.

"Sit down, Mom," says Kate finally. "Leave the kid alone."

"Yeah, don't be a jackass, Jacobi. Sit down before you fall down," says Marjorie Pearson, and nobody messes with Marjorie, so Penny stumbles back to her seat.

Kahoni puts his hand on Nick's shoulder and squeezes. "Don't worry, dude. It will come. That first kiss, it's too special to waste on just anybody."

Here we go again. Special.

"Right," Nick agrees faintly. Kahoni seems like an expert on the matter, being that his name, I remember, means "the kiss." He squeezes Nick's shoulder one final time and then wanders off to talk to some of the other guests.

Everyone goes back to what they were doing before the cake. Thankfully that includes the Jacobis. I watch Nick pick at his cake.

Unkissable.

Unfuckable.

And suddenly, I just think, *no*.

No, I think. So I do what I should have done earlier.

I stand up.

It's like an alien has taken over my body. I don't linger. I don't practice what I should say. I don't try to think of something clever. I don't hesitate. I march straight over to Nick's table and I say, "Hey."

His eyes still light up when he sees me. I didn't misinterpret him before. He likes me.

"Happy birthday," I say.

"Thanks."

"I'll do it."

"What?"

"I'll kiss you, if you want."

He stares up at me, stunned. "You will?"

"Also, do you want to have sex with me?"

"Yes." Then my words actually register. His eyes widen. "Wait—what?"

"I don't mean now, obviously," I say. "Maybe, like, tomorrow?"

His mouth opens and then closes again.

"I'll see you later," I say, and then I walk away.

21

I retreat to the bus even though it's not time to get on yet. I hide in the very back seat and try to understand why I just did that: I walked up and point-blank asked this boy if he wanted to *have sex with me*. This boy I don't know. Okay, so I do technically know Nick—I've known him since we were kids—but I don't *let's-have-sex* know him. How had I jumped straight from kissing to "Do you want to have sex with me?"

I'm just blurting shit out all over everybody here. But it's too late to call the words back.

I take a deep breath. People are filing back onto the bus now. Nick will be one of them. I need to consider what I'll say when next we talk.

The way I see it, I have three options:

Option one. *Ha ha, wasn't that a funny joke I told?*

Option two. *Sorry. I'm going through a thing. I may be losing my mind, actually. I didn't mean it.* This seems like the honest answer, but is it? Didn't I mean it? Which leads me to:

Option three. *Let's totally have sex. What works with your schedule? Because mine is wide open for the rest of the week.*

Heat floods my face. I want to pick number three because I want to be bold and unapologetic. No more shy wallflower, nice and polite Ada. Bold. I can be bold. I've screamed "fuck you" at a person in a crowded parking lot. I could be so bold again.

"Hey, Ada," comes a voice, and I stare at my feet and blurt out, "I was kidding. Obviously."

"Kidding about what?"

I look up. It isn't Nick standing there. It's Peter Wong, the second kid in the Wong family.

"Sorry," I stammer. "I thought—"

"Your sister took my seat," he says, gesturing grumpily to the front, where Afton is now sitting with Michael and Abby, Josie, and Jenny. "And all the others are taken."

I should be insulted, but I nod. "All right. Sit down."

"You don't have to talk to me, though," Peter says. He's the middle kid, between Michael and Josie—the "Ada" of the Wong family.

"Fine by me," I say. "Just sit, okay?"

He sits. The bus jerks and pulls away from the restaurant. Kahoni's voice booms over the loudspeakers, informing us that we are headed to the final stop on our tour: the active volcano part of Volcanoes National Park. Peter starts watching a movie on his phone and seems content to entirely ignore me.

I sigh. Once again, I chickened out.

I went with option one.

It's getting dark when we arrive, which Kahoni timed intentionally, since the lava from the volcano is so much easier to see in the dark.

But first the group wanders through the visitors center. We learn about volcanoes, this type of volcano in general, and Kilauea specifically, how it formed the Hawaiian Islands, how it's still forming them; right now as we're hanging out buying postcards, the Big Island is getting bigger. There's another island—I read this on the wall—a new one called Loihi that will appear to the southeast sometime in the next ten to one hundred thousand years.

I stop to examine a display of a scientist's clothing and boots recovered after he fell into hot lava from a place he thought was solid but turned out only to be a thin crust over disaster.

I think about Pop. I can't stop thinking about him. This one time we made a path of pillows all around the living room because Abby wanted to pretend the floor was lava. We hopped from pillow to pillow, Abby laughing that pure joy little kid laugh, and Pop chuckling right along with her. Pop chuckles. He's what I hear in my head when I hear the word *chuckle*, this deep rumble of mirth from his broad chest.

I take out my phone and send him a text.

I miss you a million. I'm so pissed you're not here.

We don't say pissed in our family, but I say it anyway. I also use full spelling and punctuation because Pop hates text speak. He doesn't reply. He's probably sleeping or working. I've lost track of the time difference.

"Okay, people, let's go see what all the excitement's about!" Kahoni gathers us up to take us to the overlook of the volcano. He passes around binoculars so we can get a good look at the bright orange lava bubbling and spraying at this spot in the distance.

In the far distance.

The far, *far* distance.

Hence the binoculars.

We're so far back it's hard to see anything but a bit of orange, like fire. But we can't walk any closer, because the ground isn't stable. We don't want to be that dude with the burned-up clothes.

It's underwhelming. The contrast is nice—the bloom of orange against the gray rock and sky—but it lacks definition. I don't think I could paint it, although I could try.

Abby comes bounding up with Josie and Jenny Wong. "It's lava, Ada!" she yells. "Oh my dog! I just found out I love lava!"

Maybe she's thinking about Pop, too.

"I know," I say. "Isn't it cool?"

"Actually, it's hot," she informs me matter-of-factly. "It would burn you if you fell in. It would burn you right up! Thank goodness that they don't throw people in anymore, right?"

She asks me to lift her so she can see better through the binoculars, and I do. Then she tells me she wants down and the second her feet touch the ground she runs off again with Josie and Jenny to get ice cream.

Alone again, I stand staring at the faraway glow of the volcano. It feels like I'm waiting for something. A disaster? A sign? I don't know.

Then I become aware of Nick standing next to me, the orange light accentuating the sharpness of his small, upturned nose. It's like a ski jump, Nick's nose.

My breath seizes. Oh my god, I asked him to *have sex* with me, and now what?

Am I really going to go with option one?

"Nice evening to see a volcano, don't you think?" He turns to me. "Apparently there's a tour where you can hike down to a spot where the lava is going into the ocean. That would have been pretty awesome. And there's a boat tour, too. This is still cool, though," he says.

"Actually, it's hot," I say.

He makes a sound that's a cross between a snort and a laugh. Then silence. In the far, far distance, the volcano lets out a spray of hot, liquid rock. "So," Nick says finally.

Which is how I know we're going to talk about it. It. What I said.

"So . . . ," I reply.

"I have a question about what happened earlier."

"At the restaurant?" Of course he means the restaurant.

"Yes," he confirms.

"So, what's your question?"

"My question is, why?"

"Why?"

"Why did you ask me to have sex with you?"

My heart bangs into my ribs. "I—uh—I'm kind of going through something right now."

"I noticed. But like what, exactly?"

For all of three seconds, I'm tempted to tell him. It would be so good to tell somebody. Get it off my chest. This stuff feels like it's sitting there like a stack of weights. "Well, my parents, you see . . . and then I just broke up with my—" I start, but I don't want to get into it. "I didn't—and then I saw—" Oh god, I'm going with option two, which is, I realize, even worse than option one. "I've had a lapse of sanity, I think."

He nods quietly. "So you didn't mean it."

But here's the thing: I did.

Having sex with Nick would probably be a mistake. But maybe I want to make a mistake. A huge mistake. A mind-bending, colossal, unmistakable mistake, a mistake that means I'm alive and I am a human teenage girl and I am fallible and back off, everyone. I am not a fucking square!

"I did mean it," I say, louder than I mean to. "I'm sixteen, and I feel like I've never done anything remotely risky or exciting, and it feels like everyone around me is doing things, and—well, I won't get into the details of what they're doing, but—*I* want to do things. I want to feel something besides guilt, I guess, and what do I have to even be so guilty about? Nothing. I refuse to feel guilty about the things other people do. *I* want to do things. I want to feel things. Yes. Yes, I meant it. I do. Mean it. Yes."

"Wow. That's a lot to unpack," Nick says. "But I agree."

I glance over at him. "You do?"

"Well, I didn't understand all of that, but what I did get, I agree with. My life is super boring, if I'm being honest. I keep thinking, is this it? Seriously? This is my life?"

I start nodding compulsively. "Exactly."

"I want to do things!" he says.

"So you want to have sex," I confirm.

It's dark, but I get the sense that he's turning red. "Yes," he says. "I meant it, too. At first I said yes because that's what came out of my mouth the second you asked—knee-jerk reaction, or whatnot. But I've been thinking about it for the past hour, and yeah. Yes. That's an affirmative."

Now it's my turn. "Why?"

"I'm a sixteen-year-old boy," he explains.

143

"Happy birthday, by the way."

"Thanks. Anyway, sex occupies like seventy-eight percent of my thoughts these days." He sees my expression and adds, "But it should be special, right? With the right girl. At the right place. And what could be better than Hawaii?"

There it is again, that word. Special. But I feel fluttery inside, actual physical arousal, all my lady parts revving up just talking about having sex. This sort of thing is obviously not restricted to boys. I want to have sex. With Nick Kelly, the runaway beanpole kid.

And here I thought Leo was the miracle.

"And you think I'm the right girl?" I ask slowly, taking that in.

"Well, I know you," Nick says. "I've always liked you."

So who's unfuckable now? Not me. And not Nick.

"I like you, too," I say lightly. I'd quantify it as much as I like peanut butter cups. Or almost. "But it doesn't have to be a relationship, right? I mean, we only see each other like once a year. It could be casual."

"Right. Casual," he says. "I'm okay with that. So we're agreed. We're going to have . . ."

"Sex. Yes. Agreed," I say.

"Should we . . . shake on it?" he asks.

The space alien takes over again. "Maybe we should kiss. I did say I would kiss you."

"Okay," Nick says, and then we're leaning toward each other, already moving along the path to where we'll kiss, right there in this milling crowd of tourists standing at the edge of a volcano. Our lips are zooming in, only very slowly.

My heart beats like a drum. I hope my lips aren't chapped. They get so dry for days whenever I go somewhere on an airplane. I hope my breath is okay. His smells like vanilla and cinnamon and pineapple. Like cake. I really do want to kiss him, I discover. It feels like the right call, like his kiss could erase Leo's kisses from my brain. Like kissing could make me forget the things I've seen since then. It feels right. It feels—

"Ada!"

I jerk back to see Afton standing a few feet away, hands on her hips.

"I told you not to talk to me!" I scream.

"Everyone else is on the bus!" she yells back. "Come on!" She glares at me and then at Nick and then back at me. Then she throws her hands up in exasperation and storms back to the bus.

"We better go," Nick says.

"I'm sorry. My sister ruins everything."

We dash through the parking lot. Kahoni gives us a knowing look as we clamber onto the bus but says nothing. The bus is full: there are no two seats together.

Nick leans close to me, still smelling tantalizingly of cake. "Meet me at the cabana by the Ocean Tower pool, tomorrow, nine a.m., and we'll discuss it."

That sounds very reasonable. A discussion first. Something Leo definitely should have done.

"Can we make it eight?" By nine I usually have Abby in tow, and I don't want my baby sister to be part of this conversation. Who knows what she'd come away saying this time?

"Oh, eight, wow, okay," he says.

"Tomorrow, eight a.m.," I confirm. This could be really

happening. For real, this time.

Nick finds a seat somewhere in the middle. I get stuck in the front next to Kahoni, but he doesn't launch into another history lesson. Instead he lets everyone sleep, all the long drive back to the Hilton. But I don't sleep. I've got too much on my mind.

Two hours later, as the bus is pulling into the hotel, my phone chirps with a text.

From Pop.

I miss you, too. Two million, in fact.

He has no idea.

I guess that's the problem. But I also never want him to find out.

I wish you were here, I write again. Which is half true. I wish that he'd been with us all along. Then nothing out of the ordinary would have happened. And maybe then Nick Kelly would be the most exciting thing I ever discovered in Hawaii.

22

When I was eight, Mom brought me to Take Your Daughter to Work Day at Stanford Hospital. I remember being glad that Mom wasn't also bringing Afton, and I could simply be myself without any comparison between us. I also remember being thrilled that I'd get an entire day to spend with Mom. And when we were riding the bullet train into Palo Alto, Mom tried to fix my hair, make it lie flat, but she had no experience fixing hair and soon gave up. Instead, she sat down across from me and gave me the back of a piece of paper to draw on.

"Are you excited?" she asked as I tried to capture the inside of the train car in a few lines of the pencil, although I was also looking at Mom, memorizing the angles of her face, for a portrait I wanted to do of her later.

I nodded. I wasn't sure how this was going to work. I knew she was a heart surgeon, which meant that she cut into people's chests and worked on their hearts, and my own heart beat fast if I tried to imagine myself watching her do that. All week I'd been trying to prepare myself by watching medical dramas. I'd pictured myself scrubbing in with her, capped and gowned by her side.

"Scalpel," she'd say, and I would hand her the slender silver blade. I'd peer over her shoulder as she made the cut.

The cut. Whoa. It felt like a test. Would I be tough enough to witness it? Would I puke or faint at the sight of all the blood?

Honestly, I didn't know.

The train screeched to a stop. "This is us," Mom said. "Come on."

At the hospital she took me straight to her office, where Ruthie was waiting.

"Oh, thank god, Ruthie," Mom said. "Can you do something with her hair?"

Then she disappeared down the hall, a flurry of movement in a white coat.

I sat in Mom's office in the chair behind her desk as Ruthie worked my hair into a French braid. "Did you know," Ruthie said as she tugged and smoothed, "that you were born in this hospital? Your mom was so funny. Here she was in labor, but she could not stay still. She ended up waddling over here from the maternity wing, wearing her hospital gown, to check on her critical patients."

I'd heard that story. Many times. And how, like four hours after she'd had me, she'd strapped me to her with some kind of wrap and gone back to check on her patients again. I tried to imagine what that must have been like, being so small and new, pressed tight to Mom's chest.

"Gosh, it seems like yesterday," Ruthie sighed.

"Not for me," I said. "I don't remember it."

She laughed. "Anyway. Around here we call your mother 'the Whirlwind.'"

I knew that, too. Sometimes Pop would say it to Mom at home. He'd say, "All right, now it's time to stop being the Whirlwind and come back to regular speed." And she would. Pop was magic like that.

The phone on Mom's desk rang. Ruthie answered it.

"Okay," she said into the receiver. "I'll bring her up."

I spent most of the day in the gallery, which is a room that looks down on the OR. I sat there among the med students and residents and watched, from a safe, less gory distance, as my mom did a triple bypass, opening the chest, harvesting veins from the patient's leg to connect his heart to.

I didn't faint or puke. Mostly I just read one of Pop's graphic novels and tried to look interested in case my mother looked up to check on me. Which she didn't. In there, she was laser focused. She probably didn't even remember I was there.

The surgery took five hours. It went well. I had lunch with Ruthie in the hospital cafeteria and then spent some time with Mom introducing me to the other surgeons and nurses and residents. I remember that Billy Wong told me a knock-knock joke and gave me a lollipop. He didn't have a daughter yet. Only Michael.

Afterward, on the train home, Mom said, "I'm proud of you," which confused me because I hadn't even done anything.

"I know," I said, although I didn't, really. "I'm proud of you, too, Mom."

I was.

I really was.

23

Today's the day, I wake up thinking. I've arranged to have sex. Today. And why not? I feel a certain measure of relief thinking about it. With Leo, there was a lot of pressure attached to the idea. So many feelings. A certain degree of performance anxiety. But the notion of having sex with Nick feels completely different. With Nick it feels like two nerdy people simply getting this major life event over with, so we can say we did it and move on with our lives.

Casual, I've decided. Casual is the way to go. How did Afton put it yesterday? I'm going to cash in my V-Card.

It occurs to me belatedly that maybe me deciding to have sex is a form of revenge. Revenge on whom, I can't say exactly. On Afton for trying to boss me around about what I'm ready for, or for her inexplicable ability to get any guy she wants to fall at her feet, at any time. On Mom, for expecting me to always be so good while she feels free to be as bad as she wants.

I'll show them both.

But, underneath all that, it also comes back to genuine curiosity. To know what it will be like. I feel so terrible about everything right now. I want to feel better. Sex could make me feel better. And maybe it's as simple as that.

I stretch my arms over my head. Today's the day. Or maybe tonight.

I still can't really picture it, Nick and me, becoming horizontal with each other. But I'll get there. I've decided. Today.

I'm getting out of bed when I notice the spot of red on the white sheets.

"No," I gasp incredulously. I run to the bathroom to check my pajamas. "No no no no no!"

Yes. My period has arrived. It's like four days early. I knew it was coming, and it felt unfair knowing it would happen in Hawaii, because isn't that how it always goes when you go on a trip? You have to pack the extra stuff. You have to worry about it.

But this, today, of all days, is the ultimate level of unfair. This is seriously going to mess up my life.

It's like the universe doesn't want me to have sex. Revenge or not.

"Nooooooo," I moan. Right on cue I start to cramp. Why does that always happen, too, that the pain only comes after you notice you've started? I sink to the bathroom floor. I want to scream. I want to sob over the unfairness of this world. I want to eat ice cream and feel sorry for myself and possibly die.

A shadow crosses over me—Afton, standing at the bathroom door. "You sound like you're dying in here."

"Oh, I am," I confirm. "Minute by minute, I'm getting closer to the grave. Give it seventy years or so."

She scoffs and walks away, back to hating me again.

I get up, clean up, shower quickly, make use of some feminine products, and before Mom can come in to dump Abby off on me, I run down to the pool to meet Nick.

Only now I don't know what to say.

He's there. It's nice that he's so prompt. Leo was always running late for things. "Have you tried the acai bowls from the café? They are delectable," Nick says as I approach the cabana by the Ocean pool.

He's obviously trying to impress me with his AP-level vocabulary. Like a bird flashing his brightly colored feathers. *Loquacious. Delectable*. Squawk.

"It's 'a-sigh-ee.'" I drop into the lounge chair next to him. Another passing cramp. Ugh, if I could only cut my uterus out and fling it into the sea, that'd be preferable.

"It's good." He digs around in the bowl with his spoon and settles on a huge bite of sliced banana and blueberries. "Normally, I'm not a fruit guy, but this is making me rethink my position. What is acai, anyway?"

I have no idea. "Some kind of magic berry. Why don't you like fruit?"

"My dad's always trying to get me to eat fruit and vegetables. I have to make him work at the parenting thing, you know? I hate to be so easy."

"Or, like, healthy, right?"

He shrugs his thin shoulders. "I try to be noncompliant now and then. Especially when it comes to my dietary choices."

There's an acai stain on the front of his shirt.

All morning I've been wondering if, when I saw Nick again, I would still have that almost-sexy we're-about-to-kiss feeling from last night.

I don't.

For multiple reasons, I guess.

He's looking at my face. "Have you changed your mind?"

I feel bloated. God, I love being a woman. Oh wait, no, I don't. But I say, "I'm here, aren't I?"

"You could be here to tell me you've changed your mind."

"Well, I haven't."

"So we're still on for having sex," he says slowly. "I thought I might have ingested some bad pineapple upside-down cake yesterday and hallucinated everything that happened."

"We're still on." I struggle to sound casual about it. "But we need a plan."

"Absolutely," Nick agrees. "It's common knowledge that having sex always requires a strategy."

"Right. Now be serious."

He arches an eyebrow. "I'm very serious. I'm a very serious guy."

I bite back a smile. Before this, I did think Nick was fairly serious. All my life he's been this solemn, quiet kid standing in the back of our tour group (excluding that one time in Rio). But now here he is being a wisecracker.

His gaze drops from my face to what I'm holding. "You brought a notebook. So obviously *you're* serious."

"It's my sketchbook."

"Oh, are you going to show me some of your work?" he asks, too eagerly.

"No. I use this for everything. Sometimes I use it like a bullet journal."

"*Bullet* journal? That's alarming. Is this like a hit list?"

"No," I sigh. "It's like bullet points."

He stares at me blankly.

"Like those dots you put in front of things when you're making a to-do list." I would continue to explain, but then I catch on that he's messing with me. I smack his knee with my bullet journal, and he laughs. Then I flip it open. "So, wiseass, the plan."

THE PLAN, I write across the top of the page. At the same time, my mind spins, searching for how this is even going to be possible, now that Aunt Flo has arrived. Today is out, for sure.

Nick leans over to read what I wrote. "Shouldn't it say, the *sex* plan? We don't want it getting mixed up with any of the other plans you've got written in that thing."

I snort, but put in a little ^ and print the word *SEX* between the words *THE* and *PLAN*. "Okay?"

"Okay."

His voice is quieter. I glance over at him again. His mischievous smile is gone. His face is even paler than usual. He looks scared.

Like how I felt with Leo, maybe.

I don't want to think about Leo.

"I think we should start with where this supposed sex is going to take place. Not my room," I add quickly. "I can't—" My mind chooses this moment to revisit the image of the white robe. The dark hotel room. I gulp in a breath. "I can't have sex where my mom or my sisters sleep. That would be too weird."

"All right." Nick nods thoughtfully. "How about—"

154

"Not the beach. And not a pool."

"That would be a little public, don't you think?" Nick's ears are turning pink.

"Agreed. We need somewhere private."

"Like my room," Nick says.

I frown. "What about your dad?"

"I have my own room."

I gasp. "Spoiled!"

He shrugs. "The conference pays for two rooms. There are only two people in my family. One of the perks."

"So your room it is, then," I say. "What room number is that?"

"407."

I write that down. "But it has to be neat, okay?" I think about Afton's first time, in that boy's garage, next to the washing machine. "I refuse to do it next to a pile of dirty socks."

Nick scoffs. "Do you think I'm a slob?"

"Um, no." I try not to look at the stain on his shirt, or how it's half tucked into his shorts. Or the general disarray of his hair. "Next question," I say briskly. "When?"

"Well, we could—"

"I'm not going to be ready for at least three days," I say quickly. Thankfully, my periods are fairly short. Three days should do it. I hope.

"What, do we need to take a class first?" He smirks.

"I need to prepare." I need to recover from my body betraying me.

"Three days from now is Saturday," he says. "So, Saturday?"

"Sure."

"What time? Do you have a preference for morning or afternoon?"

He makes it sound like this is a dentist appointment. "Evening, don't you think?"

"Night does seem more romantic," Nick agrees.

I'm not sure that romantic is what we're going for, but I write down, *Evening*. "But Saturday night's the awards dinner," I remember. "Maybe Sunday night?"

Nick shakes his head. "My dad and I are leaving to go to Oahu Sunday afternoon." He rubs his chin like he has a beard there instead of three ginger strands of peach fuzz. "What if we slipped away *during* the awards dinner? Then nobody would come barging in—"

"You think your dad might come barging into your room?" That's an unpleasant thought.

"He's normally good with giving me my privacy—although I've never tried to have sex before, so who knows—but sometimes he forgets and just walks in. We always have the keys to each other's rooms. But he'll be busy during the awards dinner. He's getting an award this year."

"My mom's a presenter!" I clap my hand to my forehead. "That's brilliant, actually. We could go and come back, and they'd never even notice. It's the perfect alibi!"

Nick's eyebrows furrow. "Okay, two things I want to say here. First: I really hope you don't think having sex with me constitutes a crime."

"Of course not. We're consenting . . . pre-adults."

"Great. So on to the second thing: How long do you think this is going to take, that you imagine us sneaking out of the awards dinner and then popping back in without anyone noticing we're gone?"

I stare at him. My own ears are undoubtedly pink at this point. "I mean, it probably won't take too long. What, do you want to cuddle after?"

"I don't know," he says in a kind of choked-up voice. "Do you *not* want to cuddle?"

"I thought boys didn't like cuddling."

"I didn't get the memo about what boys like. Maybe I'll want to cuddle. I guess that depends on how the other stuff goes."

"The other stuff," I murmur. I am still finding it hard to imagine the other stuff. "Right."

His eyebrows push together. "Are you sure you're okay with this? You can back out, you know."

"I'm not backing out."

"I won't think you're a coward or anything."

"I'm not scared. It's just, when I asked you last night, it was kind of theoretical sex. And now it's starting to feel real." More real than it ever felt with Leo, in a strange way.

"If you want to call it off, at any point, I'm good with that."

"I appreciate you being so flexible."

"You feel like a cup of tea now," Nick says, "but later you might not want a cup of tea."

I blink. "I have no clue what you're talking about."

He pushes his hair out of his eyes, smiling in a bashful way. "My dad made me watch this video about consent. The whole idea is that having sex is like having a cup of tea. It's a British video."

"Obviously." I press my lips together to keep from laughing at this.

"My dad's very British," Nick explains. "He adores tea metaphors of all types."

157

I know his dad is British. He strongly resembles John Oliver, I think, with his dark hair and eyes and his round glasses. Today is the first time I've noticed, though, that Nick has the tiniest bit of an English accent himself—an occasional softness around how he pronounces his *R*'s. Like in the way he just said *adores*.

I tap my pen against the sketchbook. "So, giving us possible cuddling time, and factoring in that the dinner's going to be at the Palace Tower lawn, which is fairly close to here, I'd say we could get to your room and be back in an hour. The awards dinner usually takes like two and a half hours, at least, so that should give us plenty of time. We could even stagger our coming and going, so no one would know we were together."

"Again, not a crime, us being together." Nick sounds mildly offended. "And now I'm starting to wonder if you're doing this out of some weird sort of nerd pity."

"I'm not." If I am being honest with myself, I'll admit that I don't completely understand why I'm doing it. There are a lot of possibilities, as I've mentioned: revenge, distraction, physical comfort. Maybe I want to prove something to Afton. Or I want to prove something to myself because of Afton. But when I think about her finding out, or, even worse, Mom finding out, I know I don't want to have that conversation. Because if we talk about me having sex, that would lead, inevitably, to talking about the sex my mother is having.

So I don't want anyone to know.

"It's complicated, but no, I don't pity you," I say. "Sorry. I'm all out of fucks to give about the poor unfortunate nerds of the world. Or maybe I do have a fuck to give."

Wow. I actually said that. Again, it feels like an alien has taken over.

Nick barks a laugh. Now his ears are a bright, fire-engine red. "Okay, good. Just so we're clear about our motivation."

"So we're set." I close the sketchbook. "Saturday night. Let's say eight o'clock-ish? Room 407. I'll see you then."

I start to get up.

"Wait," Nick says. Now he's really flustered. He takes a breath and lets it out. "Don't we need protection?"

I immediately feel stupid. That's twice now that a condom has been the last thing on my mind. You never see that part on the sexy CW shows when things get hot and heavy. They never have to fumble for a condom, and yet they magically manage not to get herpes.

God. Herpes. Not that either of us are in danger of that at this stage, but still. "Right. Can you tackle that department?"

He swallows. "I can try."

"Well, you've got to do more than try. I'm not on the pill, so . . . they've got to have them for sale around here somewhere."

He's nodding vigorously. "I'll handle it."

"What's your cell number, by the way?"

He arches an eyebrow. "You're asking for my number?"

"In case I get a hot tip on where to find condoms."

He blushes again and rattles off his phone number, and I enter it into my phone.

"Okay, good. I guess I'll see you Saturday night."

He jumps up and gives me a bow. "Until then, my fair lady."

"Don't do that."

"I'm attempting to be chivalrous."

"You're making it weird."

He sighs. "That's kind of my brand."

"Hmm. I consider myself warned, then."

I smile, and he smiles, and then we go our separate ways.

We try to go our separate ways, anyway. But as it happens, we're both heading back to our rooms, and those are in the same direction. So we walk together to the elevator.

"What are you going to do with your little sister today?" Because he's paying attention enough to know through all these years that I'm perpetually with my little sister.

I push the button for up. "I don't know yet." Mostly I just still want to go paddleboarding. That's what's sticking in my mind. After the sex, that is. "We're going to try all the slides." The back of the resort features a string of connected swimming pools and several water slides. In other words: paradise for a five-year-old.

"Sounds fun," Nick says.

"What are you doing today?" I ask to be polite.

"I have a date with destiny, too." He laughs like he just told the best joke ever. "Sorry. I've always wanted to say that."

"I don't get why it's funny."

"*Destiny* is a game . . . that I play . . . on the PS4. *Destiny 2.*"

"Oh."

"I could show you sometime."

I shake my head. "Let's stick to sex."

"ADA!" The doors to the elevator open and Abby and Mom are standing in front of us, Abby already in her swimsuit and goggles and arm floaties. Her nose, which bears a white stripe of zinc on it, wrinkles when she sees me. "You can't slide like that. Come on! I want to

160

go on the water slides. NOW."

"I have to run upstairs and put my swimsuit on. It will only take a minute." I glance up at Mom.

"I can't wait for you," she says tersely. "I've got to be there early. I'm presenting this morning. I've been texting you. Why didn't you answer?"

I decide to be petulant. "Did you ever think it might be nice, Mother, to ask me if I wanted to watch my little sister today? Because it feels like you're assuming I have no life."

"What?" She seems puzzled more than anything else. I have never complained about Abby before. "Look, I don't have time to—"

"Then when *will* you have time?" I interject.

She shakes her head, baffled by the sudden appearance of Uncooperative-Ada. "What's going on with you?"

I close my eyes against the image of the white robe. "Nothing. I'm just sick of you treating me like the hired help. Always me, of course, and not Afton."

"Afton's still asleep." She's not, though. She checked on me in the bathroom. But Mom obviously doesn't know that.

"Let me guess: she was out late last night," I say instead of correcting her. "You have no idea where, or what she was doing."

"She's eighteen," Mom says. "She can do what she wants. She's an adult."

"Right. And I'm sixteen, so I'm a child, and I'm stuck doing child labor."

Mom's eyes flicker to Nick, who is attempting to inconspicuously edge his way over to the stairs. Me being a brat to my brilliant mother is making him uncomfortable. "Hello," Mom says.

161

He freezes. "Hello, Dr. Bloom. Uh, nice day to—"

But she's done with pleasantries. And also, apparently, with my sass. She shoves Abby's hand into mine. "I don't have time for you to decide to be a teenager right now. I won't be back for lunch. Money's on the bedside table. Don't forget to reapply sunscreen every two hours. I don't want you two getting burned."

I nod numbly. "Yeah. Okay."

Mom hurries away in the direction of the tram, looking at her phone the whole time, stepping carefully around the tourists.

"O-kay. I'll see you later, Ada," Nick says.

"I couldn't be too compliant, could I?" I say by way of explanation.

He smiles, nods, but still ducks toward the stairs instead of the elevator.

I feel a tug on my arm. "Don't you want to go swimming with me?" Abby asks in a small voice. "Don't you like me?"

I kneel down next to her. "I love you, Abby-cakes. You know that. You are, by far, my favorite sister."

"But you wanted to give me to Afton," she says accusingly. Her bottom lip trembles. "And Afton always tries to give me away, too!"

"It's not about you, sweetie," I say. "I'm having a fight with Afton right now."

"I know that. Duh." Abby's seen Afton and me fight a few times, over dumb, insignificant stuff, though, like who borrowed whose shoes and who has to mow which part of the lawn, but this is different. Even Abby can tell. "Are you and Afton ever going to be friends again?"

"Sure we are," I say, because that's what I'm supposed to say. I hug

Abby. "You and me and Afton, we're sisters. That's an unbreakable bond, you know."

At least it was, before.

"So nothing could ever, ever break it," Abby says, brightening. "We're sisters forever."

"Sisters forever," I say, putting out my pinkie finger to hook with hers. We shake solemnly. "Now let's go do some slides."

24

Over the next few hours I voluntarily throw my body down every available slippery surface at the Hilton Waikoloa. I gave Mom a hard time about always assuming that I'm on duty for childcare, but I am grateful to be hanging out with Abby and not alone to stew in the problems of my messed-up life. I have to spend almost every minute trying to keep my little sister's head above the water.

This, too, feels like a metaphor somehow.

Sometime after lunch Abby gets tired enough to sit down for a few minutes. I reapply our sunscreen and then lean back in one of those white plastic lounge chairs that line the pools and close my eyes, feeling the sun soak into me.

My mind starts to wander back to the situation with Mom, so I deliberately choose to think about Nick instead.

Nick. The way he equates having sex with having a cup of tea. So funny.

And even funnier, our sex plan. Just the words *sex plan* cheer me up substantially, not because sex is such a cheerful subject, but because the idea sounds too ridiculous to be true. Nick Kelly and Ada Bloom—arguably the two least-cool individuals on the entire Big Island—are going to have sexual intercourse. It's glorious, in a silly yet appealing way. It'll be a good, distracting adventure.

Speaking of adventures. "How about we try paddleboarding?" I ask Abby. Paddleboarding with Abby is not exactly what I've been picturing, but at this point I'll take what I can get.

She doesn't answer.

I open my eyes. She's sprawled on her stomach over the next lounge chair, using the end of one curly wet braid to drip patterns on the concrete.

"Abby?"

"No, thanks," she says lightly. "I need some quiet time now. Maybe even a nap."

My sister is a strange five-year-old.

"But it will be so peaceful and quiet when we go paddleboarding. Just picture it, Abs, you and me on a paddleboard in the middle of the lagoon, water lapping at our feet, the sun on our faces, the wind in our hair."

"We could tip over," Abby says. "I could drown."

"You'll wear a life jacket. Plus, you're the best swimmer I've ever seen. You're like a baby shark." I try a few lines of the song, but she doesn't go for it.

She sits up and crosses her arms. "I can swim in a pool, yes. But the lagoon is like the ocean. Dark and deep, with monsters under there."

"What monsters?"

"Giant squid," she informs me gravely.

"The lagoon is not the ocean," I argue. "Water is water, Abby. We'll be fine. There are no monsters, I promise. I'll be right there with you."

"No, thanks."

"If you were going to drown, you would have done it already," I say. "And then . . . I would go paddleboarding."

Her eyes widen. "I can't believe you just said that! I'm going to tell Mom."

"You go right ahead."

She jumps up. "Look!" She points to where, not too far away, a couple has just gotten out of one of those white rope hammocks. "Let's sit in there, and you can read me my Amelia Bedelia." She reaches into our bag and pulls the book out proudly. "I packed it. I thought, you never know when you might need Amelia."

"Oh, good." I am clearly never going to go paddleboarding. I am never going to have that spiritual experience Pop talked about, whenever he talked about Hawaii.

I inspect Abby's book. It's called *Amelia Bedelia Means Business*. The letters of the title all look hand drawn, with *Amelia Bedelia* large and centered on the orange cover, and *Means Business* much smaller to one side. Abby traces her fingers over the big *A*.

"Amelia's initials are A.B.," she points out. "Just like mine."

"And mine," I say. Abby's name is Abigail Bloom-Carter. A.B.C. I always thought that was neat.

"And Afton's!" Abby exclaims. It obviously just now occurred to her that we all have names that start with the letter *A*.

"And Mom," I add.

Afton and I have conflicting theories about why Mom did this to us. Mine is that Mom likes things orderly—she likes our family to match, so we are her straight A's: Aster, Afton, Ada, Abby.

Afton's idea is that every time Mom got pregnant, Ruthie told Mom to go on a baby-naming website and make a list of the names she liked, but Mom never made it past the landing page, which was the letter A, before she got called away for a patient or an emergency surgery.

Afton is probably right.

Abby's face is all lit up now. "Holy smokes!" she yells, which is hilarious because it makes her sound just like Pop. "We all have A's!"

"Yes, we do."

"What's Pop's first name?"

"Ryan," I say. "A long time ago Pop told me his name means 'little king.' Which I guess would make you a princess."

But her face falls. "Pop's different from us. He's not a A."

"That's a good thing," I say. "It would be boring if we were all the same."

My father's name is Aaron, I realize with an inward cringe.

Dear god. We can't lose Pop.

My phone starts to ring. Abby grabs it out of my bag and holds it up. Yep. Pop. As if he could hear us talking about him from two thousand miles away. Calling to video chat.

Abby presses accept before I can decide whether talking to him right now is doable.

"Poppy!" Ada beams.

"Hi, sweeties!" He's smiling. He has a particular smile he uses almost exclusively for Abby, so big and wide it shows his back molars. I love that smile. I even tried to draw it once, but the teeth turned out kind of scary. I'm not good with teeth.

"We went swimming!" Abby cries.

"I can see that, Abby-cakes! And now you're all wet!"

"I'm getting drier, though. We went down all the slides, but I need a quiet time now so I'm going to go in the hammock, and Ada's going to read me Amelia Bedelia." Without waiting a second longer, she runs to the hammock and flings herself in. I can hear Pop's chuckles as the white rope envelops her. I gather up our bag and sunscreen and stuff and jog after her. It takes me a few tries to figure out how to get into the hammock without tipping us over. Finally I just kind of back my butt in and swing myself down.

Abby shifts the phone so Pop can see both of us.

My eyes prickle, seeing his face. This is a bad idea. I've never kept a secret like this from Pop before. I've never felt like I had to.

He's at work. He's wearing his scrubs and directly behind him there's a shelf full of medical supplies.

"Are you hiding in the supply closet?" I ask.

"It's been one of those days." He gives me a look that means, *I'll tell you later.* Pop loves to try to gross me out with stories of bizarre or improbable things that happen in the ER. But not in front of Abby, who screams like someone is murdering her whenever she sees or hears anything blood-related. "How's the trip going?" he asks.

"Great!" Abby says. "We saw dolphins, and we saw a volcano, and we rode a big bus, and we ate a lot of pineapple and pigs."

Abby often insists on calling food by the source. She calls pork *pigs*, and bacon *flat pigs*, and beef *cows*, and so on. She doesn't mind eating meat, but she wants to know where it came from.

"Awesome!" Pop says. "What about you, Ada-bean? What's happening with you?"

I force my face into a casual expression. "Dolphins, volcanoes, pigs. That's a fairly accurate description of our trip so far." I poke Abby in the side. I have an idea. "Tell her we should go paddle-boarding on the lagoon," I say to Pop.

"I don't know," he says. "Are you sure she's big enough for that? She's only five."

"It will be fine!" I rant. "She's a great swimmer! She'll wear a life jacket! I'll do all the work!" I sigh. "Never mind."

Pop is looking at me intently. Even through the phone, I can feel his dark brown eyes examining me, like I am a patient he needs to figure out a diagnosis for. "What's going on with you, Ada? What's wrong?"

Both of my parents have asked me this today. I obviously need to get better at acting like things are fine.

"Ada and Afton are having a fight," Abby volunteers.

Pop's bushy eyebrows lift. "A fight? Still?"

"Again," I say with a sigh. "Or, kind of still."

"What about? It's not like you two not to get along."

I bite my lip. I don't know what to tell him. Anything but the truth. Anything.

"I don't even know," Abby says wistfully. "But it's a doozy."

"Leo called the home line the other day," Pop says carefully.

Even my toes clench at the mention of Leo. He should have known I'd be in Hawaii. I told him weeks ago. I complained about how I was being forced to go. I moaned about how much I would miss him. Did he even listen to me when I spoke? "I don't care about Leo. Leo is a total—" I pause to modify my choice of language on Abby's behalf.

"Asshole," she fills in brightly.

"Abby, we don't say—"

"He cheated on me," I blurt out.

"What does cheated mean?" Abby asks. "Is it like when Pop cheats at Go Fish?"

"I'm so sorry, Ada," Pop says.

"Thanks."

"But how does this have anything to do with you fighting with Afton?"

"Afton broke up with her boyfriend on Friday, so they wouldn't have to do the long-distance thing at college. It was very mature of them," I report. "So clearly she and I are in a competition to see who has the most gruesomely broken heart. And I don't want to brag, but I'm winning."

"Yeah, especially now that Afton has a new boyfriend!" Abby announces, proud that she knows some of the answers. "Michael!"

Pop frowns. "Michael? Michael Wong?"

"Michael's not her boyfriend, Abby," I try to clarify. "He only got here, like, yesterday."

"No, he was here earlier than yesterday," Abby says primly.

"How would you know? Anyway, he's not her boyfriend."

"I saw them kissing," Abby adds. "Last night on the beach. It was yucky."

So they're already kissing. Wow. But why am I not surprised? Afton saw something she wanted, she went after it, and—shocker— she got it. Or should I say, she got *him*.

"How old is Michael?" Pop asks, his eyebrows dropping into a scowl. "I thought he was much old—"

"He's twenty-two," I say. "He just graduated from college."

Pop makes a face like he's bitten into a piece of bad fruit. "Now I'm starting to see why you two might be fighting. I assume that you told her no good can come from jumping right into a relationship with Michael Wong?"

I wouldn't say they're in a relationship. But I shrug. "You know how well Afton listens."

Pop's assuming that I did the Normal-Ada move here. The square thing. But I didn't tell Afton to stay away from Michael. In fact, I told her to go hook up with him. I didn't really mean it, but still. Here we all are.

"I'm sorry, honey," Pop says again. "Sometimes you just have to let people make mistakes, and love them anyway."

"Yeah, because sisters are forever," Abby intones.

"Yes." He smiles the molar smile again, then looks at me. "Don't worry about Afton. She's tough. She'll pull through. You focus on yourself right now, okay?"

God, if only I could. "Okay," I say faintly. I'm grateful, actually, that this conversation has been largely about Afton and Michael.

"Ada has a new boyfriend, too," pipes up Abby.

"I take it back," I say between clenched teeth. "No life jacket for you."

Pop's eyebrows are really getting a workout this afternoon. "Oh? And who is this fortunate and hopefully more age-appropriate young man?"

"He's not my boyfriend," I say at the same time Abby shouts, "It's Nick!"

"Who?"

"Nick Kelly."

"Nick Kelly." Pop's lips purse thoughtfully. He doesn't know Nick by name. He's never had a reason to talk about him, except— "Wait, is that the kid who got lost in Rio?"

"That was six years ago," I say in Nick's defense. "And he is most definitely not my boyfriend. We're just hanging out . . . occasionally. Okay?"

"Hmm," Pop muses. "Okay, well, I trust your judgment, Ada. I've never seen a kid with more common sense than you."

"We're just hanging out," I insist again. I wisely omit the part about us planning to lose our virginities together at the end of the week. "I see him once a year, remember? He lives in . . . Chicago? Baltimore?"

It's sad how much I still don't know about Nick. After all these years of basically going on vacation with him, I've never bothered to find out where he lives. Something I'll have to remedy this week.

"Okay," Pop says. "But promise me you'll try to relax and enjoy your time in paradise, all right? You seem tense."

"Spoken like a true hypocrite."

He laughs. "Believe me, if I were there, I'd be loving every minute of it." A loud voice blares in the background: someone calling a code over the hospital intercom. "I have to run. We'll talk more about this later, okay? Bye, sweeties."

"Bye, Poppy!" Abby yells, waving. "I loves you!"

"I loves you, too, Abby-cakes. Have fun!"

"I love you," I murmur. But he's already hung up.

25

My little blow-up at Mom this morning must have had an effect, because she doesn't insist that I come to dinner with her and the group. In fact, she offers to take Abby herself for the night.

I end up having dinner alone. I pick the little outdoor restaurant right next to the Ocean Tower. It's nice, some would even say romantic, all under a canopy with white lights strung throughout. There's a guy with a guitar in the corner playing love songs: old ones, new ones, ones he wrote. He's got a decent voice. The food's good: Mexican, addictive freshly made chips and salsa that could have been my entire meal. Sizzling fajitas to die for. I eat them glumly. It's kind of worse that they're so good.

I'm lonely, I realize.

But this is better than sitting around a table with my mother.

I think about texting Nick. He'd probably come have dinner with me in a heartbeat. But that would feel cheap somehow, like I'm using him. Maybe I am using him, I realize, but he seems okay if I'm using him for sex. There's no real romance between us. And it should probably stay that way.

My thoughts revolve back around to Pop. He seemed okay today. Maybe he doesn't know his marriage is completely on the rocks.

Dear god, I think, and then stop myself. What am I doing? I go to mass once a week during the school year, because it's mandatory at my school, but God's not someone I have regular conversations with. And even if I did—believe, I mean—I'm sure God wouldn't appreciate the fact that the only times I attempt to communicate with him are those moments I want something impossible.

I'm only interested in God when there's a crisis.

But it would be nice to truly believe in God, I think. Because then I might have someone to talk to.

That's what Mom has done to me, without even knowing it. Because of her, I'm cut off from everyone I used to turn to as a support system: my sister, Pop. And now I am completely alone.

At some point in my pity party I look up and see Afton sitting on the other side of the patio, having dinner with a dark-haired boy with his back to me—Michael, I assume. They appear to be on a real, honest-to-goodness date. She's wearing a white flowered sundress and the strappy sandals, which I wouldn't have recommended, as they are probably cursed now, after their encounter with Leo at the swim meet. Her hair is loosely braided in a long fishtail that's pushed forward over one shoulder. She's a shade or two more tan than she was only a day ago, and it makes her come off like she's glowing in the white dress.

She's perfect. Barf. If a mermaid came to shore for only one night, to have a plate of Mexican food with a handsome prince, she'd be exactly Afton.

She also looks, well, happy. The glow isn't entirely the tan. She's leaning forward slightly, listening intently to whatever it is that Michael's saying, a relaxed smile on her lips. Then she stops for a second to dip a tortilla chip in salsa, and as she's bringing it to her mouth, it drips. Right down the front of her white dress. Splat.

I brace myself for the drama. Her horrified expression. The frantic dabbing of her napkin dipped in ice water. Maybe she'll have to excuse herself to go change.

But Afton only laughs. Not a delicate, feminine titter, either, but a real, full-throated laugh I can hear over that dude's sappy guitar. She throws her head back and lets out a guffaw of pure amusement. Oh, silly salsa. Oh, silly dress.

My breath catches. I immediately want to sketch her expression, but then I realize that I already have. It's in my sketchbook from over a year ago. I reach down into my bag and pull it out, flip the pages until I find it.

Afton Laughs, I called it.

My sister has never been a big laugher. Pop says it's because she has a dignified old soul. Not that Afton is missing a sense of humor— she has that fierce, dry wit when the occasion calls for it—but she almost never laughs out loud. When we were kids we'd see something funny on television and I would crack up laughing, and Afton would be sitting next to me crisscross with the smallest of smiles on her face. That was it. The most you can usually get out of Afton is a quick, amused exhalation, a laugh-breath. If that.

Imagine our surprise, then, when she brought this boy home for dinner last year. Logan, she said his name was, there to win us all over to his side. And he did. Easily. He was handsome, tall with wavy black hair that looked like he put an effort into. He was always dressed well, too, with a little more flair than most boys bother with. A boy with style, which of course made sense, because Afton is nothing if not stylish herself. He made all the requisite charming small talk to Mom and Pop, had Abby wrapped around his finger in about five seconds flat, and then, as we were passing the green beans around the table, Logan said something to Afton, something that I didn't catch because he said it soft, just for her.

And Afton tilted her head back and actually laughed.

It was like a sudden gust against wind chimes, that laugh, an unexpected music.

That was the night of the camper trailer, I think. And I remember thinking, too, as I was drawing this sketch, lost in a feeling of being half happy for her, half dismayed because I had to suddenly share my sister's time with this guy, that this time Afton was really in love. And that was okay. That's what happens with sisters. Boys take us away from each other. But not really, right, because sisters are forever?

I frown. I don't know what to think about her laughing at Michael. She can't be in love with Michael Wong. She was still in love with Logan less than four days ago, and, in spite of what she and I seem to be fighting about constantly right now, I know that Afton's not fickle. She's not careful. But she's also not dumb.

Maybe I'm putting too much importance on this expression. Maybe Michael just said something really funny in response to her spilling salsa on herself.

It doesn't have to mean anything, this laugh.

The guitar guy starts playing a cover of "She's Got a Way" by Billy Joel. Michael and Afton get up to dance. Double barf.

I gesture for the waiter to bring the check. I was here first, but I feel like I'm intruding on my sister's date. Spying on her. Watching her now, I'm not sorry I didn't tell her about Mom's affair, because of course she wouldn't look so happy if she knew.

She spots me. Her expression darkens. I can practically hear what she's thinking—*Can't you leave me alone for five minutes?*

I look away, guilty even though again it's not my fault, give the waiter cash and tell him to keep the change, and head back toward the Ocean Tower. Afton keeps dancing, turning her face away from me. Laying her head on Michael's shoulder.

26

"It's your turn to take Abby for the day," Mom announces when she comes in the next morning.

She's addressing this to Afton.

Afton, who's standing at the mirror putting on a pair of new dangly dolphin earrings when Mom makes this pronouncement, actually gasps in outrage. "But I took her on Monday!" she exclaims. (This being Thursday.) "Remember? Hula?"

"And Ada took her yesterday," Mom says matter-of-factly. "So now it's your turn."

Afton looks stricken. "But I have . . . plans!"

I snort. Plans to get continue getting kissy with Michael, no doubt.

"Well, now you have plans with your little sister," Mom says, spritzing perfume onto her wrists. "Michael will understand. He's got a little sister, too."

"Mom!"

"Deal with it." Mom thrusts the hundred-dollar bill she usually bestows upon me into Afton's hand, then goes out in her usual hurry.

Afton puts a hand on her hip and glares at me through the mirror. "What did you tell her about Michael?"

"Nothing." It's safe to say that I haven't said more than a few words to Mom since Monday. But it's possible that Mom spoke with Pop last night, and Pop knew about Michael, courtesy of Gabby Abby. The thought of Mom and Pop on the phone together, Mom acting all innocent as she relayed the details of our trip so far, makes my stomach clench. Everyone but me seems to be so adept at pretending away the truth.

"Can't you—" Afton starts.

"I really can't. I, too, have plans." I finish rubbing myself down with sunscreen and put on my big mirrored sunglasses. "I'm sorry, but as Mom so wisely said, Michael will understand. How's that going, anyway? You two looked pretty lovey-dovey last night."

"Stay out of it," Afton snarls.

"Happy to."

From the adjoining room we both hear Abby stirring, first a yawn, and then, "I'm hungry."

"But, Ada—" says Afton.

"Deal with it." I grab my bag and go out the door.

Today it's paddleboard or bust.

For all of five minutes it feels like it's going to happen. But I've just reached the front of the line at the lagoon rental place, after waiting for more than an hour, so close to paddleboarding I can practically taste it, when I hear a familiar voice from behind me.

"Hello, dearie!" the voice says. "Hello!"

Oh no. I close my eyes and wish her away, far, far, away. Or at the very least I wish for her to be talking to someone other than me.

"Ada!" says the voice. "I'm talking to you, Ada Bloom. Hello?"

I open my eyes and turn to face her. "Hi, Marjorie."

"Oh, good. I thought that was you." She looks thrilled to see me. She's dressed in a neon-purple swimsuit, and on top of that she's wearing a blue-and-white flowered blouse, open in the front, blue Bermuda shorts, a pair of red flip-flops, a giant straw hat over her mass of white hair, and huge white sunglasses.

She beams at me. "So I see you're going kayaking."

"Well, actually, I want to go pa—"

"I want to go kayaking. In one of those nice blue kayaks they have, not a green one," she says. "That'd be nice."

She reminds me of Abby, in a wrinkled-up way. Just announcing what she wants for everyone to hear, and then waiting for people to help her accomplish those things.

"I was wondering, would you like to kayak with me? It would be a great help. I'm still sharp, but I'm not as strong as I used to be. You look strong. I've always thought so—that Ada Bloom looks strong."

I stare at her in dismay. "Uh, well, you see—"

"You'll help an old lady, won't you?"

I have to hand it to her. That "old lady" knows how to outmaneuver a sixteen-year-old girl.

So that's how I end up paddling an eighty-something legendary former heart surgeon all over the lagoon for the next two and a half hours.

"I'm sorry that your stepfather didn't come this year," she says as I paddle us to one end of the lagoon. "I quite like him. He's a peach."

"I think so, too."

"Your little sister's a doll," she says. "And that Afton's a go-getter, isn't she?"

"Yes," I agree, to both things.

"I almost feel sorry for the Wong boy," Marjorie says. "She just swept him off his feet like he didn't have a choice in the matter."

"Does everyone at the conference know about Michael and Afton?"

Marjorie purses her lips. "Everybody knows who's got eyes to see with, or ears to hear about it. It's a small world, with the STS, and people do like a little scandal now and then."

"Is it scandalous?"

"Perhaps *scandal* is the wrong choice of words. But you have to remember that we've been seeing you since you were little babies. Some of us aren't ready for you to be all grown up. Afton's a chip off your mother's block, if you ask me," Marjorie continues. "But you . . ." She taps a finger to her chin. "You I haven't quite been able to figure out. You keep your cards close to the chest, don't you?"

I'm starting to think Marjorie had me paddle her out into the middle of the lagoon so I couldn't escape her questions. But I'm not sure this is actually a question. "Cards?" I say.

She laughs. "From what I gather, you're the peacekeeper of the family. Is that right?"

I swallow. "Most of the time."

She chortles. "Classic middle child. But that can't be easy," she says. "With a mother like yours."

I stare into the water, wondering what would happen if I just dove in and swam away. Surely somebody would come by and rescue Marjorie eventually. "My mother's amazing," I feel obligated to say.

Marjorie nods. "Yes, she is. She's an amazing surgeon, that's for sure. But they call her the Whirlwind for a reason. She reminds me of myself, at that age," she muses. "I was a bit of a flurry once, too. Driven. Centered around my work. So much to prove. But you can't keep that up for too long before your real life starts to demand your attention. Something's got to give, eventually."

Or something already has. I swallow.

She reaches forward to pat my shoulder. "The trick will be for you not to smooth things over for her. You've got to let her face her own failings. Which means you've got to let her fail."

I try to decide how much she knows. Not about the affair, I think. Marjorie is only talking about Mom working too hard. "Okay," I say softly.

She gives a short laugh, like a bark. "Listen to me, blabbering on about something that's none of my business. Forgive me. I'm becoming a busybody in my old age. Because I am not, otherwise, busy."

"You're a hero," I say.

"Oh, go on."

"No, really."

"Well, yes," she says with a sparkle in her eyes. "I know. But most of the time these days I'm also tragically bored."

She shifts to talking about the weather, and how young people are using their phones too much, which seems to me to be the only wisdom adults want to impart to us lately, and ends up telling me a story about trying to find a phone booth in the pouring rain while a man on her bus had a heart attack.

"Thank you so much, dearie," Marjorie says finally as I help her out of the kayak after our time is up. By now it's past noon and it's 90 degrees out, pretty hot for Hawaii, and there's a huge line for the paddleboards.

But I am determined. *Give me a paddleboard*, I think as I wipe sweat from the back of my neck, *or give me death*.

"How long's the wait?" I ask the lady at the front as we return the kayak.

"About two and a half hours, I'd say."

Fuck! I think, but happily I don't say it out loud. I can't tell if Marjorie would be amused or offended by my potty mouth.

"You don't want to go right back out there, do you?" Marjorie says, tsking. "Why don't you take a rest and have lunch with me? My treat."

She's giving me the there's-no-way-I'm-letting-you-say-no look again.

I know better than to flat-out refuse. "Um, sure," I say slowly, fumbling for my phone. "But first I have to check in with my mom."

Do I intend to call my mother right now? Absolutely not.

I can't call Afton, either. Boo. And Pop is sleeping.

So there's only one other person on this entire island that I'm friendly enough with to ask for a favor.

THIS IS AN EMERGENCY, I text to Nick. *I NEED YOUR HELP.*

What's up? he texts back immediately.

I need you to call me and pretend to be my mother.

. . .

183

He's in that status for a while, like he's in the process of responding, but no response actually appears. Meanwhile, Marjorie is leading me over to the restaurant nearby (the one where, just a few days ago, I had lunch with Afton and Abby after walking in on Mom) and reading the menu.

"Ooh," she says. "A Hawaiian bacon BBQ burger."

My stomach lurches. "That sounds . . . delicious."

My phone rings. Thank god. It's Nick, of course.

"That's my mom—I have to pick up or she'll worry. Excuse me." I walk a few steps away, but not too far, because I still want Marjorie to be able to hear me.

Took you long enough, I want to say when I pick up. "Hey, Mom," I say instead. "You'll never believe who I bumped into at the lagoon: Marjorie Pearson."

"I don't actually have to act like your mom, do I?" Nick whispers. "I'm not on speaker? Nobody can hear me but you, right?"

"That's right!" I say brightly. "I bumped into Marjorie in the line. We've been kayaking together all over the lagoon."

"Ah, crap," Nick says.

"I know! Isn't that nice?"

"I'm sorry," he says. "I like Marjorie, but that kind of sucks. Why did you want me to—"

"Now she's so generously offered to buy me lunch."

"Oh," Nick says.

"Oh," I echo. "Oh, okay." I pretend to listen for a minute and then press the phone to my chest to talk to Marjorie. "I'm so sorry, Marjorie, but my mom wants me to meet her for lunch." I put the phone to my ear again. "Are you sure, Mom?"

"I'm sure, sweetie," Nick says in a high-pitched voice. "But seriously, maybe you should just have lunch with Marjorie, don't you think? I mean, what could it hurt?"

It could hurt my chances of ever getting to paddleboard, is what it could hurt. I like Marjorie, too, but that doesn't mean I want to spend the entire day with her. Especially because I am supposed to be relaxing by myself today. And I certainly don't want to endure another one of those burgers or another hour of her insights on my family.

"She's sure," I say to Marjorie.

"Oh, all right, dearie," Marjorie sighs. "Some other time. Although honestly, I'm not sure how much time I've got."

She's messing with me, I'm almost sure of it. Her eyes are dancing again with mischief. She probably knows I'm not talking to my mother.

"Thanks, Mom. I'll see you in minute," I say into my phone as the hostess leads Marjorie away to a table.

"Really? Are you coming over?" Nick asks hopefully.

"No," I say. "Not until Saturday. But thanks. You just did me a solid."

"You're welcome," he says.

There's a pause. "I can't find any condoms," he admits then, glumly.

"I guess that's it, then," I say. "No tea for us."

Maybe him not finding condoms is a sign.

"But I still want tea, if you still want tea. Do you still want tea?"

"Yes. I think so."

"Then I'll get the condoms. Somewhere. Somehow," he promises.

"They've got to have them in the hotel shops. This is a hotel.

People get busy in hotels. They're going to need condoms."

"I looked all over the resort," he says. "There's nothing on the shelves."

"Did you ask the cashier?"

Silence.

"You didn't ask the cashier," I say accusingly.

He grunts like I've just asked him to do something painful. "Maybe if I got the right cashier? It's hard to go right up and ask. There's got to be a pharmacy around here somewhere. Or a gas station."

I stop walking. "No gas station condoms."

"I'm sure gas station condoms are just as effective as—"

"No gas station condoms," I repeat firmly. "This is not a joke, Nick."

"Yes. We're very serious. I remember."

"Let me know," I say. "Seriously. Soon."

"Okay," he says, and I hang up.

The line to the paddleboard rental is even longer than it was a few minutes ago.

I sigh and head toward the back of the line.

But before I reach it, I spot Afton and Abby waiting in the middle of the line, both red-cheeked and sweating in the heat. Afton is, predictably, on her phone.

"I don't know," she's saying as I approach from behind them. "We're going to be here for a while, and then maybe go make those flower necklace things. Probably not until late tonight. I'll text you."

"Hey," I say loudly, startling both my sisters. "What are you doing here?"

"We're going paddleboarding!" Abby cries. "It's going to be so much fun!"

"Oh, now you want to go paddleboarding." Unbelievable. But maybe I can work this to my advantage. "Can I . . ." I lower my voice. "Cut in with you?"

Abby gasps. "You want to cut in the line?"

Now everybody in the line is glaring at me.

"No, no," I explain. "We're sisters. You were saving my place." My gaze meets Afton's. "Because that's what sisters do."

She stares at me a moment, considering. "No," she says flatly. "You can't cut with us. But if you want to swap, that'd be okay."

"Swap?"

"You take Abby. You get to go paddleboarding. I get to go see Michael. We both get what we want. It's a win-win."

Yeah, maybe, but it also sounds like a lose-lose.

"No." I reject her offer without even giving it too much thought. Pop would call this cutting off my nose to spite my face.

But this is *my* day. Mom assigned Afton to be the babysitter today, because Mom's finally recognizing—too little, too late, perhaps—that I deserve some time for myself.

"Have a good time, you two," I say to my sisters. Then I walk off. Back to the only place I can think to go.

Back to the room.

I don't want to go back there, of course, the scene of my mother's crime, but it's too hot to go anywhere else. I don't have my usual hundred dollars, so I can't go shopping, or out to eat on my own somewhere, or to the spa. So the room seems like the reasonable choice.

On the way, I stop at one of the gift shops to peruse the toiletries section. Nick was right.

No condoms.

Using my peripheral vision, I glance at the cashier. He is currently, like everyone else, engrossed in his phone. He's also, like everybody who works at this hotel, tan and tall and fairly attractive.

I try to imagine myself going up to the counter and asking this man if they sell condoms.

I picture the look on his face when I ask.

And what if they're expensive? As we've already established, I don't have much money.

"Can I help you?" the cashier asks.

"No, I'm good."

He nods and smiles politely and goes back to his phone, but I get the sense that he's also watching me now, out of *his* peripheral vision. He must think I'm going to try to shoplift or something.

I abandon the condom quest and go back to the room.

It gives me a bad, shivery feeling, entering the empty room. But it isn't dark this time. The curtains are pulled wide open, revealing the swaying palms behind them. The room is neat and freshly serviced, bed made, carpet vacuumed, clean towels on the rack, and a mint on our pillows.

I plop down in the center of my bed and turn on the television. I scroll through the channels, but there's nothing good on, until, as fate would have it, I land on an episode of some sexy Scottish show I've heard about before but never watched until now.

I watch for a while. It's not the first episode, but I think I get the basic idea of where the story's going.

It's not long before the sexy Scottish shows gets, well, sexy. And then it gets downright graphic.

After that I turn the TV off. Even here, in the air-conditioned hotel room, I feel suddenly hot. The sex scene has left me worked up—okay, I'll admit that, but it's also left me with some questions, and they're not about condoms or herpes or what kind of underwear I should wear.

I find my sketchbook and open it to the page that says *THE SEX PLAN*. On the opposing page I jot down a few thoughts I feel that I should probably sort out before Saturday night.

Thoughts I have.

About sex.

To start with, orgasms. The woman in that show made a lot of noise during sex, and she had an orgasm after like sixty seconds. I'm not supposed to have an orgasm in sixty seconds, am I? The show's just compressing things for the sake of time, right?

It isn't real life. Is it?

How long does it typically take to have an orgasm?

Is that even something I should expect?

I know about the mechanics of it all. Mom told me about the birds and the bees when I was kid. I had health class. Afton talked about it some, after it happened with her. There was even a point a few months ago when, after I made out all evening with Leo, I came home and lay down on my bed with a mirror and looked—down there—to attempt to figure out what was what and why and how could it possibly work?

I've masturbated a few times, but I've never been adept at it. It seems like a lot of work.

It's almost disturbing, how much I don't know about myself. It's frustrating to think that right now, as I'm sitting here freewriting about my sex anxiety, Nick is probably in his room playing his video game, his mind completely unworried about all of this. He can just show up and do it. Bam.

I sigh and close the sketchbook.

Boys have it so much easier.

27

My mom, like I said, was the one who first told me about sex. Because I'd asked her, once, what was going on between her and Pop in their room at night sometimes, that room that shared a wall with mine.

"I can hear you in there," I said. "You're laughing and breathing hard, and the bed makes noises. Are you playing?"

It kind of hurts to think that I was once so, so innocent. But I was like eight years old. I thought they were wrestling or having a tickle fight.

Mom's face colored, but she stayed calm. "No," she answered lightly. "We're having sex."

She said it just like that: having sex. She didn't say "making love" or try to give it some other, more romantic name. She matter-of-factly explained to me what sex was, and that it was how babies were created, and she talked for a while about the science of it—the sperm and the egg, the merging of two people's DNA, the chromosomes, the dividing of cells. She said it was nothing to be embarrassed about, that it was a good thing, a natural thing, but it wasn't something that a person was ready to do until they were older.

"Like during college," she said.

For a while I associated the idea of sex with college—a time when you learned how to be a grown-up. So I didn't give sex a lot of thought until Afton started talking about boys.

But when I think about it now—what Mom taught me about sex—I remember not the official talk, but this one night when Afton and I were sitting at the kitchen counter doing our homework. It sticks out in my mind, because Mom was cooking dinner.

This was rare—a special thing; Mom didn't cook—that had always been Pop's department. She didn't have time, obviously. She was too busy being a whirlwind and saving lives. But this was a special occasion. Their anniversary. And Mom was making ratatouille, something she'd made for Pop when they were first dating, to impress him.

She was predictably good with a knife. I kept stopping at my algebra to watch her slice the zucchini, squash, eggplant, sweet peppers, and tomatoes so neatly, her hands careful and precise as she arranged each perfectly uniform piece in the dish.

Pop came into the room. His shirt was wet—he'd just given baby Abby a bath. He took parental leave those first two years after Abby was born. He stayed home with us. It was the best, those two years of pretty much uninterrupted Pop.

"I put her on the living room floor for some tummy time," he said. "Mmm. That already smells good."

He crossed behind Mom and put his arms around her waist. She kept arranging the vegetables, but she leaned back into him.

He lifted her hair and kissed the nape of her neck. "*You* smell good," he said. "I want to eat you up."

Mom blushed. "Oh you, be good," she said, but you could tell she didn't really mean it. She finished with the veggies and pushed the dish away, then rotated and put her arms around Pop's neck, smiling. "Although I kind of like it when you're bad."

Pop's eyebrows lifted. "Do you, now?"

"Mmm-hmm."

Afton and I exchanged glances. I could tell Afton wanted to say something sarcastic, like *Hello, excuse me! You're traumatizing your daughters*, but she also didn't want to interrupt. We knew they were talking about sex. But it felt like that's what they should be talking about on their anniversary. They still liked each other. Afton and I both knew that this was something of a miracle—married people, liking each other.

It felt healthy. It felt like a role-model situation. What they had: that's what we wanted to have, eventually. That intimacy.

We didn't take it for granted.

But that was a long time ago, I guess.

28

I wake up from a nap with the urge to make art. It shames me that I didn't think of it before. What's the one thing I came to Hawaii to do, besides forget Leo, and besides paddleboarding?

I came to paint.

The sketchbook is lying next to my head on the pillow, flipped to a sketch I did of Abby a few months ago. *Puppy-Dog Eyes*, I called it, that look she assembles on her face whenever she wants something and is determined to get it by pure cuteness alone.

I grab the sketchbook. Then I go over to my bag and take out the brand-new travel set of watercolors. Then I put together a makeshift art station outside on the balcony with the sketchbook and some loose-leaf heavier paper I brought for just this purpose, some paper towels, and a few of the clear plastic cups I found next to the ice bucket.

I sit on one of the deck chairs, rearrange my supplies one final time, and lift my arms over my head to stretch.

It feels strange, that I haven't done this for an entire week, not since I drew the *Not Ready* sketch of Leo Friday night.

I avoid looking at that one, or any of my other sketches. I want to start blank. Fresh. New. Not weighed down by any past attempts.

I begin with the landscape before me, the sky and sea first, in the background, what I will later layer in shades of blue and aqua and pale clouds.

Then the shapes of the palm trees, always at an angle, blowing.

Then the foreground. The statue of Buddha, the round circles of his body and head.

Then, because I can't seem to help myself, I add a figure. Then two figures. Too distant to identify. Who are they?

Afton and Michael?

Mom and the mystery dark-haired man?

I stare at the drawing. I'm a little bit out of control, but I can't tell if this is helping or hurting me. I mean, I know it's hurting. But is it also helping?

Art can convey everything. I can pour myself in with the paint. I can bleed stuff out through the strokes of my pencil, my pens, my brush.

But at the same time, it's also static.

Art can't actually fix your life.

The man I've drawn looks like Billy Wong, I think then.

My heart starts to beat fast. I put my sketchbook down and scroll through my phone like there could be some kind of proof there, past a hundred different images: Abby in the hammock, the tight rings of her drying curls against her head. Her smile is for Poppy. For Pop.

Afton feeding a bunch of little birds at our outdoor breakfast table the first morning. Before the hula class.

The Grand Staircase, that first night.

Mom and Billy sitting at a table, leaning toward each other.

Mom smiling with her eyes.

The realization that it's Billy doesn't even really surprise me. I didn't want to consider that it could be Billy before. But suddenly it seems so obvious. He's the only man on this island who's feasible. Mom doesn't have time to mess around with someone new. But she and Billy have known each other for years. Decades, even. She's comfortable with him. They spend all their time together.

It has to be Billy.

Poor Pop, I think then, the reality of the situation crashing over me, not just Mom and some guy in Hawaii but Mom and Billy, all this time, both here and back home. All the nights she was "working late." All the excuses. *Poor, poor Pop*. I pick up my phone again and read the texts between Pop and me.

I miss you a million.

I wish I were there.

You should be here, I text now. *It's not okay, you not being here.*

I'm startled when the phone buzzes in my hand. Pop calling.

I know I shouldn't, but I click accept and lift the phone to my ear. I want to hear his voice.

"Hi," I say.

"Hi. Do you have a minute? I wanted to talk to you some more."

"Okay."

"Is Abby with you?"

"No, she's with Afton today."

196

Pop makes a surprised noise. "All right," he says. "Good. So you seemed a little off yesterday, and I just wanted to check up on you. Is everything okay?"

I consider his question.

"No. No, it's not okay."

"Why not?"

I bite my lip, and then the words start to tumble out. "Pop, come on. We're not okay. None of us are. You should be here. This is a family vacation, and you're part of our family, and you don't get to decide that you're not."

"I told you," he says. "I have to work."

"That's not going to cut it, Pop. You don't have to do anything you don't want to. You're making a choice. And this time you made the wrong choice."

"All right," he says after a minute. "I can see why you feel that way. And I'm sorry."

"I don't care," I say.

"What?"

"I don't care if you're sorry. I care if you're here. And you're not here."

"Ada . . ." He sounds tired. I don't even know what time it is for him right now. He also sounds like he's about to tell me that I don't understand, that I can't understand, but I won't listen.

So I blabber on. "I know you and Mom are going through a rough patch, or whatever," I say quickly. "You think we don't notice these things, but we do. I don't know much about love, but I have been there when people stopped loving each other; Afton and I both, we've had front row seats to that. And I just think . . ." I swallow as tears burn my eyes. "I just think that can't happen with us this time, Pop. Not with you and Mom. It's not fair. It's not right. It can't happen."

"Ada, Ada, whoa," he says. "Why do you think that— Your mom and me— It's not—"

I push on. "Mom isn't perfect. She works too much, and she . . . isn't the amazing person everyone says she is, and I know that, but I also know that Mom isn't the only member of this family, and you loved each other once, and you both made promises, and that means you have to fight for her. Are you doing that, Pop? Are you really fighting for her? And fighting for us? Can you do that? Can you fight?"

Then I'm out of breath. It should be Mom I'm giving this speech to, Mom I'm confronting, but this is the only way I can think of to keep them together: for Pop to try harder. For him to fix it.

Pop doesn't say anything for a long, long time, which is okay, because now I'm sniffling.

"Yes," he says finally. "Yes, Ada. I will do that."

"Good."

"But what happened with your mom? Did she say something that upset you? Why—"

"That's all I really have to tell you, Pop. For now."

I hang up before I can blab anything else. Because I've already said too much. I grab my art supplies and start to head back into the room.

And that's when I almost collide with Afton.

Who's been standing in the doorway for who knows how long.

29

Fuck, I think.

"Oh my god, what?" Afton exclaims loudly. "What is going on? You're going to tell me, Ada. Right now."

I glance behind her, to see where Abby is.

Afton grabs my hand. "She's watching cartoons in the other room. Seriously, you didn't hear us come in?"

I was kind of busy melting down on Pop.

Afton drags me back out to the balcony, closes the door behind us, and sits down.

"Okay. What?" she insists.

I don't have a choice now. I close my eyes. "You have to promise that you won't do anything rash with this information," I whisper. "That you won't freak out."

"I'm freaking out right now!" she says, and I shush her. We can't risk Abby hearing. "What is it?" she whispers back urgently. "Tell me."

"Mom's having an affair," I say, still whispering. There's a sour taste in my mouth. I swallow it down.

Afton's mouth opens in shock. "What? With who?"

"She's sleeping with—" God, I think, how did we ever come up with the term "sleeping with" to mean sex? Sleeping is the opposite of what they were doing Monday morning. "I don't know. I didn't really see. But she's hooking up with Billy Wong."

There. I said it. Which makes it real.

There's another long moment of silence. Then Afton whispers, "How do you know?"

I take a deep breath. "On Monday, I think it was Monday . . ." The days have all started to blur together for me. "Yeah, Monday. I had to go back to the room. I only wanted to put on my swimsuit. I saw her . . ." It all floods back. I swallow again, hard. "I saw them."

"What?" Afton says, still keeping the volume of her voice low, but much more sharply this time. "When?"

"I told you. Monday morning. When you had Abby at hula class."

"Where?"

"Here. In her bed." I gesture to the adjoining room to this one. I can't even look directly at Afton as I'm talking about this. I can't stand to see her eyes when she understands.

Neither of us says anything else for what feels like a year. When I glance up at Afton again, her face is bright red. She's just staring at the metal railing of the balcony.

I remember that numbness—I felt it myself just a few days ago. I shift in my chair. "Well, say something. Can you just say something? Anything?"

She shakes her head. "What should I say?"

"I don't know. Something."

She looks at me with the same kind of hardness in her eyes that Mom gets whenever someone does something incredibly stupid, like Afton is pissed with *me*, for some reason, like it's my fault. She sucks her bottom lip into her mouth for a few seconds, then releases it. But she doesn't speak. She's in the shocked silence stage.

I move on to the babbling stage. "I mean, I guess it makes sense, Mom and Billy. Right? They, like, touch each other all the time, pat one another on the shoulder, that kind of thing. They hug sometimes, and Mom's not exactly a hugger, is she? I always thought that was just because they were best friends." I try not to think about the white robe. The noises. The bed. "I'm so stupid! I never would have guessed." I remember last year at the awards ceremony when I saw Billy mouth the words "I love you" to his wife. And I was so naive that I thought it was sweet. "Oh, I think I hate them," I murmur. "I really do."

"Ada . . . ," Afton starts.

It's awful, reliving it, but it's also a relief to finally tell. "Maybe they planned it this way. Maybe that's why Pop didn't come. Maybe this was supposed to be like Mom and Billy's little sexfest this year, and Pop knew. I mean, he's a pretty observant guy. He's not stupid. I don't know."

"And that was Pop on the phone just now?" Afton asks, her fingers clenching into fists, unclenching, and then reclenching. "You were telling *Pop* that you saw Mom and Billy Wong?" Her voice rises again.

"No, I didn't tell him," I hiss. "I'm not totally brainless. I told him to fight for us, that's all. I told him it was a mistake, him not coming with us."

Afton stands up. "Oh my god, Ada." Her face is an even darker red. Scarlet. Partly chartreuse.

"I know. I knew something wasn't right with them, but this . . . But we have to act like we don't know," I say earnestly. "I've been thinking through it all week, and it's the only way they don't get divorced. We have to pretend like it didn't happen."

She drags a hand through her hair. Paces back and forth a few times. Stops. "No. Ada, listen to me—"

But right then we hear the door inside slam, and Mom's voice. "Girls?"

Afton and I stare at each other, wide-eyed.

"We've got to keep it together," I say quickly. I'm terrified at what Afton might do right now. What she might say. How she might unravel our entire life. "Just be calm."

I move to the balcony door and slide it open. "Hi, Mom," I say so cheerfully that that in itself is suspicious, but I can't help it. "So you're back for the day?"

"I am back for the day," she confirms. "The group is invited to a luau tonight, though."

I know this. I read the schedule. "That sounds great. Um, Abby and I would love to go, but Afton's feeling a little under the weather."

Mom's eyebrows lift. "Sick?"

"Yes. So we better let her sit out the luau."

Afton comes in from outside. Her eyes are stony in a way I've never seen, like chunks of bluish flint. My heart rate picks up.

Dear God, please don't let my sister murder my mother in broad day-light.

"Oh, you do look flushed," Mom says. "Maybe you have what Ada had."

"Yeah," I agree. "What I had."

30

At the luau I find out one key thing about myself: I'm a lightweight when it comes to booze.

I know this because I accidentally (or maybe not so accidentally) pick up my mom's mai tai instead of my fruity nonalcoholic drink from the table, and chug it down. Thinking it will help me relax and get through this meal in one piece.

A mistake, it turns out.

I think the alcohol hits me so hard because I'm stressed out over what's just transpired with Afton and worried about what will happen next. Or because I've been running around in the sun for half the day without drinking enough water, and I haven't eaten since breakfast. Or because the mai tai is heavy on the rum, which lands right on my empty stomach.

Whatever the reason, less than ten minutes after I partake of the forbidden mai tai, my brain goes fuzzy, and the world starts to spin.

The worst thing is, Mom is seated next to Billy, who is next to his wife. I try not to stare at them, but I have to look that way to see the stage.

"Are we going to eat a pig?" Abby asks.

"I think so," I answer, on account of the bunch of shiny-chested men wearing loincloths made of leaves who walk by carrying an entire roasted pig. The smell of pork hits me hot and heavy, and my stomach suddenly feels like it's filled with rocks.

Mom leans close to Billy and says something in his ear.

He laughs.

She smiles, a white flash of her teeth.

I know something with absolute certainty then: I'm going to be sick.

I lurch out of my chair and toward the restroom. I make it to the entrance to the ladies' room before I hunch forward and throw up violently into the trash can next to the door.

This has not been my best trip, vomit-wise.

Afterward I feel much better, almost normal, hungry, even, like I'm ready to eat some pig. When I return to the table, Mom has shifted our plates around, moved me over one so she can attend to cutting Abby's meat, I think.

Which means I'm now sitting between Mom and Billy Wong. And talking to Billy is slightly (and only slightly) less nauseating than watching my mom talk to Billy.

He's super chatty, too. He keeps asking all these questions about school and my art stuff and how I'm enjoying the trip so far.

"It's been enlightening," I say through clenched teeth.

"I know exactly what you mean," he says.

Somehow, I doubt that.

"I love all of these representations of East Asian art at this hotel," he says. "I feel like I'm bumping into Buddha at every turn. Speaking of which, I've been meaning to ask something."

Speaking of Buddha? "Yeah?" I say.

"I'd like to hire you."

"Hire me?" I've done some babysitting for Peter and Josie over the years, but not for a while.

"To do a piece for us," he clarifies. "I'd like to have a big painting of our family for over our fireplace. I know you can fake it these days, use Photoshop to doctor a photo to look like a painting and print it on canvas and so on, but I want the real deal. An artist. I think an artist can see beyond the physical sometimes, capture the essence of a person better than a photograph ever could. Don't you think?"

"I don't do portraits," I say briskly. This isn't at all true. Portraits are the main thing I do. I'm drawing and painting people in my sketchbook all the time. I did like three of them today.

"You don't?" He sounds surprised.

"I only do landscapes," I lie. "Watercolor, mostly."

I did do one landscape today. But I snuck in people at the end. Possibly Billy himself.

Billy is undeterred by my reluctance. "Maybe you can do a landscape for us, then. Of Hawaii, so we can remember our trip."

"Maybe," I say.

But it'll be a cold day in hell before I paint something for Billy Wong. Especially something to commemorate this particular vacation.

206

"That'd be awesome." Then he finally seems satisfied that he and I have "caught up" with each other, and he turns to talk to the other person sitting next to him, who happens to be Marjorie Pearson.

"Hello, dearie," she says.

I finish my meal in seething silence. *How dare he?* I keep thinking. The sheer nerve he has, that he would ask me to do something for him.

When he's endangering my entire world. Right now, Afton is back at the room going through what I went through, Monday night. Coming to understand that life as we've known it is over.

Billy's poisoning my family.

Smiling. Always smiling. Acting like he's such a nice guy.

My eyes fall on the small pile of salt and pepper packets I picked up when I went through the buffet line. I intended to sprinkle the salt over my pork and rice bowl.

But instead I grab a pepper packet.

I tear open a corner.

And dump the entire contents into Billy's glass of iced tea.

For a second I just stare at it, the clumps of pepper whirling in the glass, sinking, disseminating through the tea like it's meant to be there.

Then I stand up, shocked by what I've done and eager to get away from the scene of the crime. I cross to the dessert table and grab a tiny chilled plate. I pretend to be taking my time considering which flavor of haupia—those tiny gelatinous cubes that are everywhere in Hawaii—would be tastier: coconut or strawberry. I take a strawberry one. Out of the corner of my eye, I watch Billy. He's still turned to Marjorie, still talking, still smiling.

Any second now, I think.

I swivel so that my back is to him. I don't even want to be looking in his direction when it happens.

I wait for him to start coughing.

Will it hurt him, I wonder? It will be a surprise, obviously, and there's the possibility that he'll gasp and inhale the pepper somehow, and that can't be good for his lungs. But that can't be too bad, considering that the cops use pepper spray on people all the time and it never seems to do permanent damage. It won't really hurt him.

Will it?

I do a quick search on my phone. All I can find are sites listing the health benefits of pepper. Eating it, but also drinking it. Apparently it's a thing to drink hot water with pepper in it.

So I am actually helping Billy to flush his body of toxins.

If he drinks it.

I dare a glance over my shoulder at the table again. Billy is still there.

Still talking.

But his glass is gone.

I look around, but I don't see it. The only glasses on the table are my water, my mom's empty glass with a lemon in the bottom, and Marjorie's, which she is currently holding in her hand, waving it around as she talks. In front of Billy: nothing.

It's like I hallucinated the entire thing.

It's probably for the best. Some part of me still wants to make Billy suffer, even just a little bit, but it's a juvenile part. What is wrong in my life will not be fixed by Billy drinking some pepper in his tea. I know that. But still—

"Those look delicious." I startle at my mother's voice from beside me. I turn and meet her questioning blue eyes. She was sitting on the other side of me all through dinner. She could have seen me do it and snatched up Billy's glass the moment I left the table.

If she did see me do it, she will naturally be wondering now why I'm mad at Billy. And maybe she'll suspect that I know.

"Uh, yeah," I stammer. "Do you want mine? You can have it. I just figured out that I'm not hungry anymore."

"Are you feeling okay?" Her hand touches my cheek. I flinch away.

"I'm fine," I say. "I'm just . . . worried about Afton. Do you mind if I go back to the room and check on her?"

"Yes, go ahead," Mom says. She smiles. "You're a good sister, Ada. I appreciate all that you do. Your pop and I both do."

"Thanks, Mom," I mutter, and hurry to get away from her.

31

"Ada! Wait!" Nick catches up with me as I'm leaving the luau place. "Hi."

"Hi." We stand for a while, frozen in the awkwardness of what's supposed to happen between us Saturday night.

"How are you?" he asks finally. "Did you get to go paddleboarding?"

"No," I admit. "But thanks for your help with Marjorie."

"Any time," he says.

We're standing on a platform next to a tram stop, which is full of hotel guests waiting to catch a ride. I need to catch a ride myself, back to Ocean Tower and Afton. I need to talk to Afton now. We need to form some kind of game plan.

"Are you okay?" he asks.

"Yeah." I'm still feeling light-headed. "I'm fine."

"Do you still feel like tea?"

It takes me a second. "Yeah. Of course. Yes. If we can find some condoms, that is. I looked for them myself, today, and you're right. They aren't easy to locate."

"If at first you don't succeed." He smiles, but it's a queasy sort of smile.

"No gas station condoms," I repeat.

"I know. That's what you said." He doesn't sound super enthusiastic.

"What's the matter? Are you having second thoughts? That's okay, if you are. I mean, I'm not, but if you are, that's okay."

Nick holds up his hand, indicating that he'd like me to stop babbling so that he can speak. But then his lips press together, like he's unsure of what he's about to say.

"I don't know how to say this," he says.

"Just say it," I tell him. He thinks I'm ugly. He's realized that having sex with me might be a risk, as I outweigh him by fifty pounds and could squash him like a bug. He's realized that . . .

"Are you evil?" he says.

I scoff. "Say what now?"

He crosses his arms over his chest in a protective measure. "I thought I knew you, Ada, and I thought you were nice, but now I'm starting to think that you're . . ."

"Evil? Because I asked you to have . . ." I glance around. There are so many people. ". . . tea with me? Like you're Adam and I'm Eve, and here I am offering you the apple?"

"No," he says quickly. "It's not about the . . . tea . . . It's that I thought you were a good person, but . . ."

"But what?"

He sighs. "I saw you put pepper in Billy Wong's drink tonight."

Now it's me who doesn't know what to say. My brain churns with excuses, but none of them work. "You were there, and you didn't say anything?" I say, looking for some way—any way, really—for this not to be my fault. "You thought you'd just, like, spy on me?"

"I wasn't spying," Nick sputters. "I waved when you came in, but you didn't see me. You were too busy trying to poison a guy."

"I wasn't trying to poison him!" I object. "Did you know that pepper actually has many medicinal qualities? Some people drink pepper in their water every day. It helps with their metabolism."

He stares at me like I've grown an extra head.

"Oh, all right!" I burst out, exasperated. "I was trying to—well, not poison him, exactly, but yes, do something mean."

"Which brings me back to you being evil."

"I'm not evil. I just . . ." I can't tell him why. "I just don't like Billy Wong."

Nick shakes his head. "But why?"

I shrug.

"Billy's one of the nicest people I've ever met," he says.

"Maybe you should get out more."

His gray eyes flash. "Ask anybody. He's the coolest, nicest, most all-around great guy who comes to STS. Add that to the fact that he's a surgeon, and you and I both know how surgeons can be, and Billy should win an award or something."

I thought so, too. Before this week, anyway. But now things are different.

I put my hands on my hips and glare at Nick. "Maybe nobody knows the real Billy. I mean, come on, how well do any of these people know each other, really? We see each other for seven days, once a year. I don't even know *you* very well, and we're about to—"

Another group of hotel guests walk up to wait for the tram. "—have tea together."

Nick sits down on one of the benches, like he's decided to wait for the tram, too. "I guess I don't know you that well, either."

I sit down next to him. "I'm sorry. I wish I could explain why, but—"

"I saw you do it, and I thought that maybe you were messing around with your own drink. Sometimes I play with those little packets of sugar if they're on the table. I thought it could have been sugar, but the package was the wrong color. And right after you did it, you left the table."

Because I'm a coward, I think.

Nick looks down at his shoes. "So I went over there and checked, and yes, it was pepper. Billy even turned to pick it up, so I just grabbed it and gave it to a waiter who was cleaning up dishes."

"It was you! You stopped him!" I gasp, part of me angry again, that Nick would interfere. "This was none of your business, Nick. You shouldn't have—" I sigh. "Okay. That was probably fine."

The tram arrives. Everyone around us surges toward it.

Nick gazes at it thoughtfully. "This morning there was a woman who was struggling to get her stroller on the tram. Billy saw her and got off and lifted it on for her, and then he gave her and her baby his seat."

I wince. "That doesn't prove anything. Everybody likes babies."

"I saw him at lunchtime, too. He found a tiny spider on his table and he used a napkin to carry it outside."

"That doesn't make him a saint," I say stiffly, struggling to hold on to the image I most want to forget: Billy and my mom in the dark hotel room. Cheating on us all. "And now that spider is probably going to bite a person, thanks to Billy."

The tram leaves.

Nick's eyebrows squeeze together. "I don't get you. Billy's the best."

"Then maybe you should sleep with *him*!" I stand up and walk away like I'm going to leave, then change my mind and come back. "I have a good reason to not like him, Nick, and I don't have to tell you what it is, because I don't owe you anything. Can't you just—I don't know—trust me?"

But even as I say that, I think, *But why would he trust me?* He's never seen me save a bug's life or help somebody in need.

Another tram arrives. "I should go," I murmur.

We both stand up.

"I'm sorry, I—"

"I get it. You don't know me, either." I get on the tram. The doors shut between us. Nick steps back and watches as I'm spirited away.

I'm angry as I walk back from the tram to the room. Not at Nick. At Mom. Still. Again. Perpetually.

I'm quiet as I enter the room, in case Afton went to bed early. Monday night, I went to bed early. Just to get that horrible day over with.

But my sister's not in the room. She's not in the bathroom. Instead I find my sketchbook in the middle of her bed, open to the landscape I did today, the one of the beach and the two figures.

Mom and Billy. Who knows what else she saw in that sketchbook.

And my sister is gone. Still. Again. Perpetually.

32

I don't remember much concerning my parents' (my original parents') divorce. I was five when it happened. Abby's age now. I hadn't even been aware that my mom and dad were unhappy with one another, although I did know that they yelled a lot.

I thought that's just what grown-ups did.

They told Afton and me separately. Afton first. They left me in the playroom with a new dollhouse I'd received for my birthday, Ruthie's idea, I'm sure. I was playing obliviously, moving tiny wooden people around a meticulously decorated miniature three-story model while they sat my sister down in another room. When they were satisfied that she understood what they were trying to tell her, they swapped us and brought me into their bedroom, where I immediately knew something was off because I wasn't normally allowed in their bedroom. It had the quiet, austere presence of a church to me, a place I entered without shoes so I wouldn't sully the cream-colored carpet.

The air smelled like sandalwood, although of course I didn't know it was sandalwood at the time, just a bright, piercing scent that to this day makes me summon up the word:

Divorce.

We all sat on the upholstered bench at the end of my parents' king-sized bed. Mom's face was a picture of calm, like one of those masks from a party store, completely expressionless.

Dad's face was red. His eyes were also red. Bloodshot. Puffy. His voice shook as he tried to tell me that he was moving out. Finally he stopped trying, and Mom stepped in.

I didn't get it. Not really. But I nodded like I did.

Then they brought me back to the playroom, where Afton was waiting. Her expression was set exactly like Mom's. I can still see it in my mind's eye. If I did a drawing, I would title it *Determined*.

It's wild to think she was only seven years old.

Mom and Dad were out in the hall, yelling again.

Afton took my hand. "It's good," she said.

"It feels bad," I said.

She shook her head. "They don't love each other anymore."

That was a terrifying thought, that people can love you, and then they can stop.

She didn't let go of my hand. I don't know if that was for her, or for me. We were still clutching hands when Dad appeared in the doorway holding a suitcase. He was crying. I'd never seen him cry before, or since. I felt so bad for him I started crying, too.

Then he was gone.

"Don't worry," Afton told me, squeezing my hand so tight it hurt. "I'm still here."

33

I wake up to yelling. I open my eyes to see Afton and Mom standing at the foot of my bed, squared off like boxers.

Dear god, I think. *Here we go.*

"That is unacceptable, young lady!" Mom says, in as close to a shout as she gets. "You can't simply not come home at night!"

"This isn't my home!" Afton hollers back.

"You know what I mean!"

"I'm eighteen!" Afton yells. "I'm legally an adult. I can do what I want!"

"This is my house—" Mom pauses, jaw clenching. "My hotel room, and as long as you're part of this family, staying in our rooms, you'll do what you're told. It's not unreasonable for me to ask you to come home at night, and for you to let us know where you are. Who you're with. What you're doing."

"No," Afton says.

"No?"

"No. And what are you going to do about it? Ship me home? Lock me up?"

"I'm considering it," Mom says. "I'm surprised at you, Afton. Normally I can trust you to be responsible. Think about the example that you're setting for your sisters."

"Oh. That's nice," Afton says. "Coming from you."

I scramble out from under the covers. "Hey, you two, let's—"

"Stay out of it, Ada," they both say at the same time, with the same exact inflection.

They are too much alike.

"So I assume you spent the night with Michael Wong," Mom says. She gives a humorless laugh. "I knew you had a crush on him, and I thought he must be humoring you. But staying out with him all night, that's—"

"That's none of your business," Afton says.

"Everything you do is my business," Mom argues. "I created you. My body assembled the cells that made you a person. That makes you my business."

"Doesn't the human body replace every single cell over the course of seven years?" Afton says.

"And the Wongs are my business," Mom continues like she didn't hear. "Billy Wong is my closest colleague. My partner at work. My friend."

My breath freezes. This would be the most opportune time for Afton to confront Mom about Billy, and I don't know how to stop her. I don't know how to stop any of this.

"Stop," I say, but they ignore me. "You're going to wake up Abby." My little sister is a deep sleeper. She's literally slept through a fire alarm before, without so much as stirring. But still. She's just in the next room over.

Afton scoffs. "Oh, so you're afraid I'm going to make you look bad in front of your work buddies."

"No, but having a fling with Michael Wong reflects badly on all of us," Mom says.

Afton shakes her head, a tumble of long blond hair. "Why? Who cares?"

"There's too much of an age difference," Mom says stiffly.

Afton cocks her head. "Tell me again how much older you are than Pop?"

Ooh, ooh, I know the answer. Six years. Which is more than the four-year difference between Afton and Michael Wong.

"This is different. Two weeks ago, you were still in high school. This is inappropriate."

Afton scowls. "Don't you dare lecture me about what's inappropriate."

Mom's cheeks color. "Don't talk to me like that. I'm only trying to protect you."

"Well, you're doing a stellar job," Afton snaps.

"Hey," I try to interject again. "Let's just calm down, okay?"

"Michael has a girlfriend," Mom says then.

Afton's expression goes blank. "What?"

"I've even met her," Mom says. "Michael brought her in to the hospital to have lunch with Billy, about six months ago. Her name is Melanie."

Afton's breath becomes funny, irregular. "Six months ago is not now."

"One month ago he was buying her an engagement ring."

"A lot can happen in a month," she says.

"If they'd broken up, I would have heard about it."

Afton sucks her bottom lip into her mouth and holds it there, between her teeth, for a long time. "You ruin everything," she says finally.

"Oh, don't be so melodramatic. I'm sorry, Afton," she says, more kindly. "I know you just broke up with Logan and . . ."

"You don't know anything," Afton says. "Like you have anything to say about relationships. Look at you and Pop."

"I'm not talking about Pop," Mom says.

Afton's cold blue eyes flicker to me. "Well, maybe you should. Maybe we could get some of this shit out in the open, am I right?"

Thankfully at that exact moment Abby appears, bleary-eyed and clutching her nubby blanket to her chest. "What's going on?" she asks. "Why is Afton swearing?"

Afton turns toward the door. "I'm going out."

"There's another group trip today," Mom says. "They leave in an hour, and you're going with everyone else."

"Yes, ma'am," Afton says with a petulant smile, and then she's out the door, wearing the same clothes she was wearing yesterday.

I follow her. "Afton!"

She stops. Turns.

"Thank you," I tell her.

She scoffs. "For what?"

"I know you're mad, and this thing with Michael sucks, but

thank you for not telling her that you know about Billy. I don't think I would have had so much control." I know I wouldn't have. It didn't even seem like Afton was mad about Billy. Her anger seemed focused solely on Mom.

But Afton's looking at me now like I am the worst. "This is all your fault," she says, and turns to go.

Today's field trip this time is only a half day. The first stop is a place called Pu'uhonua o Honaunau. Kahoni makes us practice pronouncing the words several times.

"Back in the ancient days," he tells us as our bus winds its way into the parking lot, "if you broke a law, any law, the penalty was death. Hey, you!"

He points at Marjorie, who is lifting a cracker to her lips.

"No eating on the bus!" Kahoni says as sternly as if she's stolen a car. "You have broken a law."

"If I don't eat every two hours, my blood sugar gets iffy," Marjorie says in her defense.

"Your reasons do not matter," Kahoni says. "You broke the law, so you must die."

"He's not really going to kill Marjorie, is he?" whispers Abby from the seat next to mine. "Wait, is this the part where he throws her in the volcano?"

"No. He's just making a point," I whisper back.

"You're in big trouble now, Marjorie," Kahoni says. "If we can catch you, you're dead. But if you can escape and get to the nearest pu'uhonua, you'll be saved."

"I'm faster than I look," Marjorie says, and we all laugh.

Kahoni goes on to talk about how the place is a temple where the chiefs' bones are buried, and still holds their mana—their power. We file off the bus and look around. To one side is a huge L-shaped wall made of palm tree trunks, cutting the area off from everywhere else, down to the black rocky beach.

"Go explore," Kahoni says. "But remember, this place is filled with the spirit of peace and forgiveness. Treat it with respect."

I keep a careful eye on Abby as we wander—through the royal grounds, into several thatched-roof structures with people inside demonstrating how to make nets from a certain kind of leaf and con- tainers out of gourds. We didn't even discuss whose job it was to look after Abby today. Mom just handed me the hundred dollars.

Nick's with us, as usual, standing in the back. He keeps a respect- ful distance. He probably thinks I'm mad at him, but I'm not. I have a lot of other, more pressing things on my mind than having tea.

Afton, true to her word, is here, too. She stubbornly sat with Michael and the rest of the Wongs on the bus. Avoiding even so much as looking at me.

I don't know why she's so mad at *me*, but I kind of get it. I was mad at her over it, too. I don't know what to do about it, so I try to act like things are normal, for Abby's sake. I take a lot of photos with my phone so I can go back and do some watercolors off them later. I love the wooden ki'i statues with their gaping smiles and wide grimaces. The place reminds me a little of Notre Dame, when the conference was in Paris four years ago. Pop wore Abby in a baby carrier strapped to his chest, and she went totally quiet in the cathedral, her little rose- bud mouth forming a silent O as she stared up at the stained glass. This place feels the same, like the sand we're standing on is holy, the air charged with an ancient and wise energy.

It's peaceful, I think, being here.

"YOU'RE A DOUCHEBAG, YOU KNOW THAT?"

Afton's voice echoes off the walls and the rocks and the trees. Everyone—even the people who aren't part of our group—stop to stare at her and Michael standing in the coconut grove. Afton's face is red, her fists clenched at her sides.

Michael's looking down at his flip-flops. "Hey, look, I'm sorry," he says quietly.

"Save it," she snarls, and stalks off down the beach.

"I guess that honeymoon's over," says Marjorie from somewhere in the back.

I stare after Afton. I bet this outburst has to do with the infamous Melanie. I happen to know exactly how that feels. Like screaming, "Fuck you, Leo!" in a crowded parking lot.

"Is Afton okay?" Abby asks. "Is she winning?"

"Winning?"

"You said you were in a competition to see who had the worst broken heart," Abby reminds me.

I snort, then nod. "Yeah. I think she might be winning now."

"Everyone's yelling all the time," Abby says with a sigh. "I wish it would stop."

My heart squeezes. "Well, I won't yell anymore, okay?"

"Promise?" She holds out her pinkie.

I take it with mine. "Promise. And remember what Pop said. Afton's tough. She'll be okay." It's the rest of us I'm not so sure about. I try to mash Afton's words down in my brain: *This is all your fault.* Blaming me the way I blamed her for taking Abby to hula, which led

223

to me discovering Mom and Billy. It wasn't Afton's fault. And it's not mine.

"All right, people," says Kahoni in disgust. "It's time to go."

The next (and final) stop is a coffee plantation. That word—*plantation*—makes me uneasy and wonder about the situation of the people who worked there, both in the past and now. White guilt at its finest, I guess. I wonder, but don't ask about it. Then the tour guide—a woman who's employed by the plantation, not Kahoni—explains that in this case the word means "a place where trees have been planted," because obviously she gets that question sometimes.

But that gets me thinking about the nature of words. Sure, the word *plantation* has a dictionary meaning that has nothing to do with the word *slavery*. But the two words are connected now. It's impossible to totally untangle them.

Like the word *sex* and the word *affair*.

Sigh. If things were going normally, I'd hang out with Afton at the coffee place. If there is one thing that bonds us as sisters, it's our mutual love for coffee. But she avoids me after we get off the bus. Michael also lags behind in the back of the group, sticking close to his mom, who seems on edge herself.

For all of my never-ending love of coffee, I find I didn't know that it starts out as a bright red berry that grows in a bunch on the branch of a tall, leafy bush. Inside each berry, like magic, are two pale little beans, which are roasted in huge drums and dried and then ground and turned into sweet, sweet coffee—also known as the nectar of life.

They give out samples of the different roasts. I try them all.

Abby is hot and bored and predictably hungry, but I am in coffee heaven.

Then heaven hits a bit of a snag after the official tour of the plantation is over, because there's no lunch.

"What do you mean, there's no lunch?" Marjorie asks the tour guide in a huff. She pulls out the STS trip itinerary and waves it under the coffee lady's nose. "It says, right here, 'lunch will be provided.'"

"There's been some kind of mix-up, I'm afraid," says the coffee lady coolly. "The restaurant's not open today. We'd be happy to provide you all with free mugs instead."

"It says lunch will be provided," repeats Marjorie.

The coffee lady wants to sigh, I can tell. But she says, "I'll see what can be done," and disappears into the building.

The group congregates on the back patio area and on the lawn, which has a spectacular view: coffee bushes as far as the eye can see, stretching all the way down to the hazy blue ocean in the distance.

My fingers close around an imaginary paintbrush. I wish I'd thought to bring my watercolors and some paper, but I assumed that we were going to be on the move all morning.

"I'm hungry," Abby whines again. "I'm going to starve to death if I don't eat soon."

"And I will miss you," I say, then smile to show her I'm not serious. "We won't starve, Abby. Did you know that the human body can go three whole weeks without eating before starving to death? Anyway, we could always eat Peter if we get desperate."

She giggles.

My own stomach is rumbling, and a bit heartburny on account

of all the free coffee I drank and no food. "Let's sit down." I lead us over to where there's a metal table and some chairs. Abby sits for all of two minutes before she pops up again and runs to do cartwheels in the grass with Josie.

I watch Afton slip into the gift shop, where everything is of course coffee-related. Coffee in bags. Coffee grinders. Chocolate-covered espresso beans. Coffee cups of various shapes and sizes.

I sigh. The thing is, I'm starting to really miss my sister. Even though I assume, from what I saw, that she looked through my sketch-book last night. Which is the equivalent of reading my diary.

Still, she needs me today. I've always been her support system whenever she had boy trouble. I'm there for her. I listen.

Except not lately.

I sigh again.

"Is this seat taken?" Nick is standing next to the table, red-brown hair windblown, his cheeks and nose a bit sunburned. His eyes match the gray-blue ocean behind him.

"Let me think." I pause, smile. "Okay."

He sits.

"How's it going?" I ask.

"Very well, thanks. I wanted to say I'm sorry," he says. "About last night."

"Oh, you mean when you accused me of being *evil*?"

"Yeah, that. I thought about it, and you're right. I believe you, if you say you have a good reason not to like Billy. And you're also right that I don't know you, not that well, anyway. But I'd like to."

I stare over at him. "You must really, really want to have tea, huh?"

He flushes. "No. I assume we're not doing that anymore. Even though I . . ."

Well, now I'm curious. "Even though you what?"

He clears his throat. "I got condoms."

I sit back. "You did. How?"

He scratches at the back of his neck. "From my dad."

"You . . ." I lower my voice. "You stole condoms from your dad?"

"No. He gave them to me, because I told him."

My mouth drops open. *"You told your dad?"*

"He figured out that something was going on. He asked, so I told him. Don't worry. He's cool with it."

"He is?" I can't imagine either of my parents really being cool with it.

"He actually gave me some tips."

I cringe. "Don't tell me. I don't want to know. But good job, I guess."

"Yeah," he says. "Even though we won't be . . . having tea anymore."

"Who says we're not having tea?"

"Uh, well. I thought . . ."

"I still want tea," I tell him, and right in that instant I feel like it's the truth. Life is short. Bad things are happening all around us. There's no better time for us to live for the moment. "Do you still want tea?"

"I think I would love tea," he says.

"Okay, then. Tomorrow night's still on."

"Really?"

Something about the way he says the word *really?* reminds me of Leo. It's been a while, I realize, since I even thought about Leo. Which is progress, I guess.

"Look," I say to Nick, "if I say something, I mean it. I wouldn't tell you I wanted to have sex in order to trick you."

"Okay. Good, I guess." He coughs into his fist. "Good. I've been doing a lot of research."

My eyes fly to his face, which is slowly but surely going as red as the coffee berries. "You have?"

"It's been very interesting." He stares off at the ocean for a second. "I didn't know girls were so . . . complicated."

"Don't feel bad. I didn't, either. I haven't done this before, you know."

"I kind of figured," he says with a shy smile.

But he doesn't say it like he thinks I'm unfuckable or anything. Just like he recognizes that this is as much of a big deal for me as it is for him.

"I did see this really sexy episode of the Scottish show yesterday," I tell him. "So that's probably all the research I need, right?"

"Oh, the Scottish show?" he says lightly. "I've seen that. I get why the ladies like it. That guy is ripped."

"Agreed. He's almost unbearably hot."

"How am I supposed to compete with that?"

"Better do some push-ups," I say.

The corner of his mouth twitches. "But does this mean you like redheads?"

I bite my lip against a smile. "Go team ginger."

Our eyes meet. Then we laugh, and the tension between us dissolves. We're both blushing.

We're flirting. I am surprisingly into it.

Abby comes running up. "Josie's mom says the coffee lady said that the chef is whipping something up for us, but it may take a while. Which is bad because I'm so hun-gry!" She suddenly seems to notice I'm not alone. "Hi, Nick."

"Hi, Abby. Hey, I've got something you might like." He heaves his backpack onto the table and rummages around in the front pocket before he produces a granola bar. "Here. It's chocolate chip."

"Oh my dog! Thanks!" Abby gasps. "You just saved my life!" She tears off the wrapper and takes such a huge bite I worry that I'm going to end up doing the Heimlich.

"That's me," Nick says. "Casual superhero."

"Thank you," I say.

"Do you want one? I've got one more."

My stomach makes a pterodactyl sound. "I shouldn't. I mean, don't you want it?"

"I'd be happy to give it to you."

I take it and wolf it down. Nick sits watching me. I narrow my eyes at him. "What's different about you?"

I scan down his body. Same long, messy hair. Same wrinkled video-game-themed shirt. Same baggy shorts and dirty white sneakers. Then I figure out what's missing. "Where's your phone?"

"My dad made me leave it back at the room."

"Oh my dog!" I exclaim for Abby's benefit. "Are you okay? Are you going through withdrawal yet?"

He smirks. "Ha ha. I'm surviving . . . barely. I don't get to take any pictures, though, which sucks." He gazes around at all the fabulous scenery that surrounds us.

"I can text you some of mine," I offer.

"That'd be awesome. Thanks."

"Are you Ada's boyfriend?" Abby asks, propping her chin in her hand.

He glances from me to her. "No. But I am a boy who's her friend."

"But you like her. Like kissy like," Abby says.

He looks at me again. "You got me. I guess I do."

"And she likes you."

"Does she?"

"Yep." Abby takes another enthusiastic bite of the granola bar. "Trust me. She likes you a lot. Her last boyfriend was an asshole."

"Abby!" I exclaim. I'm blushing. I rub the back of my neck. "She's right, though."

"That's . . . good to know."

"So you should be her boyfriend, and she should be your girl-friend," Abby says. "Have you kissed her yet?"

"No," he says slowly. "Not yet."

"You should," Abby says.

"I will if she wants me to."

Shit. I want him to. The magic is back: my palms are sweaty and my heart is racing and there's a suspicious fluttering in my stomach. Or maybe I've just had too much coffee.

He has nice lips, I observe. Not too small or too big. A good pro-portion between the top lip and the bottom. They look soft, too. I wonder what they would feel like.

I make a mental note to start our time tomorrow night with kissing.

"A-duh. You're not listening to me, are you?"

I blink. I've been zoning out. Worse, I've been daydreaming

about kissing Nick while I'm sitting right in front of him. "I'm sorry, Abby-cakes. What did you say?"

"I said, I'm still hungry. Almost enough to eat Peter, I think."

"Oh. Well, you're just going to have to—"

"Lunch is served!" calls out the coffee lady from the patio. "It's a simple spaghetti and meatballs, but I think you'll find it quite satisfactory."

The group assembles into a line in record time. In a minute we're all back at the table with our plates piled high with spaghetti and meatballs. Abby starts shoveling it into her mouth. She doesn't even bother to try to talk anymore.

"What do you think?" Nick asks as I try not to pig out myself. "Satisfactory?"

It's easily the best spaghetti and meatballs I've ever tasted.

"Delectable," I say, and he laughs.

He has sauce on his chin. "So what are you two going to do when we get back to the hotel?"

"Ukulele lessons," I tell him.

Abby claps her hands together. "Yay! Uku-lei-lei!"

"You've probably got to rush back to your lonely, utterly abandoned phone before it implodes from lack of use," I rib him.

"Stop." His mouth splits into that crooked smile he has. I know, all the guys in romance novels have crooked smiles. But when I say that Nick's is crooked, it's because his teeth are crooked. And I'm starting to get why that's a thing people like.

"I'm feeling the call of duty this afternoon," he says.

It takes me a second, but I catch on. "Which is a game that you play on your PS4."

"You should really try it with me sometime."

I can't imagine myself doing that, pretending to shoot people. Although maybe, given how angry I've been feeling lately, it could be therapeutic.

"I have a better idea," I say. "Come to ukulele lessons with us."

His mouth opens in surprise. "Why?"

"So we can hang out more. Because you're a boy who's my friend."

Abby immediately understands what needs to be done here. "Please, Nick, come with us! Please!"

"You need to get uku-lei'd," I say with as straight a face as I can manage.

"Okay."

"Yay!" Abby jumps up and down.

"Yay," I say, too.

34

Abby ditches me on the ride home. She wants to sit with Josie again, so I pick a seat in the back of the bus. I'm flipping through my photos, deciding which ones I will send to Nick, when someone says, "Can I sit here?" and I smile and say, "Go right ahead."

But it isn't Nick. It's Michael Wong.

I frown up at him. "Don't you want to sit with my sister? Work things out?"

He makes a quick little grimace. "She and I need to give each other some space."

We ride for a while in silence until I can't hold back the obvious question. "What'd you do?" Although I feel like I can guess. Like Leo, Michael Wong's a cheater. And he made Afton an accomplice.

"Do?" Michael repeats, like he has no idea.

"To get Afton mad at you?"

He shakes his head. "Nothing. I told her—" He stops himself. "She's crazy, that's all."

I sit up straighter. "Don't call my sister crazy. She may be a lot of things, but crazy's not one of them."

"Okay, yeah, sorry," he says, although he clearly doesn't mean it. "She can just be a little intense, is all."

Normally, I'd agree.

But not today. "What is it with guys saying girls are crazy, just because we have feelings and sometimes we dare to show you what they are? That doesn't make us crazy. Crazy is a messed-up, ableist word, anyway. I mean, guys act like they're clueless morons half the time, but we don't go around saying you're stupid, do we?"

Okay, maybe we do.

Now Michael's looking at me like I'm the crazy one.

"I'm just saying, if Afton called you a douchebag—although I don't approve of douchebag as an insult, either, because it's misogynistic, but that's fine, whatever—if she called you that, it's probably accurate."

I'm pleased with myself that I even had the guts to say this.

Kahoni is coming down the aisle handing everyone a paper-wrapped coffee mug, an apology gift from the plantation for the mix-up with lunch. I take mine with a mumbled thanks and lean down to put it in my bag. When I sit up again, Michael has switched places with the guy in front of him. He's putting headphones in—the fancy wireless kind that make it look like snot is dripping out of his ears. Then he starts bobbing his head to some music I can't hear.

I kick the back of his chair.

* * *

The ride back to the hotel goes quickly this time, since we didn't go far. When I stand up to exit the bus, Nick stands up, too, from the seat directly behind mine.

I didn't even know he was there.

He's staring at me. He clearly heard everything I said to Michael.

"Oh, great," I moan. "You're going to call me crazy now, too."

"I would never." He presses his hand into his chest. "No, I thought that was totally badass." We lumber down the steps of the bus, and Abby comes running up.

"Hi, Nick," she says almost shyly, gazing up at him through her eyelashes.

That was obviously some granola bar.

I notice Michael is standing with the rest of his family. He notices me, too, and actually turns his back so he won't have to look at me.

"I think Michael's scared of you now," Abby says observantly.

Nick nods. "You owned him. I am both frightened and admiring, trust me."

"Yeah, well, he deserved it." I ruffle Abby's flyaway hair. "Nobody gets to mess with my sisters but me."

35

When I was in first grade, I had a bully. It's a rare thing these days, actually. Back when our parents were growing up, kids were expected to sort out that kind of problem themselves. Pop loved to talk about this one kid who used to take his lunch money every week, until Pop finally couldn't take it anymore and went to the principal, not to tell on the bully, exactly, but to report that he was going to be punching someone next week, because he could see no other option. "I'm just going to hit him once," Pop said. "Really hard. In the nose. I think that will do it."

Then, of course, the principal tried to talk him out of it, and tried to get him to tell which kid he was planning on hitting, but Pop wouldn't. "I was no snitch," he said when he told the story.

And then he did. He punched the bully in the nose. Hard.

Pop got suspended for three days. But the bully didn't rob him again.

Now, though, the grown-ups are so determined that nobody will get bullied. They talk to us constantly about it. Not just face-to-face bullying, either, but text bullying and bullying on social media and all forms of harassment and public shaming. We have assemblies about it and lectures on it and the word *bullying* has a powerful zing now. No tolerance for bullies. No way.

Anyway, back to first grade. My bully was a girl named Chloe. Her bullying wasn't very subtle, but she did it quietly: with a well-timed, super cutting remark. The same one pretty much every time:

"You're ugly," she'd whisper.

I always wanted to say something clever back, but I could never think of anything in the moment better than, "It takes one to know one," which didn't make sense. I also thought about saying, "No, I'm Ada. *You're* ugly," but I wasn't brave enough.

So I didn't say anything. Not to anybody. Looking back, it seems wild that for more than a year this girl called me ugly almost every single day, and I didn't do a thing to try to stop her. I just tried to keep my head down. I tried to ignore her. But it hurt. Every day, every time, the word hit me like a rock she was throwing at me.

Ugly.

Ugly.

UGLY.

But then, one day, as I was waiting in line to get on the bus after school, Chloe stepped right behind me and pushed me—just a small push, something nobody would notice—and then she said, "You know what?"

I braced myself. I did know, was the thing. That's why it hurt.

"You're ugly," she said. Louder than usual, this time.

I nodded. Like, yes, okay, I know that's what you think. I accept that you think that.

But then another voice said, "*What* did you just say?"

Afton's voice.

Chloe and I both turned. My sister had been standing behind us the whole time. A mighty third grader.

She handed her backpack to one of her friends. "Hold this for me," she said. "I've got to tear this girl's hair out."

Chloe didn't wait for her to act on the threat. She started to scream for our teacher. "Mrs. Yowell! Mrs. Yowell! I'm getting *bullied*!"

"Not yet, you're not," Afton said grimly, and then BAM—she punched Chloe in the nose, a punch that would have made Pop proud, but we didn't know Pop then. A single heartfelt punch.

"AHHHH!" bellowed Chloe. Her nose was bleeding. Mrs. Yowell was running over. All the kids around us were yelling.

Afton took my hand then, and we ran, past the grown-ups who tried to intercept us like a game of football, dodging and weaving, along the school's driveway and out onto the street, then down the street, running as fast as we could, until we ducked down a side street and hid behind someone's trash cans.

"Why'd you do that?" I panted.

Afton rubbed her fist. "Because I'm your sister. Nobody gets to pick on you but me."

I smiled. "You *hit* her."

"It kind of hurt."

"We're going to be in so much trouble," I said.

She nodded. "I will be. I'll explain that it was all me."

"No." I put my hand over hers. "I want to be with you."

"Okay," she said.

We waited for a while and then went into a store and asked to use their phone and called Ruthie to tell her where we were and what had happened. And we did get in trouble, but Chloe got in trouble, too—in fact, the entire school had to go through another no-bullying assembly again—so it felt like justice had been served. And I learned another valuable lesson.

Afton was with me. And I was with her.

36

Everything feels different, Saturday morning. For real this time. Fingers crossed. It seems like birthdays sometimes do: you wake up, one year older, and ask yourself if you're different now, or if you're going to be different after today.

After tonight, I think, I won't be a virgin.

Will nonvirgin me be more of an adult? Will people sense that and treat me like a grown-up? Will I think more mature thoughts? Will I finally understand the ways of the world?

I kind of doubt it. But at least I'll get to check the event off my life's to-do list, so I won't have to worry about it anymore.

It's just sex. Millions of people in the world are probably having sex right this minute. It can't be that hard. I'd say that Nick and I are above average intelligence when it comes to most things. We'll figure it out.

I check on the period situation. It seems like I'm done with that, just in the Nick of time.

"Abby's going to spend the day with Josie," I tune in to Mom saying. "There's a kid day on the beach, and I said she could go with the Wongs. Jenny should be here to pick her up in just about—"

There's a knock on the door: Jenny. Abby squeals and goes off arm in arm with Josie. Afton slips out as the door is closing, muttering something about shopping. She was in a foul mood all last night, tossing and turning and keeping me awake, too. This morning there are dark circles under her angry blue eyes. Maybe I should be concerned, but I am relieved to see her go.

"It looks like it's just you and me today," Mom says, after they've left.

"Don't you have to be at the conference center soon?"

"I have the day off," she says, rolling her neck from one side to the other. "I could use a break. You girls have been having all the fun without me this week."

I bite my lip to hold back the words, *Well, not all the fun, though, right?*

"You should call Pop," I say instead. That's my new strategy: to remind Mom that she still has Pop to think about, that he loves her, that we are all counting on her to love him back.

She smiles obliviously. "I'm going to the morning yoga class in the wellness center in a few minutes. Come with me?"

I try to think of an excuse but come up empty. One-on-one time with my mother at this juncture is a terrifying idea, like walking around with a lit match into a room doused with gasoline. But if I go to yoga with her, at least we won't have to talk.

"Okay," I say.

Thirty minutes later we're each sitting on a mat in a cool, sunlight-dappled room, celestial music rolling over us as we twist, flex, stretch, and roll.

"Breathe into your feet," the instructor says.

"My feet don't breathe," I whisper to Mom.

"Don't be a smartass," she whispers back.

"My ass isn't smart" is my reply.

She snorts. "Just relax, all right?"

"Fill yourself with silence," the instructor says a bit sharply. "And reach."

Here's what I learn at yoga when I'm supposed to be finding my inner calm and lifting my heart and acknowledging and exhaling my pain: first, my mother is incredibly flexible.

I am not.

I could call that a metaphor, too.

Second, my mother is at peace with herself. She doesn't act like a woman who's betraying her husband, like she's hiding anything, like she's lying. She's as relaxed as I've ever seen her. Like her conscience is completely clear, so much so that I feel doubt bubbling up again, that what I saw on Monday morning was real.

But it *was* real, I tell myself.

I know what I saw.

So Mom being so completely chill about it means that either she's a magnificent actress (which I know she isn't) or that the affair has been going on for a long, long time, so long that it feels normal to her. She doesn't feel like she's doing anything wrong.

"Are you okay?" she asks as we wander, loose-limbed and woozy, out of the yoga studio.

I really wish people would stop asking me that. Especially if they're not really interested in finding out.

"I want you to know, I heard what you said to me before, about the child labor thing. I have been taking you for granted. I'll stop doing that."

"It's fine. I like hanging out with Abby," I say.

We reach the front desk of the wellness center. "Will you be paying with a card?" the woman there (who's wearing a name tag that reads Malia) asks my mother.

"Can you charge it to the room?" Mom asks.

Malia nods and takes down our room number, and Mom signs to accept the charge.

Her signature, like most doctors, is an illegible, hurried squiggle. Pop calls it her "chicken scratchings." I've seen Ruthie sign it for her a bunch of times, just the big loop of the *A* for Aster and another shape that could be a *B* for Bloom.

"Be sure to take a brochure and check out the services that are available from our spa." Malia hands the brochure to my mom.

"Services?" I take the brochure out of Mom's hand and scan down it.

"We offer massages, facials, waxing, threading, eyelash extensions, a full hair and nail salon, body scrubs, cleanses—you name it, we've got it. Plus if you pay for a service, you are allowed access to our exclusive relaxation area and hot tubs."

"No, thank you," Mom is saying to Malia, but then I blurt, "Yes, I'm interested."

Mom turns to look at me, frowning quizzically.

"I'd like a . . . massage," I say brightly.

243

If Mom knew me, really knew me the way a mother is supposed to know her child, she would be suspicious. I've had exactly one massage in my life, and vowed never to do it again. I was so weirded out by the feeling of a stranger touching me that I giggled through the entire thing and ended up weirding out the masseuse.

But Mom has never heard that story.

I have a good reason to lie to her, and no reason not to, right? If I tell her what I am really after—namely, hair removal and general beautifying—she'll definitely find that suspicious. And if she finds out what I'm up to tonight, she'll put a stop to it. She isn't going to be good with it, like Nick's dad. She isn't one of those no-sex-before-you're-married types of mothers, but she's definitely a wait-until-college one. Not that we've ever talked about it outside of that single conversation about sex we had when I was a kid. Apparently she was cool about the topic of sex when Afton told her about her experience, but I doubt she'll be similarly chill with me. In fact, Afton's not-so-great sexual encounters might even make Mom more protective, now that it's my turn.

"We have an opening for a hot stone massage in about ten minutes," Malia says.

Mom is still frowning.

"Come on," I plead. "We're on vacation. Don't I deserve some pampering?"

Mom's lips purse the way they do when she's weighing her options. "All right, if that's what you want. I just envisioned us having a day together."

"The *entire* day?" I say, aghast. I don't know how I could stand to be with my mom for an entire day, knowing what I know.

"We could head back to the room and change into our swimsuits," she says. "Then maybe you and I could go paddleboarding. Word is, you've been wanting to do that all week. I thought we could do it together."

There's nothing in her eyes, no accusations, no awareness, just a kind of hopefulness. She wants to hang out with me.

"When your stepdad and I got married, we came to Hawaii for our honeymoon, and we went paddleboarding this one morning," she says, because she doesn't know that I already know this story. "It was beautiful. Almost magical. This would be different, I know. It's more a tailored experience here. But I'd like to share something like that with you."

It feels good, being around her, hearing her say she appreciates me, that she's listening, that she's not going to take me for granted anymore. It's what I've wanted for such a long time, for my mother to see me. To value me. To want to spend time with me.

But I can't.

It's too late, I think bitterly. No amount of her being interested in me now will ever make up for what she's done. "I have plans today." I look away before I can see the disappointment flare up in her expression. "By myself. Sorry. Yoga was fun, but now I have to go do my own thing. But I'll see you at the awards ceremony tonight, okay?"

"Oh," she says softly. "Ada—"

"You should call Pop today," I add. "He misses you."

"I will," she says.

Malia, the lady at the counter, moves off to straighten some of the items that are for sale around the front desk: fluffy white robes and smelly lotions and jars of face masks. Because she can tell we're about to be in the middle of a serious conversation.

"Good," I say. "This thing where you're missing family nights, and you're not talking to each other as much, and he's not here, it's bullshit," I gather up the guts to say. Her telling me that she'd call him makes me feel hope. That maybe it isn't over.

Maybe I can fix this.

"It's complicated," Mom says stiffly.

"No." I refuse to let her get away with that. "It's not that complicated. Pop is the center of our world, you know. More than just Abby. Afton and me, too."

"I know."

"You said we'd always come first."

She sucks in a breath. "I know."

"So deal with it," I say. "Soon. I'll see you later."

Mom looks like she's ready to argue. But maybe she's had enough of her daughters reaming her out for one day. She nods once, quickly, and then hurries toward the stairs, not because she has anywhere to be, but because Mom only has one speed: fast. Always the Whirlwind.

I take a few deep breaths. That was close. I almost cracked. I almost mentioned Billy.

When Mom's out of sight, I turn quickly to Malia, ready to shift my focus to something else. Something that's not so serious, but at the same time is pretty freaking serious. "Actually, can I switch the massage to waxing?"

"Of course. Which areas would you like to be waxed?"

"All of them. It's kind of an emergency."

She gives me a knowing smile. "No problem. I think we'll be able to fit you in."

***

I can sum up the next hour in one word: ouch.

The result, though, is very smooth legs, and underarms, and bikini line. I am even willing to brave waxing that spot that no man has ever gone before, but the torture expert—aka the wax specialist—asks me, "So you have big plans tonight?"

And I tell her. I tell a total stranger that in less than twelve hours, I am planning to have sex for the very first time.

"That *is* big plans," she says, and I say, "I know, right?" and we laugh awkwardly and then she rips another swath of hair from my thigh.

"Do you think I should wax . . . all of it?" I ask. "I mean, I don't want to look like a cavewoman down there, but I also don't want to look like a little girl."

"I wouldn't recommend it, actually," says my torturer. "Waxing that area isn't great to do right before—uh—intercourse. It can make the skin red and irritable and leave tiny microscopic tears, which could lead to an infection if you . . . you know."

"Well, that would have been helpful to know about a half hour ago," I say.

"It's in the fine print." She rips off another strip.

"Okay, so no crotch waxing, then," I say, blinking away tears. I don't want to risk an infection. "Just do the bikini line."

My skin feels hot and tight all over, like a sunburn, as I hobble out of the waxing area. The same woman—Malia, I remember—is still at the front counter. She smiles when she sees me.

"I hear you have a big night planned," she says.

Heat rushes to my face. Or maybe that was just from where I've had my upper lip waxed. "I think that classifies as a violation of my patient-waxer confidentiality," I gasp, outraged.

"In Hawaii, we have a saying," she says. "*A'a i ka hula, waiho i ka maka'u i ka hale.* It means, 'dare to dance, leave shame at home.'"

"Okay. Thanks, I guess?"

"Just make sure he's a good boy. Respectful, yeah?"

"Yeah," I say, calling up the image of Nick at the coffee plantation, being so understanding, giving my little sister a granola bar, making us laugh. "I think he is."

"Good." Malia taps her pencil against her scheduling book. "What else?"

I glance up at her. "I don't think I have much hair left on my body."

"No, we could work on the rest, give you a makeover." She thrusts the brochure at me again. She's already circled a bunch of things in pink pen: a haircut and styling, deep-conditioning treatment, a pedicure, manicure, facial, and a makeup consultation.

I do some quick ballpark math and realize that all of the things she's circled add up to more than three hundred dollars.

"We have another saying," Malia adds. "*Kahuna nui hale kealohalani makua.* It means, 'Love all you see, including yourself.'"

My jaw tightens. What the hell, I think. Malia is right. Tonight is going to be about sex, but it's also going to be about doing something for myself.

"Okay," I say breathlessly. "I'll do all of it."

"Wonderful," Malia says, beaming, but then she, too, seems to realize how much it's going to cost. "Are you sure you want to do *all* of it? Maybe just pick one or two? Otherwise it will be a lot—"

I'm two steps ahead of her this time. "I'll charge it to the room," I say.

She looks hesitant. It's a normal thing for people my age to charge things to our parents' rooms, but she must need some sort of permission.

"Trust me, my mom's okay with it," I lie smoothly. "The waxing is less than the massage anyway, right?"

Malia relaxes a bit. "Right. I'll charge it to your room."

37

"I want you to know," Mom told us the day we met Pop, "that you girls will always come first."

She was saying this because she was already serious with Pop. She already suspected that he was "the one" for her, that she'd marry him eventually. But she'd never brought a man home to meet us before. She hadn't included that part of her life with ours—dating, romance, sex. She actually had never been big on dating after she got divorced from Dad. She didn't have time. She joked about getting Ruthie to create a dating site profile for her, but she never went through with it. She met Pop as a fluke. They'd both been waiting for takeout at a Chinese restaurant when they'd noticed that they'd ordered the exact same thing. I could always picture it perfectly when Pop told the story, love born out of some shrimp egg rolls they both had passionate feelings about.

And then at some point she'd decided it was real, what she felt about Pop. So she introduced him. She brought him over for dinner.

He was funny that night. I remember it well. He even had Afton giggling. He seemed to know everything about everything—how many bones were in the human body, how old the pyramids were, what Italian salad dressing was made out of, what the rules were to backgammon. He'd brought a set of four laser tag guns, and we ran all over the house sniping each other.

At the end of the night, he gave me a stately bow and Afton a high five.

"What did you think?" Mom said.

"He's all right," Afton said.

"He's the one," I said.

We both approved.

"Good," Mom said. "I like him, too. But you girls are the most important thing to me. More important than anybody else could ever be. I want you to be happy and safe. So if he comes over more, and you don't like him, for any reason, you can tell me. I'll listen. Because you girls come first. That's my promise to you."

This worried me a little, because I liked him, but I could see how the power she'd just given us could be misused. Afton could say she didn't like him, just to test Mom's loyalty. It seemed like a thing she might do.

"Don't mess this up," I whispered to her that night, after we'd been put to bed. "I like this guy."

"Me too."

"So we agree, then," I said solemnly. "This is our chance to have a normal family again. He's the one."

38

"Mom, come quick! Something's happened to Ada!" Abby yells after she and Mom come into our room later.

I'm standing in front of the mirror, wearing a new dress. This afternoon, just as I was ascending the stairs from the spa, buffed and polished and primed and filled to the brim with the cucumber-infused water they serve there, something in a store window caught my eye: a dress, floor length and black, with three red, pink, and orange tropical flowers printed on the front.

It's strapless, held up by elastic stitching all around the bodice. I've never worn a strapless dress before. I've been too self-conscious of my cavewoman shoulders. But this is pretty. Simple. Elegant. It's formal, but not too formal. The tag says one size fits all, and it does. It fits like it was made for me. I finger the light cotton fabric. It feels like wearing a cloud.

I already had a dress for the awards ceremony. Ruthie picked it out for me: navy blue, short sleeved and knee-length, with a V-neck. It would have been fine for the stupid dinner and schmoozing.

But this dress—this flower dress—is special.

So I bought it. The ridiculous one hundred and fifty dollars of it. And, like with the spa treatments, I charged it to the room.

Now I'm standing in front of the mirror, assessing the new dress, loving how it clings and flows in all the right places. I've got a new pair of fancy black flip-flops on my feet, my toes painted a saucy red, a new shell bracelet around my right wrist, French-manicured nails, and earrings of tiny white hibiscus flowers.

But Abby's talking about my hair. It's glorious, shiny and smooth, cut to just below my shoulders and blown straight, then curled again into soft, beachy waves. It's easily the best my hair has ever looked. Ever.

I'm wearing makeup, too. Eye shadow and blush and lip liner.

"Ada, you're a princess!" Abby exclaims.

I do kind of feel like one. Part of me feels silly, like I'm trying to act out the make-over scene in a romantic comedy and now I expect everyone to find me suddenly, irresistibly gorgeous, and I know I'm not. A nice dress and good hair and makeup can only get me so far.

But I do look good. I feel good, too. Like I am taking charge of my life.

Mom comes into my room to see what all the fuss is about. "Well," she says softly. "Don't you look grown up?"

"That's what I was going for."

She clears her throat and turns and bustles back into her own room, crossing quickly to the closet to retrieve her own long black dress. I entertain Abby as Mom pulls her straight blond hair into a simple chignon, briskly applies a minimal layer of makeup, spritzes her wrists with perfume, and, finally, steps into her dress.

She looks beautiful and classic and fierce. But that's how she always looks. Whenever I picture her in the operating room, it's the same.

She's flawless.

Except, I think, for this one glaring flaw that almost nobody knows about.

"Zip me?" she asks.

I hurry around behind her to zip the dress.

"Is it all right?" she asks.

"It's great. Ruthie picked a good one."

Abby appears at Mom's hip and gazes up at her adoringly. "I wish Poppy were here. His eyes would go boing, seeing you so pretty, Mom."

She spins away, twirling in her own sky-blue gauzy sundress, her curls long and loose around her heart-shaped face.

"Yeah, Mom," I echo. "Don't you wish Pop was here?" I wonder if she actually called him today, like I told her to. And if she called him, what did she say?

"Of course I do," Mom says.

I hate the way she smiles just then. A secret smile. It makes me want to tell her that I know.

That smile isn't for Pop.

But I'm learning to stuff the secret down inside me. I can manage it. I can pretend.

Mom puts on pearl earrings and a delicate gold chain with a

single pearl that sits in that hollow spot of her throat. She steps into her simple black heels.

"I'm going to break my ankle in these things tonight. If I weren't presenting I'd go for flip-flops, too." She glances at herself in the mirror, dabs at her lipstick with a tissue, and sighs. "All right. Let's go."

"Where's Afton?" Abby asks.

"She texted me that she's going to meet us there," Mom says.

Abby frowns. "Did you make up yet from your fight?"

"Not yet," Mom says. "But we will."

"She's tough, though. She'll get through," Abby says.

I hold the door open, and Abby runs out. My mother stops in the doorway to look at me.

"I think I understand what your plans were this afternoon," she says, taking my wrist and holding it out as she looks me over.

"I charged it all to the room," I say, my chin lifting without me being able to stop it.

A little line appears between her eyes, but only for an instant. "All right. Like you said, you deserve to be pampered sometimes. But next time you should ask me first. Okay?"

"Okay."

She lets my wrist drop and takes a step back. "There's something different about you this week. More than the hair and the dress."

I smile and shrug my bare shoulders. There's no way to explain to her that what's changed about me this week is everything.

It seems that all 2,300 members of the STS conference are milling around on the lawn of the Palace Tower like a swarm of formally dressed ants. There's a large stage set up at the far edge, where a live band is performing the song "Beyond the Sea." The lawn is a huge square, the stage serving as one side, with three long buffet tables making up the other sides, the dining tables and chairs all boxed inside.

I pick at the food. If I never see another buffet table in my life, I'll be fine with that.

"Eat your dinner," Abby scolds me. "You're a growing girl."

I take three more bites.

Mom demolishes her dinner with that speedy-eating efficiency she says she picked up in med school. Then she abandons us to go backstage with the other presenters and prepare. I push my plate away and survey the scene for signs of Nick.

"You look very nice tonight, dearie," Marjorie says from across the table.

"Thank you. You're beautiful, too." She's wearing a long-sleeved, floor-length lavender gown with chiffon butterflies at the neckline. "Not everybody could pull off that dress, but you do."

"Don't I know it," she replies. "If you've got it, flaunt it, I always say."

"If you've got what?" Abby asks, tilting her head to one side.

"Pizzazz." Marjorie finishes her glass of red wine and gazes around us almost sadly. "You should be somewhere more lively, my dear, dressed like that. Not stuck with all of us old farts."

Abby giggles. "Farts." That's a new word. Pop will be thrilled.

Marjorie's sharp brown eyes widen slightly. She's looking at something over my shoulder. "Here comes trouble in a red dress."

I turn. Marjorie gives a low whistle as Afton materializes from amid the crowd. She's wearing a dress I've never seen before, scarlet to match her lipstick, the front cut almost down to her belly button.

Holy shit.

For the first time since we arrived, I am sincerely glad Pop isn't with us. He would have a stroke if he saw Afton in that dress, at one of Mom's work functions, no less.

"Look at you, girl," crows Marjorie as Afton approaches. "Aha! That Wong boy is going to rue the day he let you slip away from him when he sees you gussied up like that."

"I think that's the point," I mutter.

"What's gussied up?" Abby asks.

Afton shoots me a cool glare and sits down in the seat next to me, which we saved for her. When she crosses her legs, she reveals another titillating feature of the dress: a slit that runs up the side to the middle of her thigh.

I can feel the attention of the people around us shifting toward Afton.

My phone buzzes.

Nick.

Your dress is really pretty.

I scan the tables around me until I find him sitting with his dad, closer to the back. He waves at me and then pantomimes being shot in the heart. Like my good looks are killing him.

He's wearing a dark gray suit and a tie, as well dressed as I've ever seen him. He's also gotten a haircut—not short, exactly, but neater, no longer in his eyes.

For me. He gussied up for me.

Suddenly the primping and pain from earlier feels worth it.

You're pretty, too, I text. I want to write something sexier, something clever and bold and fun, but I can't think of anything. I search the emojis for the tea one, which is some green steaming liquid in a white mug, but I end up going with a GIF of Morticia Addams drinking tea instead.

I watch the smile bloom on his face. We spend the next several minutes sending tea GIFs to one another, and then the band abruptly stops playing and the awards ceremony officially starts up.

Dr. Asaju gives a speech about how informative and productive the conference has been. He makes the team who had organized the trip come up in front of everyone, and we all clap. That's what awards night is really about: clapping for how great the conference has been, and then clapping for the people who organized it, and clapping for every person who wins an award, and the people who present the awards, and for the entertainment, and for the food and the people who serve the food, and the fine hotel that hosted us, and finally clapping because we are so happy that the awards are over so we can rest our weary hands.

My mom and her black dress sweep onto the stage. We all clap for her.

"I'm now going to present the Earl Bakken Scientific Achievement Award," she says. Her voice is slightly sharper than usual—the only indication I can see that she might be nervous up there with thousands of eyes on her. "This award was established in 1999 to honor individuals who have made outstanding scientific contributions that have enhanced the practice of cardiothoracic surgery and patients' quality of life."

Clap clap clap.

Your mom is so boss, texts Nick.

I can't explain that I would rather have a mother than a boss, and it seems that Aster Bloom, for all her great badassery, is not capable of being both.

"The award is named after Mr. Earl Bakken, who, among his many great accomplishments, developed the first wearable artificial pacemaker," Mom continues smoothly.

Clap clap.

"This year the award will go to Dr. Max Ahmed," Mom says with a smile, because she considers Max to be a friend. Max, who's been waiting off to one side, joins her on the stage. Mom tells us about his work on a new device that help patients awaiting heart transplants, which sounds complicated, but important and cool. She lists off where Max went to college and medical school, where he did his residency, all the different hospitals where he practiced, and the research he did and papers he contributed to. She closes with talking about how, in his spare time (which I can't imagine he has much of, considering what I know about heart surgeons and everything my mother has listed so far) he plays bass violin in an orchestra in Seattle, how much he loves hockey and sailing, and what a loving and dedicated husband and father and grandfather he is.

We all clap again.

Mom hands Max a plaque and an envelope that almost certainly contains a large check.

Clap.

The official event photographer stands up and takes their picture, and then Mom takes Max's arm, the two of them walk off the stage, and we're on to the next award.

Abby looks bored, so I give her a pencil and a paper napkin to doodle on. Afton uncrosses her legs and recrosses them the other way. Michael Wong is openly staring at her from the next table over. She doesn't look at him.

After the next award there's a break for hula. It's less formal than the other night's hula dancing had been, this time done by girls about my age instead of the seasoned performers who hula five nights a week for the hotel. I find myself captivated by the dancing in a way I wasn't at the more polished luau. This is more powerful—more heartfelt, even though it's just a drum played by one man and their teacher calling out the words in Hawaiian while the girls move gracefully in the center of the stage. Each dance a story, every move representing an image.

Dare to dance, I think, *and leave shame behind.*

"I can do that," Abby says matter-of-factly. "I can do it just like that."

"That's awesome, bug." I smirk at Afton. "You can do that, too, I guess. Since you also did the hula class."

"No, she can't," Abby says. "Only I can. And Josie. And Josie's mom is pretty good at it, too, since she has nice big hips."

"It's not nice to talk about people's big hips," I say.

"Why? Mrs. Wong's hips are really good ones."

"I'm going to get a soda." Afton stands up. "I'll be right back."

She breezes past Michael like a model on a catwalk, head high, spine straight, hips swaying.

"Afton has good ones, too," Abby observes. "It's too bad she doesn't know how to hula."

This surprises me. Afton is a dancer, after all. She's done ballet since she was Abby's age, practicing her plies while she's washing dishes at the kitchen sink, jeté-ing across our yard. I've been to countless performances of Afton playing Clara in *The Nutcracker*, and Odile in *Swan Lake*, and so many other things. She's a swan, my sister. A scarlet swan in a wicked dress who'll slap you silly with her powerful wings if you tick her off. And she'll be graceful doing it.

"Afton wasn't good at hula?" I ask Abby, but then we're all clapping again, because the hula is over.

My phone chimes with an alarm I set.

Eight o'clock.

From a few tables behind me, I see Nick stand up. He leans and says something to his father, who claps him on the back. Then he looks over at me, a question in his eyes.

I give him a nervous smile.

He nods and starts walking toward the Ocean Tower, his strides quick. Then he's gone.

My heart thunders. This is it. Time to make my move.

I wait about ten minutes before I follow Nick. As is the plan. But then I can't just leave Abby for like an hour with no explanation, and I can't locate Afton, so first I go looking for her.

I find her in the restroom.

She's standing in front of the mirror, pressing some powder to the space under eyes. Her smeared mascara and swollen eyelids tell me that she's been crying—my fierce and tough older sister, crying, and over a stupid boy, no less.

"Are you okay?" I ask.

She blows her nose on a paper towel. "I'm fine."

"I'll help you beat him up."

Her red-rimmed blue eyes meet mine in the mirror, startled. "No, it's fine. It's not his fault. Or maybe it is a little, but . . . I screwed up."

"That's okay. You'll fix it."

"Maybe I can't."

"Well, look on the bright side. Whatever you did wrong, it can't be as bad as Mom's situation."

She sucks in a breath. "Ada, I need to talk to you. About what you saw that day—"

"What about what you saw?" I remind her.

"What I saw?"

"My sketchbook?"

"Oh." Her eyes lower to the floor. "I shouldn't have looked at that. I'm sorry. I was losing my mind a little."

"And what did you . . . learn, by reading what is essentially my diary?" I say.

"You're really talented. I don't know how you capture people like you do."

"Afton, be serious."

"I am. That was the biggest thing I learned."

"And?"

"And you're a good sister, Ada," Afton says softly. "I know you're trying to hold all of us together, for Abby. Which is why I need to say—"

My phone chimes with a text.

All clear.

I have to go. "Speaking of being a good sister, would you be in charge of Abby for a while?" I ask Afton. "Like maybe for the rest of the awards?"

"Sure." Afton's eyes narrow on my face. She probably saw the page of my sketchbook with the words *THE SEX PLAN* in big letters across the top. And all my humiliating questions.

"I'm going to hang out with Nick Kelly," I say. "Could you cover for me?" After all, I've covered for her, so many times.

She thinks about it for a minute. "You're going to hang out in his room?"

"Yes." This time, unlike a week ago (god, was it only a week ago, with Leo?) I don't offer up the details of the plan, even though she probably already knows. I don't ask her advice. I don't insist that I'm ready.

Her forehead rumples, but she says, "Okay."

"Okay, you'll watch Abby?"

"Yeah."

"Thanks." I give myself a final once-over. Fluff my hair. Reapply the lipstick.

"You look really nice, by the way," Afton says. "I hope you have a good time."

"That's the plan," I say. To have a good time. To feel good. To feel better.

We leave the restroom, and my sister returns to our table and Abby, and I make my way toward the Ocean Tower again.

And find my way to room 407.

39

When I get there, I hear music coming from inside the room. Bag-pipes.

I text Nick. *407, right?*

Correct.

I'm standing outside the door. But—

The door opens. There's Nick. "Hi."

"Hi."

"Come in."

I step inside and kick off my flip-flops. It's dark in the room, the shades drawn, a lamp glowing dimly in the corner and a few lit candles around the bed, which seems like a fire hazard. My stomach does a little flip of anticipation. I take a shaky breath.

Dare to dance, I tell myself silently. *Leave shame behind.*

"Are you okay?" Nick asks.

"Yes." I swallow. "Can we maybe turn on a few more lights? And open the curtains? This is romantic—no doubt—but I want to be able to see what's happening."

He crosses quickly to the window and pulls back the drapes. A warm light floods the warm. Behind the balcony, the sun is sinking into the ocean, all red-and-gold fire as it plunges into the water. The sky has a pink hue, which makes everything a bit surreal. As if it isn't already surreal enough.

But I can breathe again. "Thank you."

"Anything else I can do?"

I shake my head and step farther into the room. My foot touches something cool and smooth: a petal. There are rose petals everywhere, leading from the door to the bed, which is sprinkled with them.

"Where did you find roses?"

He gives me a bashful smile. "I ordered the honeymoon package for the room. It came with your standard red roses, champagne, chocolate and strawberries, and something called a 'sensual bath bomb,' so we're set. Whatever you want."

A nervous laugh slips out of me. "Very smooth, Mr. Kelly."

"Thank you, Miss Bloom. I just wanted it to be nice."

"Nice," I repeat.

"Well, I want it to be epic," he says. "But I know we can't expect ourselves to be pros, our first time, so I decided that epic was overly ambitious. So let's start with nice."

"Nice is nice."

I look at him.

He looks at me.

We both blush. Neither of us moves.

"Can we kill the bagpipes?" I wrinkle my nose.

"It's supposed to be a joke," he explains. "I was going to wear a kilt and call you Sassenach, and that was going to make you laugh, and laughing would break the ice. But the kilt didn't get here on time, and so I thought I needed something else Scottish, so I went with bagpipes, but then you got here and I totally forgot the point." He fumbles with his phone, and the bagpipes cut off abruptly. He looks up at me hopefully. "You want to hear my second choice?"

"Do I?"

He touches his phone again, and the deep voice of Barry White rumbles out of the speaker on the bedside table.

I laugh.

"I'm just kidding." He turns Barry off, too.

"Quiet is good." I take a step in his direction, and he takes a step in mine—one step and then another, until we're standing in front of each other at the foot of the bed.

"You really ordered a kilt?" I suppress a smile.

"I did, lassie," he intones.

I laugh and reach up and smooth down the edge of his lapel. "The suit looks good. The gray matches your eyes. And the haircut is a nice touch."

He tucks an errant strand behind his ear. "And let's talk about that dress. I love the bird-of-paradise."

"Bird-of-paradise?"

"That's the type of flower this is." He points to the top flower. Then he realizes he's basically pointing at my breasts, and he drops his hand. "Anyway, I like them."

"I'm glad it meets with your approval."

"It's perfect."

Perfect seems like a dangerous word. My hands are trembling. I close my eyes for a second and try to focus, try to remember that this is no big deal, that it's just fun with our bodies, in essence, and nothing to be frightened of. Nick isn't scary. So I shouldn't be scared.

This isn't like it was with Leo. This is Nick and me, mutually deciding.

Come on, I tell myself. *Dare to dance.*

"Maybe I should take the dress off," I say.

"Holy geez." Nick shivers visibly. "I might spontaneously combust if you were to get naked right now. Maybe we should try kissing first?"

I nod and wet my lips. He steps closer. His hand touches my bare arm, and it's my turn to shiver.

"Is this okay?"

I nod mutely.

We move toward each other.

"I haven't done this before, either," he says suddenly.

"I know."

"Should I close my eyes? I don't want to miss you somehow—this feels like one of those keep-your-eye-on-the-ball sort of moments. But if I keep my eyes open, will it be creepy, like I'm staring? In movies they always close their eyes."

"I think you should do whatever feels right to you," I say.

I close my own eyes.

His hand touches my waist. I put my hand out and reach for his shoulder. It's nice, warm and solid and with more meat on it than I thought he had. All that video game playing must have some positive effect on his delts.

I can feel his breath on my chin.

This is fine, I think. We're fine.

"So to be absolutely clear here, I can kiss you now?" Nick asks.

"Oh, for god's sake, Nick, yes. Please do."

He leans in, angling up, and I bend a little to meet him. His lips brush mine, soft and brief. It's like a whispered hello.

So far, so good.

"Now can I kiss *you*?" I ask.

"Yeah."

I put my mouth on his more firmly this time, and try to stay there a bit longer, so it will resemble less of a peck and more of a romantic kiss. I know how to do this. The one good thing about my relationship with Leo, I think, is that I got in some good practice kissing.

We kiss a few more times, until I take a step back. "That was . . ."

Definitely not epic.

Not that I expected the earth to move under me, kissing Nick Kelly. And it wasn't bad, at all. It was . . . "nice."

But the problem is, it wasn't anything more than that. Kissing Nick didn't make me lose myself in him or tremble with desire or go weak in the knees.

I refuse to give up, though.

I'm ready. For real, this time.

"Maybe we should . . . ," Nick starts to say, but I blurt out, "Let's take our clothes off," and pull his suit jacket off his shoulders and fling it onto a nearby chair.

Something works in his throat. "Ada . . ."

"If we're going to do it, we should just do it," I say quickly.

He scratches the back of his neck. "I don't think—"

"Don't think," I say. "That's the key. We can't overthink this." I start working on the buttons of his shirt, undoing them, peeling back the fabric to reveal the white tee underneath. "You must have been boiling at dinner in all these layers. Let's get this off."

The resistance leaves him. He helps me take his shirt off, laying it gently across the chair to join his jacket, and then pulls his tee over his head. His hands come around to my back, smoothing the fabric of my dress. "Does it have a zipper or something?"

"No, it's stretchy. It—" I freeze.

It pulls down. And I'm not wearing a bra. I didn't have anything strapless, and I didn't want the straps to show.

I take a step back. "Uh, maybe—" I glance at the bed. "Would it be more comfortable if we got under the covers?"

He nods quickly. We both slide under the smooth white sheets, sending a cascade of red petals to the floor. Nick wriggles around and finally tosses his pants out his side, followed by his socks. "I'm going to leave the underwear for now," he announces.

"Okay," I rasp. I slide my dress down and off my hips and lay it on the floor next to the bed. Then I turn so we're facing each other. "Eyes up here," I bark as he starts to look downward. His gaze jerks up to mine. His eyes in this light are a strange contradiction: warm gray—a color I could make by watering down black and mixing in a drop of blue and then a bit of peachy pink.

He's looking into my eyes, too. "Hi, again."

"Hi."

"This is wild."

"I know."

"It's a lot."

"Right?"

"What now?"

I think about it. "Maybe we should touch."

Without waiting, I reach across under the covers and put my hand against his chest. It's hairless and warm. His heart pounds under my palm.

He sucks in a shuddering breath.

"Now you touch me," I whisper.

He lifts his hand and then hesitates, his fingers curling into a fist and then uncurling as he decides where to go. Then he closes his eyes and follows the line from my shoulder to my neck.

I let my hand wander down (too chicken to go straight down, of course), moving across the small juts of his ribs to the outside of his hip.

He responds by tracing back down my arm to my waist, my hip, the outside of my leg down to the very soft skin behind my knee.

"Your legs are really smooth," he murmurs. (They are also splotchy and red and pretty tender, on account of the wax, but he doesn't need to know that.)

His legs are long and lean and slightly fuzzy.

We take turns touching each other, cautiously, slowly, avoiding any area that feels too private, until I have a moment of bravery and grab his hand and put it on my breast.

His Adam's apple jerks up and down. "Wow. These are . . ."

"Round?" I supply.

"And soft. And I'm pretty sure they have superpowers."

He must be feeling braver, too, because he squeezes gently.

I feel a jolt low in my stomach. My breath catches. I am feeling very firmly centered in my body right now. No sense of disconnection. No floating out of myself.

Maybe I'm finally past the fear.

I scoot nearer in order to kiss him. His arm goes around my shoulder, pulling me even closer. Our legs bump, tangle. Our mouths open and our tongues touch tentatively. Heat flares all along my nerve endings.

He makes a sound like a laugh mixed with a groan.

"Can I touch you?" he asks hoarsely.

For a minute I'm confused. He is already touching me. But then I understand what he means.

"Yes," I whisper, because I want him to.

He doesn't, though. He touches my legs, up the insides of my thighs and down again. He brushes gently over my naval, my hip, back to my thigh. He touches everywhere but the spot I most want him to. Which only makes the sensation build up even more.

I sigh in a turned-on frustration. Then I realize that he's doing it deliberately.

I pull back, my heart hammering. "You've been researching this, haven't you?"

"Well, I aim to—" He can't make himself finish the joke. "Is it okay?"

"Yes." I shudder. "I want to touch you, too." I'm distraught because I don't have any moves, no special techniques that are going to make it better for him. "Can I touch *you*?"

His hand catches mine before it can. "I'd like that, but I don't think I could handle it," he says. "I don't want it to end before we even really get started."

"So let's get started."

His eyes flash up to my face. "Are you ready for that?"

My skin is hot and tingling, my insides made of boiling liquid, and I can feel my pulse in a part of my body where I've never felt it before. This is so much more than what I felt with Leo. If that isn't ready, I don't know what is. I take off my underwear and let it fall to the floor. "Yes," I say simply. "Do you have the condom?"

He nods quickly and rolls to one side of the bed to get a packet from the bedside table. He turns his back to me briefly. I hear him take a deep breath, the kind a person takes when they're swimming and about to go underwater. Then he's under the covers again, and we start kissing. He's getting much better at it. His hand, which is in my hair, smells like plastic and blueberries.

I shift to the center of the bed, where I discover that he's laid down a towel. Because he knows I might bleed, this time. This small act of consideration brings the beginnings of tears to my eyes. The terry is rough against the skin of my back. He moves closer, kissing me again.

I pull at him so he's hovering over me.

Nick breaks away, breathing hard. "If you want to be on top, you can. If you think that will be more comfortable."

I can't help it: I see a flash of the white robe in my mind's eye. My mother straddling Billy.

"I don't think so," I pant. "If I'm on top, it'll be like—I don't know—like impaling myself. Have you ever tried to do something to yourself that you think might hurt?"

272

"Oh. Yeah, I guess. This one time I dropped my laptop on my big toe, and it got all swollen, and my dad said we had to relieve the pressure . . ."

"The point is," I say before he could get any further with that story, "I think you should be on top."

"Are you sure?" His eyebrows are worried again.

Suddenly I just want it to be over with. If there's pain, fine. I can handle being hurt.

"Just do it," I say. "It'll be okay. Maybe it will even be nice."

His gaze drops to my chest, because he's a boy, after all. "Okay," he says softly.

I arrange my legs, and he braces himself on his arms so he won't squash me (as if he weighs enough to squash me, but okay, he's considerate, even now). I look up at him and try to think about how I will remember this moment, the sketch I will hold in my mind, Nick with his hair a mess again, his gray eyes still worried, his arms framing me.

But then I make the mistake of putting myself there, too, there naked under him, looking up at him, my waiting face.

What am I waiting for? Sex. Possibly pain. But underneath all of this, the confused signals my body's giving me, the insecurity and arousal, the curiosity and sweetness, I am angry. I can feel it, like a tight ball of pain at the very core of me. I am pissed off. And I'm suddenly afraid, not of sex or pain, but that this won't do what I want it to, after everything. It won't erase Leo. It won't help me understand my mother better or help me accept what she's done. It won't fix me. It isn't even really distracting me, because here I am about to have sex for the first time, and I am thinking about her.

The white robe. The dark room, identical in every way to this one. I am stuck in that room with her, and having sex isn't going to get me out.

"Okay," Nick murmurs from above me. "Okay, here we go. Okay."

This is wrong. It is all wrong.

"Stop," I whisper. "Stop. I don't want tea."

40

Nick pulls away from me so quickly I feel cold, missing the heat of his body. His face hovers over mine, like he's searching for an injury.

"Ada?" His fingers touch my cheek. Shit. I'm crying. I try to hold it in, to keep the broken pieces together, but they crumble. The tears start to pour. I clap my hand over my mouth as I start to sob—a full-on ugly cry, right there in the middle of the bed.

Nick shifts to lie next to me, still hovering. "Are you hurt? I didn't . . . What's wrong?"

I can't answer. I just cry.

Time passes—I can't perceive how much. Outside the light fades from the sky. When I return to myself, slowly, Nick is still beside me. He brushes my hair out of my damp face. "Hey. Welcome back."

I squeeze my eyes closed, then blink the last of the tears away. "Oh my god. I'm sorry. I don't know what happened." I sit up and pull the sheet around me to cover my body. "I'm fine."

He scoffs.

"No, really," I say with an embarrassed laugh. "I'm sorry. I didn't mean to . . . Just give me a minute. We can still—"

"Yeah, that's not going to happen," he says, and hands me a tissue.

I take it and blow my nose. When I look up again, he's put his boxers back on and is sitting at the edge of the bed.

"I'm so sorry," I say again.

His eyes close. "You've got to stop saying that. There's nothing for you to be sorry for."

"But this was our first time, and it was going to be . . . epic, or at least nice—I think it was going to be nice, and then I had to go and—"

He shakes his head. His face is brick red, from his chest to the lobes of his ears. His heart is beating fiercely in his neck. "I couldn't have done it, anyway."

"What?" I'm confused.

"I don't know what happened. I was fine while we were kissing and stuff, and I think my back is an erogenous zone because when you ran your fingers down it—wow. I was . . . good to go. But when it was time to actually do it, I don't know. The little guy just wasn't up for it." He looks away. Coughs. "I think I got scared."

This makes me feel somewhat (but only slightly) better. I try to cover my utter humiliation by being funny. "I see. So the little guy got stage fright."

"Hey, he's not that little. I just said little by comparison with the rest of my body. I believe him to be a perfectly average size, as penises go." He smiles.

I do like that smile.

But I've made a mess of everything.

"It just wasn't the right time," he says. "Maybe we're too young, you know? There's a reason why grown-ups are always saying we should wait until we're older."

I nod.

"Maybe we could try again next year," he says.

"Okay. Maybe next year." I blow my nose again, and glance at the clock on the bedside table. "We should probably get back to the awards ceremony. We've been gone for more than an hour."

My mom will have noticed my absence by now. But I try not to think about how I'm going to explain myself. Another lie, probably, which I am getting so sick of.

Nick leaps up and puts his pants on. He runs around and picks up my dress and underwear from the floor and hands them to me. "I can turn my back, if you want to go use my bathroom."

"Thank you," I say awkwardly. "I think I will."

In the bathroom I pull on my dress again and smooth it down my legs. It isn't too wrinkled. I wash my face with cold water. The mascara is supposed to be waterproof, but it's no match for my torrent of tears earlier. I use the handy package of makeup remover that's sitting next to the soap on the kitchen counter, and scrub all the makeup off my face. In the mirror I look like myself again, a blotchy, obviously-having-a-rough-night version of myself, but me.

Still a virgin, but okay with that.

Nick stands up when I exit the bathroom. He's wearing his suit again, jacket and everything, but without the tie.

"You still look really pretty," he says after a minute.

"So do you."

It's awkward between us as we go out.

And awkward as we wait for the elevator.

And as we ride the elevator to the bottom floor.

And as we shuffle back toward the Palace Tower.

But then Nick stops walking, so suddenly that I bump into him.

"What?" I ask.

"Do you hear that?" He tilts his head slightly to one side. "What is that?"

I hold my breath, listening. "Music?"

"Yeah." He looks around.

"Probably from the awards," I assume.

"No, it's that song . . ." We're quiet as he listens again. Then he starts to sing along. "Somewhere . . . over the rainbow . . . way up high . . ."

"Uh-oh, are we about to end up in Oz?"

"It's coming from over there," he says, and takes my hand. "Come on."

I don't argue as he tugs me toward the music, away from the Palace Tower and the awards and my family, in the direction of the beach. It's fully dark now, but there's a space lit by lanterns and strings of white lights on the other side of the chapel. The music gets louder and louder, and suddenly we come upon the source: a large man with a ponytail playing a ukulele and softly singing "Over the Rainbow" mixed with "What a Wonderful World" to a crowd of people dressed in formal wear. They're chatting and laughing and drinking tall glasses of champagne.

"It's a wedding." Nick frowns. "No, it's the party after the wedding. What's that called?"

"The reception." And he's right. At the end of the crowd is a woman in white—the bride—holding the arm of a man that I can only hope was the groom. Behind them is a table bearing a classic white wedding cake with a topper that reads, *Happily Ever After.*

My chest feels tight. The anger bubbles up again. Everywhere I look, people are getting married, while the one marriage I most want to be doing well is falling apart.

"We should get back," I whisper.

"Yeah. But what if we don't?" Nick says then.

I tear my gaze away from the cake to look at him. "What?"

His eyes dance with the reflection of a thousand tiny lights. "Let's not go back," he says. "Let's stay here. We're wearing the fancy clothes. We'll fit right in."

"You want to crash these strangers' wedding reception?"

"Hey, could you say that a little louder?" He glances around. Nobody gives us a second look, because, like he said, we fit right in. "I don't want to crash anything. I just want cake. And the hors d'oeuvres look tasty."

We shouldn't, I think. I check my phone, where there's a single text from Mom (*Where are you?*) followed by a text from Afton (*You'd better get back soon. Mom is freaked*). And I find I'm not ready to go back just yet.

"Shall we, my lady?" Nick offers me his arm.

I take it. Why the hell not? "We shall, good sir."

41

We crash the wedding reception with style. Kind of by accident, Nick says he's a friend of the groom, while I say I'm a friend of the bride, and so we end up pretending we just met, which in some ways, it feels like we have.

We listen to the toasts, eat cake, and watch a video that shows the bride and groom as babies, as kids swimming and camping and doing various sports and performances, as lanky awkward teens, then young adults studying and having fun, and finally, as two people who found each other—this couple so very in love. The video makes it feel like their entire lives were a series of moments that has led up to this one night. This moment. Now.

Maybe that's true. I can't hold on to being cynical about their chances at happiness. They seem like nice people. Normal people. They seem happy. In spite of everything, I can't help but wish them well.

Then the music starts up again, and everyone is dancing.

"I've never been to a dance before," Nick tells me as we sit eating a second piece of wedding cake, watching people pair up on the dance floor. The cake is vanilla with vanilla frosting, but it's one of those cakes that proves that simple can be amazing. "I asked this girl at school, Lola, if she wanted to go to homecoming with me, but she didn't think that was a good idea."

"She said no?" I lick frosting off my fingers.

"She said, 'I don't think it's a good idea.'"

"Ouch."

"Agreed. It could have been worse, though. She could have said, 'No way, loser! Get away from me!' I think she was at least trying to be polite. And anyway, my friends and I beat the Dragonstar Arena on veteran that night, and that wouldn't have been possible if I'd been at homecoming with Lola, so, I figure it was destiny."

"Destiny, like the game."

"No, the real thing." He hands his empty plate to a passing waiter. "As in fate."

"I go to a private Catholic school. All girls."

"You're Catholic?" He sounds surprised. Maybe because he thinks Catholics prefer to wait until they're married to have sex, and that doesn't exactly seem to be my modus operandi.

I shrug. "I am for the purposes of school, which basically means I go to mass once a week."

"So you've never been to a dance, either," he says.

"Well, yes, I have," I admit. "I went to prom this year."

"Oh. With the asshole."

"Yes." I remember the way my prom dress burned when I tossed in the fire in my backyard. It was pretty satisfying, watching it go up in flames like that. I turn my focus back to Nick. "So you're a dance virgin."

"I guess so."

I stand up. "Not if I can help it. Not anymore." I hold out my hand. "Dance with me."

He takes my hand and jumps to his feet, like he's been waiting for me to ask. "All right, let's do this, doll."

I stifle a smile. "You're so weird."

"You know it." He catches his bottom lip in his teeth and does what could be interpreted as a disco move. "Now this is a first I can handle."

I follow him onto the dance floor. The guy's singing about a full moon rising, and dancing in the light, but there's only a white sliver of moon in the sky above us. Nick spins me and then pulls me close to him, his feet moving steadily from one spot on the floor to another and back again. He isn't a great dancer. But he tries. That counts for a lot.

I wind my arms around his neck. I am too tall to lay my head on his chest, like Afton did the other night with Michael, but I kind of lean my head against Nick's. Not cheek to cheek, exactly, but close enough. I close my eyes and feel the tension slowly drain from my shoulders.

"It's been a good night, hasn't it?" Nick says. "Even if it had a bumpy start."

"I'm sor—" I stop myself from apologizing. Sigh. "I think we managed to salvage it."

"And we always have next year, right?"

"Right," I say softly, but I don't believe that, deep down, because I can't imagine that what was wrong this year is somehow going to be right, next year. But I don't want to think about that now. I want to dance. Breathe. Be myself. "Crashing the wedding was a good idea," I admit.

"Yeah, well, I'm pretty smart," he says.

"Humble, too."

"Of course. And you forgot to mention that I am smoking hot."

"How could I forget that? I can't even think straight, right now, because you're so blindingly attractive."

We both laugh. Then silence falls between us.

"I want you to know, it wasn't about you not being sexy," I say after a long moment.

He doesn't answer, but his Adam's apple jerks in his neck.

"I did think you were sexy. I mean, I still do. It wasn't about that."

"Okay."

"It just didn't feel right. That's all."

"I know. I really didn't know what I was doing."

"No, the thing is, I just found out that—" The words catch in my throat. The secret is stuck there, and suddenly I want nothing more than to get it out. So I make myself say it: "My mom's having an affair."

He stops dancing for a second, but I hold on and continue moving, keeping us close so he can't see my face. He falls into the rhythm again, the slow back and forth of our feet.

"How did you find out?" he asks.

I tell him everything. About me blundering into the hotel room that day, yes, but also about Mom and Pop and how solid I thought things were between them until recently. I even fill him in about Afton and her drama. It takes dancing to two more songs.

Nick doesn't say much. He's the epitome of a good listener, quietly taking in all that I have to say. Then he simply says, "No wonder you put pepper in Billy Wong's tea."

I bark a humorless laugh. "That was a mistake."

"Was it, though? I'm almost sorry I stopped you."

"It was stupid. I'm glad you stopped me. It wouldn't have fixed anything."

"Yeah, but maybe it would have made you feel better."

"Probably not."

He clears his throat. He has something he isn't saying.

"What?" I ask. "What is it?"

"It's nothing. It's just, I'm disappointed in Billy. And it makes me remember when . . ." He trails off.

"Remember what?"

"No, we're talking about you," he says. "Not my drama."

"Please, let's stop talking about me. I just spilled all the sordid details of my life, so it's only fair for you to get to do the same. Tell me. What did you remember?"

He takes a breath. "Okay. I was thinking about when my mom came to see me."

"Your mom? I don't think I've ever met her."

He shakes his head. "You wouldn't have. She was a resident when she and my dad had their thing. And you know, it's not like how they show on TV, with surgeons hooking up with residents all the time. That doesn't usually happen, right?"

"I don't know. My mom's life strongly resembles a soap opera right now. But yeah, I get it. So your mom was a resident."

"She dropped out. She had me. And then she quit medicine." He pauses. "I think because she was an addict. She had to have a C-section when I was born, because I was trying to come out backward, and then afterward she went downhill, like a lot, started talking about how she was fantasizing about throwing me in the pool at her apartment, so my dad came and got me. And then later she got caught stealing pills from the hospital, and she got kicked out of the program, and she just kind of left. Until this one night. When I was ten." He drops his gaze to our feet. "She showed up at our house really late. I didn't even know her. I wouldn't have known she was my mom except she kept calling me 'sweetie' and touching my face. Her eyes were like black, black holes. I guess that means she was high or something."

"Wow, that sounds like it sucked."

He nods. "The worst part was, she wanted to come back. She asked my dad if they could try again. She said it just like that. 'Please, let's try again.'"

"Oh god. What did he say?"

"He said no. And then she left."

"Wow. I'm sorry."

"He was right to say no. I understood that, later. She was a mess. She's still a mess."

I grab his hand, and we intertwine our fingers.

He bows his head for a minute. Then he says, "It was two days after that that we went to Rio."

"Oh. Ohhhh," I say.

"I was with the group, shopping at the street market, the one with the word *hippie* in it."

"I remember." Afton and I were fascinated by the embalmed piñatas.

"And there was this lady selling bracelets—bahia bands, they're called, made out of different colored ribbons. She explained that I could wrap the bracelet around my wrist and tie three knots, and I could make a wish for each knot, and then I had to wear the bracelet until it fell off on its own, and then my wish would come true."

I see where he's going with this.

"So I bought three bracelets, two white ones and a dark blue one—the colors had different meanings. I thought I would wear one myself, and give one to Dad, and then, if I ever saw my mom again, if she came back, I'd give one to her, and she could wish to get better and then maybe she really could come back and be my mother."

"Oh, Nick."

He clears his throat. "So, yeah. That's what I was doing. I was buying wishes. And when I looked up, everybody was gone. I wandered around for a while calling for my dad, and then this man tried to help me, I think, but I got scared and I ran away from him, and then I was really lost."

"Everyone totally lost it when they realized you were gone. Your dad was frantic."

Nick nods. "Finally I sat down in a corner, next to a stray dog, and I tied that bracelet around my wrist and I used up all three wishes wishing I was home."

I squeeze his hand.

"And then Billy Wong found me," Nick says softly. "He said, 'Hey, buddy,' and he sat down next to me, and I recognized him as someone from the group, and threw myself into his arms. He just held me for a while. While I cried. He hugged me, and he said I was safe, and he said, 'I got you.' I never forgot that. And then he carried me back to my dad, even though I was kind of too big for that."

I pull away. "No wonder you thought Billy Wong was the best."

He sighs. "Right? I guess the moral of the story here is that a person can't be summed up by a single action."

I don't know what to say to that, except, "Well, I'm glad he was there for you."

"And I'm sorry he was there, for you."

We stop dancing. Then, at that exact moment, the singer with the ponytail taps the microphone to get our attention. "And now the bride would like to dance with her father, while the groom dances with his mother."

I immediately feel tears start to well up. I cast a desperate look at Nick, who also looks stricken. "Oh shit. We have to get out of here."

He takes my hand and we just run, away from the reception, away from everybody, away, just away, until the grass under our feet gives way to sand and we reach the ocean. Nick takes off his jacket for me to sit on. Then he produces a rumpled tissue from his pocket. He hands it to me. "It's clean."

I dab at my watery eyes. "This trip is going to kill me."

But then I look up. Away from the lights of the party, the sky has cracked open over our heads. I gasp. I have never seen stars so bright.

"It's because there's no light pollution," Nick says as we gaze raptly upward. "We're on a largely uninhabited island in the middle of the Pacific Ocean. So everything's very clear."

"That feels like a metaphor," I whisper.

He laughs. "I don't know what it'd be a metaphor for, but it's beautiful."

"I could never paint this." I close my eyes and breathe in the sweet salt air.

Nick takes off his shoes and socks and buries his toes in the cool sand next to mine. "You'll just have to remember it."

"I will."

The breeze ruffles his hair. "Me too."

This will be the beach I remember from now on, when I think of beaches. This beach and this night.

"Thank you," I say.

"You're welcome, but for what?"

"For telling me your story. And for being my friend tonight."

He gazes out at the water, smiling sadly. "I was hoping I'd get to be more than a boy who's your friend. But that's okay. I could use a friend, too."

I understand. He thinks I'm giving him the let's-be-friends speech. I shake my head.

"You're more than that. I don't know what we are, exactly, but we're more than friends."

He turns and looks at me, his smile happy again—I can tell, even in the dark. At the exact same moment we lean toward each other, closing the distance between us until our lips meet somewhere in the middle.

It's the perfect kiss. It isn't too long or too short, too dry or wet, too soft or firm. It's simply two people who want to tell one another what we feel without having to use words.

At some point we come apart again. I touch his face, his smooth boyish cheek, and smile at him. He tucks a strand of my hair behind my ear.

"That was epic," I whisper.

42

Next morning. Mom wakes me by poking me in the foot. Because the rest of me is still buried under the covers.

"Wake up," she orders in her usual drill-sergeant style. "Get dressed."

I groan. "We're supposed to be on vacation. Doesn't that mean sleeping in?" But the vacation is almost over. We have one more day in Hawaii, and then we'll be going home.

I still haven't figured out how I am going to keep myself together around Pop.

"Rise and shine," Mom says. "We're all having breakfast together."

I sit up slowly. "Who's we in this scenario?"

"The core group," she answers. "The Wongs, of course, and Marjorie and the Jacobis and the Ahmeds." She is suspiciously cheerful, when I've been expecting her to be furious. I've pulled an Afton, after all. I up and disappeared last night, and I never answered her texts, and I still don't intend to provide her with any explanation as to where I was. To top that off, Nick and I talked on the beach until like two in the morning, which put me back at the room about two thirty.

I sink back against my pillow. "I need a vacation from this vacation," I moan.

She actually smiles. Here I was thinking that she was going to shouty caps things like WHAT'S GOTTEN INTO YOU? and I THOUGHT I COULD RELY ON YOU and NORMALLY YOU'RE SUCH A GOOD, RESPONSIBLE CHILD but she just stares down at me for a minute, smiling this very weird smile, and then she pokes my foot again. "Get up. Put your swimsuit on under your clothes, because we're going swimming directly after breakfast. Get a move on."

I get up. Afton and Abby are already showered and ready to go. I was sleeping so hard that I didn't hear them getting ready.

"Come on, Ada," Abby whines as I pull my board shirt over my head. "I'm hungry."

"What else is new?" I say.

"Be nice," Mom says from the bathroom mirror, where she's paying extra special attention to her hair. She's wearing a flowery sundress I haven't seen before, and makeup, too, I notice. "Oh," she adds, "and I also invited Nathan Kelly to breakfast, and his son. What's his name again?"

My eyes dart to Afton. What did she tell Mom?

Afton raises an eyebrow. "Nick, I think," she answers for me.

"Isn't that the boy who got lost in Rio?" Mom says.

I think of Nick sitting on the street in Rio, tying wish knots into a bracelet on his bony wrist. The image leads me, as all things seem to do now, back to Billy Wong.

Mom's phone chimes. She puts it in her purse and then claps her hands together, a call to order. "All right, girls," she says with the enthusiasm of a cheerleader. "Let's go."

The restaurant where we're meeting the group has a large outdoor deck that overlooks the ocean. The entire group is seated along one big table, and sitting in the middle are Nick and his dad. I stop when I get to him. "Hi."

"Good morning," he says, and yawns.

"Are you as tired as I am?"

He doesn't get to answer me, though, because right then Abby starts screaming.

It isn't a scared scream, I quickly figure out. It's an excited, loud, over-the-top, earsplitting squeal. Because there's a familiar smiling figure sitting at the very end of the table, jumping up now, opening his arms and lifting Abby up and kissing her chubby cheeks.

Pop.

"Surprise!" he says, and Abby yells, "This is the best surprise ever!" and they keep kissing each other's faces, big smacks: Mwa mwa mwa!

"Ada, breathe," Nick whispers, touching my arm.

It feels exactly like I've had the wind knocked out of me. I watch in a daze as Pop puts Abby down and hugs Afton, who looks nearly as stunned as I am, and then kisses Mom—a quick kiss, but still intimate. Then he frowns and his eyebrows rumple and he glances around, his gaze finally landing on me.

"Hi, Pop," I wheeze.

"What are you waiting for, silly? Get over here," he says.

I stagger over and into his arms. He squeezes me a couple of times, then pulls away and looks at me. "There's something different about you."

"That's what I said," Mom exclaims. "I can't put my finger on what it is."

I look at Afton. *Help me,* I say with my eyes, *help me, or I'm going to wreck us all.*

She shakes her head quickly. "She got a haircut, you guys. That's all."

"Oh, I see," Pop says, tilting his head one way and then the other to check out my hair. "That's nice, Ada."

"I also got a manicure, a pedicure, and a facial," I mumble. I leave out the waxing for obvious reasons.

"Wow. Well, you look great," Pop says.

I do not look great. I have dark circles under my eyes, and some leftover puffiness from the previous night's cry fest, and a secret burning me from the inside out.

"Thanks," I croak. "What are you really doing here?"

"I'm fighting," he whispers back.

I take a second to dash away some quick tears. He heard me. He listened.

The details of the surprise come out after we all take our seats. Mom called Pop yesterday, and he said he wanted to join us. They moved around some flights. Pop took the red-eye to Hawaii, to surprise us. We're going to stay tomorrow, as previously scheduled, but then we're going to go to Kauai.

"So we'll get another whole week in paradise," Pop says. "Together. As a family."

"Hooray!" Abby yells. "And it will be so much better with you, Poppy!"

"Hooray," I say weakly. It's good news. I know this. But it still feels bad.

"And that reminds me," Mom says. "Happy Father's Day."

The table erupts in a chorus of "Happy Father's Day," aimed at Max, Jerry, Billy, and Pop. Yep. It's June twenty-first. Which means, this year anyway, we're supposed to be celebrating our fathers.

Just five minutes ago, I was fine. I wouldn't call myself happy, maybe, but the pleasant aftereffects of last night's decompressing dancing and soul-spilling with Nick still lingered in my system. I was calm, relatively speaking. I was ready to go home and figure all of this out.

But now everything's been turned on its head.

Pop's here. He's sitting on one side of Mom, and Billy Wong is sitting on the other side of her. From my angle the three of them are in a perfect triangle.

The waitress comes and takes our orders, but I don't order anything but fruit. Watching Mom has made me lose my appetite. She's being uncharacteristically affectionate toward Pop, even holding his hand, leaning in to whisper things in his ear, smiling, smiling so hard, with all of her teeth, her eyes squinty.

She's putting on a fine performance, and it makes me want to throw up. Or throw something at her. Or I could throw a fit. Whatever I do, I decide, should definitely involve throwing.

My phone buzzes. Nick. I glance down the table at him. His face is the quintessential expression of sympathy. He feels bad for me. He knows.

I feel bad for me, too.

I can hardly hear the words everyone is saying. It's like I'm underwater. But suddenly I hear Billy say, "And tell him about last night."

"Last night?" Mom repeats. "What happened last night?"

Billy turns to Pop. "Your wife, as I'm sure you're aware, is simply amazing. She was the star of the awards ceremony."

"Oh, well, she's always a star in my book," Pop says. She puts her hand over his and smiles at him.

But Billy's not done. "But she wore heels. All night."

Pop turns to Mom with a kind of mock surprise. "My wife wore heels?"

"I regretted it, trust me," Mom says. "I'm still regretting it."

"You were pretty, Mama," Abby says. "You talked good, too."

"Thank you, bug," Mom says. She looks at Billy again. "But I wasn't the only one who was amazing last night. You, if I remember correctly, won a 'distinguished service' award last night."

Oh god, I think. *I'm glad I missed that.*

Pop raises his eyebrows. "Congrats, Bill. What did you win it for?"

Billy waves his hand, like it's not important. "It's complicated," he says. Like maybe Pop isn't smart enough to understand it. He looks at Mom knowingly. "Let's just say, I won it for my 'distinguished service' in my field."

My blood starts to heat. Every sentence, every flirty word that passes between my mother and Billy Wong right in front of Pop like this is transforming me from girl into volcano, filling me with white hot magma, the pressure building.

My phone buzzes. Afton this time.

Be cool. You don't want to freak in front of everyone.

My thumbs whips across the surface of my phone. *Mind your own fucking business*, I write.

Down the table, I see Afton turn her phone facedown.

Mom is still talking about the stupid award. "I don't know if I'd call it distinguished, though. I'm just saying."

Billy's still smiling that nice-guy smile. "I will have you know, Aster, that I am extremely distinguished. Ask anybody."

"No," says Peter. "I don't know what distinguished is, but I'm pretty sure you're not it, Dad."

"Yes, he is," says Josie.

"He is," Jenny agrees sweetly, because everything Jenny does is sweet, poor dear Jenny who has no idea.

All eyes then turn to Michael, who has until now been texting on his phone. He glances up. "Uh, I plead the fifth, Dad," he says. "But I do think you're a great guy."

"Gee, thanks, son," says Billy.

Mom pats Billy arm. "Aw, now, everybody's always so hard on Billy."

He smirks at her. "You most of all."

She puts a hand to her chest, her blue eyes widening. "Me? I would never—"

I clutch the edge of the table. "Stop," I murmur.

Nobody hears me. They just keep on talking, laughing, making light of everything. Mom is still holding Pop's hand, while she's joking about being hard on Billy.

It's too much. Vesuvius is about to erupt.

I stand up. "Stop!" I yell as loudly as I can.

Conversation at the table fades to silence. Everyone, not just the Wongs and my family, but Marjorie and the Kellys, the Ahmeds and the Jacobis, all turn to stare at me.

But I am focused on Mom.

"Stop talking to him," I say, my entire body quivering with rage. "Just stop with your stupid games already."

Mom frowns. "What is wrong with you, Ada?"

"What is wrong with you?" I scream. "I mean, come on, Mom!"

She shakes her head, still acting puzzled. "I don't know what you're talking about."

"I know about the affair!" I burst out.

Silence. It's like I've turned everyone at the table to stone.

Afton is the first to break the spell. "Ada—"

"It's my turn to talk now," I say. "I've been trying not to talk about it all week, but I just . . . can't pretend it didn't happen. I'm sorry. I'm not built that way."

"Oh, honey," Mom says after a long moment of silence. Her expression is weird, like she's surprised but some part of her was also expecting this. "I didn't know that you knew."

"Of course I didn't know!" I glance at Pop wildly. He doesn't look surprised, either; he looks deeply embarrassed. "How would I have known?"

"We just wanted to wait until you were old enough to understand. We didn't want you to be hurt," he says gently.

"Oh, god." I glance from him to Mom to Billy and back to Pop. "So you . . . this is so messed up. I mean, I've heard of people swinging and playing fast and loose in their marriages, but this is *messed up.*"

"Now wait just a minute, young lady," Mom says, back to her no-nonsense voice. "That's not what we—" She composes herself. "We don't need to talk about this here."

"It's all right," comes a voice from farther down the table—Jerry, who has never looked more ready to take charge of this kind of social emergency. Beside him, Penny gives a nervous giggle, and Kate is buried in her phone, probably live tweeting the entire exchange. "I'll talk to the waiter," Jerry says. "We can get a different table, maybe inside. It's too bright out here anyway."

Without waiting for confirmation, everybody gets up, the chairs scraping as they hurriedly push them back. They all start to file out, except for Marjorie, who stays right where she was.

"Margie?" Nick's dad asks.

She waves him off like a pesky fly. "No way, sonny. I want to see how this turns out."

I boil over again as the Wongs also start to slink out. "Wait, you're not leaving, are you, Billy?" I ask loudly.

He stops. "Me?"

"Don't you think you, of all people, should stay?"

His eyes are wide. The fear I see in them gives me courage. "You're an excellent actor," I go on. "You missed your true calling by becoming a surgeon."

"Oh my god, Ada, stop," says Afton, standing up.

"I mean, you've got balls, I have to admit," I continue like I didn't hear her. "The way you dare to sit here, next to her, when she's here with my *father*. You absolute fucking bastard."

Now everybody at the table is saying the words *Ada* and *stop* and *don't*. Then, above them all, comes the high, reedy voice of my little sister.

"What's an affair?" Abby asks. "Why is everyone so upset?"

Shit. I forgot about Abby. I am officially the worst sister in the universe. "I'm sorry." I glance at Afton, whose face is pale as milk under her tan. "I'm sorry. I just couldn't do it anym—"

"It was *me*," Afton says then, loudly and clearly and slowly, like she's speaking to a person who doesn't speak English well. She draws herself up to her full height and looks into my eyes. "It. Was. Me."

I don't understand.

"It was me you saw that morning," Afton says. She closes her eyes for a moment, and a myriad of emotions cross her face in quick succession. Anger. Guilt. Relief. Then she takes a deep breath and turns to our parents. "Ada thinks Mom is having an affair, because earlier this week she came back to the hotel room, and she saw me—"

I'm shaking my head. "It couldn't have been you. I saw—"

"It *was* me," she insists fiercely. "Trust me. I was there."

Now I feel sick for an entirely new reason. "You and Billy Wong?"

"Ew!" Afton exclaims. "Ew, no! No, stupid. Me and Michael."

Everyone in the group swivels to stare at Michael. He'd almost made it to the door of the restaurant, attempting a half-hearted escape, but at his name he knows he's caught. He freezes for a second, like maybe if he doesn't move, we won't see him.

"Well, son?" pipes up Marjorie. "Was it you?"

He sighs and turns to face us. "I would just like to say that—"

"But it happened Monday morning," I argue. "Michael wasn't even here on Monday."

"He came in late Sunday night," Billy corrects me gruffly.

"But how would you have known that?" I ask Afton. "How did you even have time to—"

"When he wasn't at dinner on Sunday, and I heard that maybe he wasn't going to come this year, I texted him," Afton says stiffly. "And he texted back, and said he *was* coming, after all; he was actually on the plane, heading over. And so then we were texting back and forth . . ."

"He's who you were texting all night," I murmur.

She nods. "He gave me his number last year. We had a little . . . thing, at last year's awards dinner."

"Thing?" This time it's Michael's mother, aka Jenny, asking the questions. "What thing?"

Afton ducks her head, blushing. "A kiss," she says, at the same time that Michael says, "It was just a kiss."

"No." I press my hands to my head because it feels like my brain is going to explode. "It still couldn't have been you, Afton. You went with Abby to hula class that morning."

"But when we got there, we ran into the Wongs," Afton explains. "I left Abby with Jenny and Peter and Josie, and Michael and I . . ." Her face colors even more. "We went back to the room."

"And you put on Mom's new robe."

"Hey!" Peter glares at me, his hands planted on his hips. "Not all Asians look the same, you know."

"It was dark in there!" I protest. I swallow. "I didn't actually see Billy's face. I just assumed it was him. He's the only guy Mom really talks to."

"What did you see them doing in there?" asks Josie.

Shit.

"Hey, I have an idea," comes a familiar voice from next to the door. Nick. He's been standing there, listening to the entire exchange. I want to think it's his form of being my moral support and not just sheer curiosity. "Why don't you kids all come with me?" he asks. "This is grown-up talk, and it's kind of gross. Who wants to play a game in my room on my PS4?"

Mom and Jenny nod at him gratefully. He nods back. For once, his video game addiction is going to come in very useful. Abby, Josie, and Peter all follow him out without another word.

I turn to Afton. In that little break with Nick and the kids, the facts have settled in my brain, and the facts are these: Afton has screwed up everything. She even said so in the restroom last night during the awards dinner. But I hadn't known that I was supposed to take her *literally*. "Why didn't you tell me?" I fume. "For, like, two days you let me think that it was Mom hooking up with Billy? How could you let me think that?"

"I tried to tell you!" she cries, her hands clenching into fists. "But you were so mad, and you kept talking and talking, and I couldn't get a word in, and then Mom came in, and then the stuff with Michael happened . . . I was going to tell you. Just as soon as I could get a moment to think about what I'd say."

I sink into my chair. "You should have told me."

"But wait," interjects Marjorie. She finishes the last of her glass of orange juice. "Didn't you tell us, Billy, that Michael has a serious girlfriend?"

All eyes go back to Michael. He doesn't say anything. He just puts his hands into the pockets of his shorts and sighs. "I don't have a good excuse. I messed up. In my defense, though, your sister—"

"My sister is not crazy," I spit out.

"Your sister is . . . kind of irresistible," he says.

I can see his point. If Afton decided that Michael was going to be her rebound—the first cute guy *she* saw—and went after him with her typical Afton-like tenacity, Michael didn't stand much of a chance. My sister is a force to be reckoned with.

Still, though. Douchebag.

The waitress arrives with various plates of food. She already looks stressed out, what with half the group moving to a different table, inside, and now the kids are gone, but their food's here. Then Billy says, "Look, we'd like to move, too, if that's okay. We have some things we'd like to discuss with our son."

"Sure," the waitress says, in a voice that conveys how very weary she is with all these freaking tourists. "Just pick a clean table, and I'll bring your food there."

Billy and Jenny thank the waitress, nod at Mom and Pop, and walk out, Billy pulling Michael behind them by the arm. "Do you know how old that girl is?" I hear him mutter.

"She's eighteen," Michael says. "I know, but Dad—"

Then the door swings closed behind them, and they're gone.

Marjorie heaves a sigh. "This has been very entertaining," she announces. "But I should go, too."

She picks up her plate and sees herself out.

So it's finally down to Mom, Pop, Afton, and me.

Which is a good thing, because something else has just occurred to me.

"Wait," I say. "When I said I knew about the affair, you acted like you knew what I was talking about. But you didn't know about Afton and Michael, did you?"

"No," Mom says grimly. "I didn't know they had sex in my bed. I wish I'd never found out about that, honestly. But everything makes so much sense now—how you were acting out all week, why you were so angry."

"So what affair did you think I meant?" I ask.

Silence.

Then Pop sighs. "We thought you meant *our* affair."

"Your affair," I repeat stupidly.

Mom clears her throat. "When your pop and I met, I was still married to Aaron, and Pop had a serious girlfriend."

I blink a few times. This means that Mom and Pop had an affair while they were both committed to other people.

"Oh," I say numbly.

"We weren't trying to deceive you, honey, or keep it a secret from you forever, but you were very young at the time."

"Oh." I glance at Afton. Her face is totally unsurprised by this revelation. She must have known somehow, too. Which is why she was saying those things, in her fight with Mom, about not being a good role model herself. "I see."

"We always meant to explain how it happened to you, someday," Pop says. "We should have. You're old enough to handle it now."

Or not.

I stand up. I've been so wrong about everything. In all of human history, it feels like there has never been anyone so spectacularly wrong as I have been.

"I have to go now," I say, and then I run.

43

When I finally stop running, I am, once again, at the rental shack for the paddleboards. It's early enough that there's very little line. I don't even really think about it; I rent a board, collect it, and paddle myself into the exact center of the lagoon.

Where nobody will be able to find me.

Where I can be alone with my thoughts, with my wrongness, with the way I obliterated any semblance of dignity for me or my family, with all that I've been so clueless about, all that I didn't know, because no one bothered to tell me.

I sit there on the board, legs in the cool green water, the sun beating down on my back, and I wish that the world would swallow me up. But the world cruelly refuses.

After a while I see something swimming toward me: a head, followed by a long, lean body in a red bikini. When she reaches me, she starts treading water. Which feels like a metaphor.

"I need to talk to you," she says softly.

"You've been saying that all week."

"Maybe now you'll listen."

"Fine. Come aboard, then." I try to counterbalance so she won't tip us over as she pulls herself up onto the board, water pouring off her. She arranges herself to face me, but then it seems like she loses her nerve.

The water laps at our legs. The wind stirs our hair. I can hear the agitated in and out of my sister's breathing—I can almost see the words forming in her head, the excuses she wants to give me about what she's done.

But I don't want to hear it.

And she knows that. Because she knows me.

So here we are, having a non-conversation while, around us, kids splash and play, and couples pass by in kayaks, and the world goes about its business as usual.

I want to say, *You said you need to talk. So talk.* But I can't be the one, this time, to break the silence.

Her jaw shifts. She's chewing on the inside of her cheek, a habit I hate. Her breath, in and out, in and out. Until she finally says: "I'm sorry, Ada."

"Apology not accepted. I can't believe you let me think that it was Mom." I swallow back tears. "Do you know what that was like for me? I felt like my life—our life—was over."

"I made a mistake," she murmurs.

I scoff. "Obviously. But guess what? You don't just get to say you're sorry and have it be fine."

"I know!" she cries, and then, to my total horror, my tough big sister starts to cry, not just movie star tears, but red-faced bawling her eyes out that shakes the paddleboard.

"It's just, I felt so broken," she says between sobs. "I didn't think I was fragile like that. I didn't think I would feel so . . . empty after."

My teeth grind together. I want nothing more than to kick that boy in the balls right then, no matter how mad I am at my sister.

"He's an ass," I say. "Which is a letdown, honestly, because I always thought Michael was okay."

She blinks at me, her eyebrows drawing low over her wounded blue eyes. "Michael? I meant Logan." Her face contracts into a grimace again. "This was always about Logan. The thing is, I loved him. I still love him. I wish I could stop, but every time I check, it's still there. But he's right that it wouldn't be feasible for us to keep seeing each other from across the country. We're moving on to a new part of our lives. I get that." She wipes at her nose with the back of her arm— the most un-Afton-like gesture I've ever witnessed.

Now I am chewing on the inside of my cheek.

Afton shudders. "I was so embarrassed that I was such a mess," she says, not looking at me but out to the horizon, fat tears still rolling down her face. "And then you were so ready to have sex with Leo, and we started talking about my first time, and . . ." She pauses. "That first time, in the garage, with that guy. It shouldn't have happened."

"Then why did it?"

"I was angry at Dad."

"Dad? As in . . . Aaron?"

"Yeah." She sniffles again. "Up until then, he always came to my ballet recitals."

"I thought you hated that."

"I did, but . . ." She almost laughs, or sobs. "But then, this one time, he didn't come. And I thought, okay, that's it. He's not ever going to come again. And I knew I shouldn't be so broken up about it. Dad is such a small part of our lives, and I told myself I didn't care. But it upset me, him not coming. And this boy was there, and he kind of offered, and I felt so bad about Dad. I just wanted to feel better. I wanted to feel good. So I did it."

I nod. Of course I know exactly what she means. It's possible that she and I, in spite of our differences, are cut from the same cloth.

"The second time was even worse. I got drunk at a party. I wasn't so drunk that I passed out, or I didn't really know what was happening, but . . . I wouldn't have gone through with it, if I'd been sober. And there was no condom and I was so scared after. Oh my god. So scared."

I remember the train ride we'd taken to the Planned Parenthood for Plan B. Afton hadn't seemed scared. She'd just seemed pissed off that all of that was necessary.

"So that's why you tried to warn me, when I was talking about having sex with Leo."

"Yeah. After that I just felt kind of gross about sex. Until Logan. It was good with Logan. Because I loved him. That's the thing, Ada. If you don't love the guy, sex can complicate things in a bad way. And you didn't love Leo."

"No," I admit, easily now. "I didn't."

"I loved Logan. But then that fell apart, too, and I was right back where I started. It's like I didn't even remember my own advice. I heard that Michael wasn't coming, and I felt disappointed, and then

I found out he *was* coming, and I thought, he's cute, and he's funny, and he knows me so it's safer than it would be with a stranger, and if I have sex with him, maybe I'll feel something else besides heartbroken. But it didn't work." She sniffles. "Of course it didn't work. If anything, it made me feel worse. And then you saw us, and you thought I was Mom. I wanted to tell you the truth—I swear I did—but I was too ashamed of myself. If I said it was me, it'd be like I was just as bad as you thought Mom was."

"Well, not *just as* bad," I say reluctantly. "Michael's not married. And you didn't force him to cheat on his girlfriend. He did that all by himself."

"He's been with Melanie since his junior year of college. He was planning to ask her to marry him. I knew that, actually." She takes a deep breath. "I didn't even really care, honestly. I was thinking about myself, and how if I could get Michael to like me, not just this one time hooking up but really like me, like we were falling in love or something, then it would somehow be worth it." Her nose wrinkles, like she hates her own bad smell. "I was so stupid. I could see that Michael did love Melanie—he was just freaking out because he's getting to that time in your life when all the big decisions happen, the ones you have to live with. It was, like, cold feet."

"You're not going to get me to feel sorry for Michael. And you're far from stupid, Afton. You just got your heart broken and did some stupid, stupid . . . *really* stupid things," I say.

She smiles at the three stupids, her eyes finally meeting mine. The broken pipe that has busted loose inside her slows to a trickle.

"I know I don't act like it," she says. "But I'm jealous of you, Ada. You're always so good, so goddamned perfect at everything, with your sketchbook and your to-do lists and your plans. You've always got things figured out."

I give a disbelieving laugh. "What."

"Really. You do."

"I don't."

"You do. Tell me the stupidest thing you've ever done."

"Um, have you forgotten that less than an hour ago I accused our mother of having an affair with her business partner, in front of a bunch of her colleagues, and also in front of our little sister and our dad?"

"But that was my fault."

I snort. "Okay, let's go with that when they sit me down to talk to me about it."

"If I'd just fessed up as soon as you told me, it wouldn't have happened. It was my stupidity, rubbing off on you."

I bite my lip, then release it. "Fine. How about this: I asked Nick Kelly to have sex with me. I thought, *he's cute, and he's funny, and he knows me so it will be safer than it would be with a stranger*, and I thought, *if I have sex with him, maybe I'll feel something else besides heartbroken*."

She doesn't look surprised. Because of course she already knows this.

"Oh, so you did read that in my sketchbook," I confirm.

She cringes. Nods. "Sorry. To be fair, I wasn't expecting to find anything like that. But did it happen last night? Did you two . . ."

"No. I freaked out at the last minute. I tried to. But no. It didn't happen."

"Wow. That sounds . . ."

"Humiliating? Yes. But it actually turned out all right. Afterward we crashed somebody's wedding, and we danced and talked and looked at the stars, and I did feel something else, for a little while, at least." I sigh. "And then this morning happened."

"Yeah, well, we were blindsided by Pop."

"He really could have warned us. Of course, I basically told him to do something exactly like that, the last time I spoke to him."

Suddenly Afton laughs, a choked-up, husky laugh—a kind of sound I've never heard come out of her before. She puts her hand over her mouth to try to hold it in, but it just keeps tumbling out, making the board underneath us tremble.

"I bet he never tries to surprise us again," she titters.

I laugh, too. "Let's hope not."

"And Marjorie was just sitting there like she was at the movies having popcorn," Afton says, wiping what I hope are laugh tears from her eyes. "Did you hear her? *No way, Jerry. I want to see how this turns out.*"

We laugh and laugh, until we're tired and our sides hurt. I sigh and put my hand on Afton's shoulder.

"I can't say I forgive you," I say.

"I can't say I blame you."

"I want to forgive you, though."

"Okay."

I nod solemnly. "I'll probably only hold this over your head for another twenty or twenty-five years, tops."

"That seems fair."

"The thing is, I get it. I don't like it, but I get it. Also, we're sisters, and that, unfortunately, is an unbreakable bond. Like forever." I hold out my pinkie to her.

"Sisters forever," she whispers, shaking my pinkie with hers.

We hug then, because of course it is a requirement of sisterhood, but it turns out that hugging is more than we can manage while still balancing on the paddleboard. We go right over into the water.

I come up sputtering. "Shit." I grab for the paddle, which is floating away.

"Ada, look!" Afton says excitedly.

"Get it!" I order.

But she isn't looking at the paddle. She's gazing down in the water below us. "It's a turtle," she says in a soft voice, like it will disappear if it hears us.

I stop. "Shut up," I say, the affectionate kind of shut up, though, meaning, *you can't be serious.*

She points down.

There, only a few feet beneath us in the pale clear water, is a massive sea turtle.

"Oh my dog," I whisper.

Its shell is a red-brown color, segmented into thirteen large sections that each bear a starburst pattern with hash marks of golden and lemon and white. Its fins and head are darker—almost black, and threaded with pure white, which makes it look like it's paved with cobblestones. It's gorgeous. I'll never be able to do it justice in a painting in a million years.

As Afton and I tread water, staring at it, it's looking at us, too. Then, slowly, lifting and dropping its huge front fins like it's flying instead of swimming, it ascends to the surface. Its head is less than a hand's stretch away from me. Its eye as it gazes back at me is an inky, fathomless black.

We aren't supposed to touch them. It's illegal, in fact. There are signs posted all around the lagoons saying not to touch or ride them, that you could be fined up to fifteen hundred dollars for harassing a Honu—the Hawaiian word for a green sea turtle.

So I don't touch. I tread water, holding the board with one arm and trying to stay as still as possible in the presence of this creature.

It stays for a minute. Maybe two. Then it lowers its head and drifts downward again, turning in the water toward the mouth of the lagoon, and with a few sweeps of its powerful fins, it disappears into the darkness of the ocean.

Afton and I don't say anything. She swims over and fetches the paddle, and then we climb carefully back onto the paddleboard and, together this time, we paddle toward the shore.

44

I meet Nick in the lobby that afternoon, as he and his dad wait for the taxi that will take them back to the airport, and from there to Oahu for a few days, and then to Boston.

"Keep in touch, okay? Deal?"

"Deal," I say.

"I will hold you to that."

"I'll text you. I promise. Prepare yourself for an onslaught of cheesy GIFs."

"I consider myself warned," he says. "And maybe we can even play some games together, sometime. It's fun. I think you'd like it, if you tried it out."

"Don't push your luck. Oh," I say, remembering. I set down my bag at my feet and pull out my sketchbook. And then from the sketchbook, I remove a drawing.

It's a beach at night, the long stretch of sand, the waves tumbling in. Stars sprinkled liberally all across the sky. And two figures, sitting on the beach, leaning back against their arms, looking up. One of them me, a rare self-portrait, with the bird-of-paradise dress pulled up over my knees.

The other, Nick, who is both lanky and handsome in his suit.

It's nowhere near as beautiful as that night was. But it is still one of my best sketches ever.

"Oh, wow," Nick breathes. "This is . . . wow."

"Thanks." I feel a tad embarrassed. But also good.

"I'm going to frame this," he says. "And when I look at it, I'll think of you." His dad says his name, and he turns. "I have to go."

The breath whooshes out of me. "I need to say thank you," I gasp. "You were a lifesaver. You were my, like, sanity."

He makes a quick, scared face, like perhaps *sanity* isn't the right word, since I'd so clearly gone insane. I laugh and fake-punch him.

"Okay, okay," he says. "Now give me a hug, so I can get out of paradise."

I throw my arms around him. My breasts press tightly into his skinny chest. My chin drops to rest on his shoulder. "Don't be a stranger," I murmur close to his ear.

"I was about to say the exact same thing." He pulls away. "Uh, don't look down," he mutters, his cheeks going red. "I've got a situation."

Oh. He has a boner.

I don't laugh, because I don't want him to think I'm laughing at him. So I just give him a friendly pat on the back.

"Maybe next year," I say cheerfully.

He grins his crooked smile. "Maybe next year."

45

After that it's just the main squad—Mom and Pop, Afton, Ada, and Abby—although now there's a sense that we've been through something and survived it (if only barely), and we shouldn't take our family for granted again. We do a lot of talking that week, about what transpired and what we can learn from it—i.e., what we should never do again. And Mom and Pop go off together, to discuss how things really are between them, and how they can make them better. Starting with Mom working less. And Pop maybe moving to the day shift so they'll have more time to be together.

Then there is Kauai, which is as relaxing and low-key as the Big Island had been fiery and upscale. There's our hotel right on the beach where roosters crow us awake every morning and huge snails slowly cross the grass. There are golden sand beaches, and Abby chasing sand crabs as the tide goes out.

We ride in a helicopter over the island, and we ride bicycles along the coast with the wind whipping us. We fill our stomachs with acai bowls and seafood and shaved ice that tastes of coconuts and cream. We buy a chopping board made of koa wood for Pop, a crap ton of Kona coffee for Mom, a bright yellow sarong for Afton, and a ukulele for Abby and me to share. And through all of that, we talk. We stitch ourselves back together, so that by the time the week is over, we feel like a solid unit again.

We don't fix everything. But we make a start at it.

The last day in Hawaii, a baby seal appears on the beach a few steps from our hotel room door. A man in a uniform shows up and puts caution tape and warning signs around the area, to keep tourists from "helping" the baby seal by pouring water on it or covering it with towels, trying to feed it, or dragging it back into the water.

Because humans are dumb.

Abby is, naturally, distressed. "But where is its mama?" she asks the man. "Why did she leave her baby?"

"Her baby got too tired to swim, so the mother seal brought it here, up to the beach, to rest. The mother will swim around and get some food and then return to pick her baby up later. The beach is kind of like baby seal daycare."

Abby bites her lip. "But what if the mother gets lost and doesn't come back?"

"The mother always comes back," the man says. "She remembers exactly where she left her baby. Trust me. They'll find each other again."

Afton snorts and rolls her eyes. She's irritable today—she forgot to put on sunscreen before our bike ride yesterday and now her skin is

317

the approximate color of a ripe tomato.

"Come on, let's get some more aloe on you." Mom lifts Abby into her arms. "And let's get you a snack, bug. Ada, do you need anything?"

"I'm good."

They start back toward the room. Pop and I stay on the beach, listening to waves crash into the sand and watching the seal pup—from a safe distance, of course.

"It doesn't even look like it's breathing," I say.

The man from the park service stakes a final *Don't touch!* sign into the sand and stands up. "Seals can hold their breath. In the water they only come up to breathe about every three minutes."

"Oh. Cool. Well, it looks . . . dead," I observe.

The man sighs. "That's why people are always trying to help them. They think there's something wrong, so they try to intervene, when the best thing for everyone is to leave it alone."

Pop looks over at me with knowing eyes. "There's a metaphor in there somewhere," he says.

Acknowledgments

In the summer of 2017, my mother, Carol, and my stepfather, Jack, invited me to go along with them to the annual conference of the American Society of Mechanical Engineers, a week-long event they attended every year. That year it was held in Hawaii at the Hilton Waikoloa Village on the Big Island. I said yes, of course. It turned out to be one of those vacations of a lifetime—it was beautiful and relaxing and fun every minute. I will always be so grateful they asked me—and Jack paid my way, I should add. While I was there, I bought a Hawaii-themed blank book (it had palm trees on it) and started jotting down an idea, something about a girl propositioning a boy she'd spent a week with every year for almost her entire life. It was set in Hawaii, of course. Thank you so much, Carol and Jack Ware, for that amazing vacation, and for all the ways you've supported me and my writing over the years.

On that trip I was looking at my phone a lot—too much, really, an embarrassing amount. I'd just met a man I thought I might be in love with. He was smart and nerdy in the best possible way, and also kind, thoughtful, and funny, and I could not stop texting him. And video chatting with him. And thinking about him. He's my husband now. Thank you, Daniel Rutledge, for being my best friend and lover and all-around good man.

Writing the book was tougher than I expected it to be. I thought at first that the story was going to be this light and funny examination of teenage sexual awakening. Then I got Ada on the page, and with Ada came these two sisters, and her brilliant whirlwind mother, and her bedrock father figure, and before I knew it, I was basically writing a family drama with the funny sex stuff as more of a side note. And during the entire process, Jodi Meadows talked me through the ups and downs and offered her invaluable insights about plot, pacing, and the perils and joys of sisterhood. Thank you, Jodi. Words truly can't express how thankful I am to have you as my friend and writing partner.

At one point I was feeling stuck, and I spent a few hours one Saturday reading the first several chapters out loud to Amy Yowell, my best friend since I was thirteen years old; Ben Yowell, her awesome husband; and Kathleen Yowell, their amazing daughter. They laughed so hard at every joke that I instantly felt my confidence return—maybe I could write this book about (eek!) sex and not fall flat on my face. Thank you, Amy, Ben, and Katie—my favorite! And hugs to Gwen, the younger daughter, even though she wasn't there, because that would have been totally inappropriate. . . .

On that note, thank you, Allan, my brother, for the conversations we had about this book that probably made you wildly uncomfortable. And thank you, Will, my son, who had to endure the sudden onslaught of "the talk" when I was reading up on how teens approach this subject differently than they did when I was sixteen.

Thank you, Katherine Fausset, for your continued encouragement and sound advice as my agent for almost sixteen years now. You're the very best. A big thank-you also to the people at Curtis Brown: Holly Frederick, my film agent, and Sarah Gerton, especially.

Thank you, Erica Sussman and Stephanie Stein, my editors, for all the work you do to make my books as good as they can be. I'd also like to thank the entire team at HarperTeen and everyone who contributed to the book's production: Alexandra Rakaczki, Jaime Herbeck, Louisa Currigan, Jessie Gang, Jenna Stempel-Lobell, Kristen Eckhardt, Sabrina Abballe, and Anna Bernard; Helen Crawford White, the amazing cover artist; and Joy Osmanski, the narrator of the audiobook.

And finally, I'm beyond grateful to my readers, both the new ones and those who've stayed with me for the past ten years (and ten books!), for all your emails, letters, and comments on Instagram that make me feel so validated as a storyteller. You're the reason I sit down to write every day. Thank you so much for reading.